RED GUITARS IN HEAVEN

Tom Morton lives in the Shetland Islands, where he devotes himself to motorcycle maintenance, roofing repairs and seeking a cure for baldness. He was formerly Highlands and Islands reporter for *The Scotsman*, and writes a weekly column for the paper. In 1994 he received the Columnist of the Year prize in the Bank of Scotland Press Awards.

Red Guitars In Heaven

TOM MORTON

MAINSTREAM
PUBLISHING

EDINBURGH AND LONDON

Cover montage and photograph by Pinhole Observatory:
  1962 Red Fender Stratocaster courtesy of David Mitchell, Glasgow
  Sheep courtesy of Glasgow Museums

First published in Great Britain in 1994 by
MAINSTREAM PUBLISHING COMPANY (EDINBURGH) LTD
7 Albany Street
Edinburgh EH1 3UG

ISBN 1 85158 653 9

The publisher gratefully acknowledges the financial assistance of the
Scottish Arts Council in the production of this book

A catalogue record for this book is available from the
British Library

Typeset in 10.5 pt Palatino by CentraCet Limited, Cambridge

Printed and bound in Great Britain by
Biddles Ltd, Guildford and King's Lynn

To Susan

Acknowledgments

Significant Other, JP and JM decamped to Gaza, Shetland, while this book was being written in Cromarty, Ross-shire. Significance-in-law looked after them, bless her apple-and-blackcurrant pie. John McNaught and Gillian Jones, Steve and Christine Johns, Gillian Bowie and Dave Newman all helped look after me.

At Mainstream, Peter Frances and Janene Reid performed wonders; Bill 'n' Pete bought the requisite drinks. Post-Cromarty, Willie and Nancy, Elaine and Scott, Ross and Jim the Singing Builders, Duncan and Jimmy the Human Hurricanes all helped facilitate the Morton family's survival.

A lunch between Campbells Bobby and Bill sparked off *Red Guitars in Heaven*, which could not exist were it not for the likes of John Nelson Darby, Peter Hynd, George Muller, Billy Graham, Revd Willie Still, Clive Calver, Leo Fender, Mick Jagger and Keith Richards.

This is, I would like to stress, a book of lies.

Tom Morton
Shetland

Contents

PART ONE

White Settler	11
Born Again	26
Animals	43
Immersion	55
Gospel	76

PART TWO

Cash	99
Ghosts	122
Rock	134
Success	158
The Rats of Fear	165
Heaven	184

. . . there's no bottom, none,
In my voluptuousness. Your wives, your daughters,
Your matrons, and your maids, could not fill up
The cistern of my lust, and my desire
All continent impediments would o'erbear
That did oppose my will
Macbeth, Act IV, scene iii

Blues falling down like hail
And the days keep on 'minding me
There's a hellhound on my trail
Robert Johnson

There is no other sound
In the darkness but the sound of a man
Breathing, testing his faith
On emptiness, nailing his questions
One by one to an untenanted cross.
R.S. Thomas, 'In Church'

PART ONE

White Settler

True love, perfect sex and a certain faith. These were the objects of my craving.

And a red guitar.

A red electric guitar. Lacquered that deep, glossy, dive-in, suck-it, eat-it, fuck-it, worship-it red. Shaped in sinuous, sensuous curves. And loud, capable of singing sweetly, sure, but with that huge, erupting power, the power to deafen and destroy parental disapproval, the power to attract people, seduce them, force them to love the master of the red guitar. Convert them. The power to confer fame and fortune and riches, to channel a resounding spirituality. In the guitar itself, I realised, was the potential for belief, for power, sex and true love. Oh, there's simply no question that old Sigmund would have revelled in the throbbing, holy symbolism of Leo Fender's three-pick-up masterwork: the Freudian Stratocaster.

But at first it was a Watkins Rapier, glimpsed in a shop window one bitter Sunday night as the man and I, giant Revised Standard Version Bibles clutched in gloved hands, walked through Kilmarnock to a gospel rally in the Bethesda Hall. I was the man's miniature, his familiar: 11 years old, converted through the good offices of an evangelistic film in which most of the adults died of cancer just after confessing Jesus Christ as Lord. Made by the Billy Graham Organisation, it had been shown in shaky 16mm in our own gospel hall, in the Ayrshire coastal town of Bittermouth. I was terrified into tears and the loving arms of the Lord. I had to have hot, sugary Sunquick orange before I went to bed, and the man bought me a special RSV Bible. Uncle Andy gave me a New English version of the New Testament, which was regarded as slightly suspect. Even liberal. But Uncle Andy was very intelligent, and could read – but not speak – Greek, the ancient variety.

In the Brethren, this was regarded as both an immense achievement and potentially fatal to fundamentalist faith. The Brethren was a resolutely working-class movement, born, unlike its English equivalents, in mines and steelworks and fishing villages, committed to the priesthood of all male believers and the silent domestic power of women. Uneducated men, awesomely self-taught, could memorise not just the entire Bible, but commentaries on the Holy Word, reams of symbolism, especially about the second coming of Christ, which was, of course, imminent. Tomorrow maybe. Or not, but expect it, live as if today is your last day, hour, minute. Soon, He is coming, He is coming, to gather His jewels . . . precious jewels, His loved and His own . . . I once heard a man, a missionary, refer in a sermon to the great philosopher Socrates, pronounced to rhyme with dinner plates. God (oh forgive me Jesus, forgive me), how I giggled, furtively and superciliously, while bald men, and women smelling strongly of mothballs sighed agreement and murmured, 'Amen.'

I must have been about 14, gawky and stretching towards a dumbfounded, awkward adolescence. Longing, longing to share my superiority: 'So,' I said to the man later that evening. 'Crates.' He had come to collect me from the Youth Fellowship in his white Vauxhall Velux, a middle-class source of jealousy among his fellow brethren. The man. My father. A chiropodist, he was doing well from the veruccas of Bittermouth. He didn't look like a chiropodist, or talk like one. Big, well over six foot and broad, but permanently stooped, his prematurely bald head topped a brooding, tense face. Much like mine is now, except the alcohol and other things have smoothed and blotched away the tension you could see in his. In his heart he was a missionary, on fire for God, trudging through jungles with the Gospel of Light and Life. But there wasn't much call for chiropodists in New Guinea or Peru. 'God has called me to serve the feet and soles of my fellows in the homeland,' he would sigh, dreaming of blowpipes, poisoned darts and witchdoctors. At least, that's what I dreamed he dreamed of. He pulled the car into the side of the road, switched off the engine and turned to me.

'You have the privilege of an education,' he said, drumming his fingers, smooth and white from the perpetual washing-away of other people's footsweat, from his shiny, rather freckled head. 'Something I had to struggle for, and that holy brother tonight never had. He's probably read Socrates, which you haven't. He had no one to tell him how to say the writer's name. But you know how to say his name, so that makes you bigger and more clever and holier than the preacher is, does it? That man, who gave up all for God to become a missionary, who has suffered, become diseased . . . when you've clothed a hundred naked natives in the dark, sin-seared lands and seen them turn to Christ, you can boast then. But you won't, though. Because saints are humble.' It was an important moment, the crestfallen silence which followed, just before he started the car and we drove off for our secret, Sabbath-busting bag of potato grease in a bad chip-shop far from other brethren's prying eyes. It was then, amid the aromatic incense of hot, vinegar-sodden newsprint, and the man's gentle, complete, hard, God-like forgiveness, I realised that knowledge came second to spirituality, and that someday I would be an evangelist, a preacher, perhaps a missionary to the naked natives, clothing them, healing them, converting them, bathed and bathing in their grateful love, in God's gratitude too. Although I had a sneaking suspicion, burrowing faithlessly up through my guilty mind, that the mispronouncing missionary had not picked up his Socrates quote from the great Greek's own tomes, but from the Paternoster Press's *Preacher's Dictionary of Quotations*, a copy of which my father used when he was called to give 'the message'. He was fond of quoting from Kierkegaard, whoever he was. Pronounced Keer-ki-gard. Correctly.

But that was when I was 14. When I was 11 I wanted that red guitar so badly it hurt. The window of the music shop glowed on to the dark Sunday street like the illuminated, full-size Christmas stable scene the man and woman took me to see every year, despite its Romanist overtones. In an Ayr park, black as sin, Mary and Joseph, the donkey, the three kings and the baby Jesus shone from within in rich red, blue, green and white plastic. The promise of Christmas: expensive presents, favourite relatives, vast quantities of wonderful food – it was all there in those cheap plastic statues. The music-shop window blazed with light, and shimmering in the middle of the display was the red guitar. My own personal rock'n'roll Golden Calf. Oh, smite me, God! Smite me, punish me, forgive me. But first, let me play it. Let me possess it. Let it possess me.

I had no idea if a Watkins Rapier was a good guitar or not. It was the shape, the colour, the potential of it, just sitting there, silent. A friend at school had an electric guitar. He'd brought it to my house one day, with an old valve radio his father had converted into a crude amplifier. The noise it made was vast, unimaginable, terrifying – but so joyful it made me laugh uncontrollably. 'House of the Rising Sun' he played, the chords progressing magically, A-C-D-F, no one in my family knowing, fortunately, just what purpose the house in the song actually served. The woman rushed in, skillet in hand, glasses steamed up. 'Turn it off! Turn it off! You'd think it was the Last Judgement!' She was nearly right.

I stood in the street, transfixed, my hand tightening on the big Bible. 'Look. Look at that.' My breath condensed on the window, clouding my view of that six-string divinity. I reached to wipe the glass, and my Bible dropped on to the icy ground, its fine, expensive Oxford India paper whispering like a footfall in old, tiny leaves.

'Pick that up, pick it up,' hissed the man. I bent to do so, my eyes still fixed on the Rapier. 'What is it, anyway?'

'The red one,' I said, knowledgeably. 'A Watkins Rapier.' That's what the label said. The price tag was in guineas. Eleven guineas, 11 shillings and 11 pence. The red guitar radiated something totally alien to that deserted Kilmarnock street. I didn't know what it was, but I wanted it. I wanted it with my whole being, with a hunger, a thirst. The kind reserved in the Bible for righteousness. But that guitar was something much more and much less than righteous. It grinned, two giant red lips, glittering with a promise I was too young, maybe, to understand. The man was tugging at my shoulder, his Bible tucked under his arm, his black Crombie overcoat slightly creased from the car journey. He wore a homburg, black and final. I had only hair, short, Christian, to protect my head. My ears were already numb.

'We'll be late,' he said. 'Come on, now.' He smiled, hesitated. 'There won't be any red guitars in heaven, you know.' We walked away, into the darkness, towards the gospel, the true, clear Light. But my Bible was stained and dirty from the street, and would never completely recover. The whole of First Kings was stuck together. Which, I later concluded, wasn't much of a loss, even if you were born again.

A bell rings. The tinkle of a potential customer entering Worms, the second-hand bookshop, junk antique emporium, and excuse for lounging around all day which occupies the ground floor of Number Seven, The Street, Mollydish. It is winter in the West Highlands, and customers are few enough even when the summer sun strokes touristic necks into bubbling cauldrons of purple flesh, only for the cooling evening to bring giant midges capable of driving the Special Air Services – who frequently practise living rough in the hills behind Mollydish – into a whimpering madness of itching. There are bats in the eaves of Number Seven, and I encourage them as much as I can. They are the only creatures whose staple diet is midges. They are, as far as

I am concerned, God's little rodents, bless 'em. I did think of trying to tame a couple and train them to hang from one or other of my physical appendages as I paraded out of a summer evening, perhaps to the Incomers, the public bar of the Mollydish Hotel. Midge-free, bat-protected, I would sink a couple of pints in unbitten peace and comfort while all around, batless drouths would splash stout on their lumpy features. However, our local representative of the Royal Scottish Society for the Prevention of Cruelty to Alsatians and Pit Bull Terriers said the bats might suffer. I use Old Spice aftershave instead. And smoke.

The tinkling stops. Someone is inside the shop, examining my PVC-bound collected Reader's Digest *Abridged Complete Dickens* in three volumes, my Biggles books (bestsellers, especially to German tourists), my vintage *Beano* annuals and bound *Spiderman* comics. Not to mention the dozens of absurd books by the English travellers who have patronised Scotland over the past 300 years. They're the real tourist sellers. Tourists like precedents for their patronising. Though it's fun, sometimes, to tell some sheltering browser that the hardback of Dick Francis's *Dead Cert* in the locked, glass-fronted cupboard is £1,000. A tad steep for holiday diversion.

It is 11.00 a.m., a Tuesday, and I am, fortunately if somewhat approximately, dressed. I leap down the narrow stairs, peering through the join in the curtains which guard the shop from my sordid personal habits, such as raspberry-jam-and-vinegar-crisp sandwiches. The unmarried bookseller. The weirdo who plays the guitar at midnight and scares the sheep. Me. It's icy. The potential customer has brought the frosty, dull-bright chill of the shifting morning into my already cold shop. I decide to dislike him. That doesn't turn out to be difficult.

It is not a tourist. Of youthful middle age, male, Gore-Texed for the winter, booted by Scarpa, socked by some elderly granny with shaky hands, this is a creature bent on something more or less than leisure. A small, expensive rucksack bobbles on his shoulders. He is thin, very tall and crew-cut. Even his moustache. He reeks fitness and soldiering. In his non-combatant clothes he invisibly wriggles, a Dobermann pinscher with a stick-on poodle cut. 'Yes, Colonel,' I say, loudly and insolently, as has been my wont when dealing with people whose souls wear uniforms. He looks up, startled. I smile inwardly. I have startled an SAS man, some secretive would-be defender of democracy who's not sup-posed to admit who or what he is. He grins.

'Hallo there! Wrong rank, old chap. Major Blenheim, it is, Major, of the Royal Greenjacketed Fusiliers Highland-Lowlanders. I'm looking for some pornography, actually. Anything in stock in that line?' It is my turn to look startled. I pull aside the velveteen curtains and walk into the shop.

'Pornography? No, I'm afraid I don't, although you may find the odd Jacqueline Susann or Nancy Friday in the paperback bin by the door.' I fold my arms and look disapprovingly at his gormlessly hardened face, like Stan Laurel's set in granite and then hit with jaggy, solid metal things, frequently and powerfully. The essential stupidity is still there, impossible to discipline or batter out. He winks at me.

'Oh come on, old chap. Must have a back shop with some interesting bits and pieces. Come on, it's for the lads, for Queen and country, in a manner of speaking. I have to inspire leadership, you see. Dole out some fleshly delights up on the moors, along with the orders and the Bovril.' I look at him, my jaw dropping. Do they do this kind of thing in Northern Ireland? Right, chaps, just off to sort out Paddy, so watch out for bombs, and by the way, here's a copy of last month's *Playboy*. You've got five minutes, so packs off, trousers down, wrists, ten-SHUN! Get ready for possible death. Jolly good show. Surely not.

'No, I'm sorry.' I shake my head, sorrowfully. 'The garage has one or two videos, *Emanuelle in Aldershot*, that kind of thing. But I'm fresh out of masturbatory aids.' He looks momentarily crestfallen.

'Damn. Now I suppose I'll have to make up a few stories for them.' Is he winding me up? If he's joking, he's clearly a few steaks short of a mad cow, or vice versa. 'Actually, I was only joking,' he says, not smiling. 'I'll take this.' And so, for £10, pretty extortionate actually, even for the hardback, I sell him *Biggles of 266*, with its manly bonding and stiff upper lips and Sopwith Camels. He leaves smartly, without small talk, and I realise he hadn't been joking at all, that he'd really been looking for some wank-inducing literature with big pictures, for the delectation of 'his boys', who were probably making his life a living hell for him out on whatever grim, plain-clothes exercise he and 'his boys' were engaged in. 'His boys.' Sex as leadership aid. Sex as winter warmer on the Highland hills. I shake my head in disbelief. On a Tuesday morning in winter, it's all a bit hard to take.

Back upstairs I make myself coffee with my one-and-a-half-cup cafetiere: frustration, either too much or not enough. In the corner sits the red guitar, my pride, my joy, my hope, my dream, my comfort. It is a 1962 Fender Stratocaster, red. It is old, battered, with the original finish worn through to the wood in numerous places. But I keep it polished, and its remaining redness over-whelms the room. It is a cheap, garish sort of red, redolent of fairgrounds and the leatherette seats of big American cars, of the tops of ballpoint pens, of cheap PVC book bindings, candied chocolate drops, seaside rock, Chinese toy rockets. It is a red of cheap ecstasy. Hendrix playing 'Voodoo Chile' with his teeth. Suddenly shadowed, it is cheap and tawdry and deceitful, like Hendrix's stupid, needless death.

But this is not a cheap guitar. On the contrary, it is very valuable indeed. Leo Fender later sold his company to CBS, and the quality of guitars plummeted. The pick-ups were wound with cheap copper, the wood was unseasoned. Then Fender became Japanese, and nothing was ever the same again. Leo Fender, just before he died, formed a new company called G&L (Good and Loud) and was allowed to put, in tiny letters, 'by Leo Fender' on the head stock. But they looked like cheap copies of the original Stratocasters and Telecasters, and then he died. My red Strat was Leo at the peak of his abilities.

I have an old Fender amplifier, a Twin Reverb, all ragged silverised cloth, torn plastic and a big, red neon pilot light. The guitar lies against it, connected by a curly lead. The strings glisten in the bright, hollow winter light from outside. In this strange morning of mad or foolish soldiers, Biggles and pornography, it is an antique combination. A dead dream, a picture of someone else's past, not mine.

I play the red guitar. In public, too. In Mollydish, the taste is for country music, and I'm happy to oblige. I love country of a certain kind. It is the only adult popular music where raw emotion can be expressed without irony, without deceit. I hate these post-modern bastards like Lyle Lovett who take the piss out of it. So it's sentimental. So what? Life is sentimental. The straight-faced sneering of art-college dickheads in cowboy hats is a blasphemy, for this is a holy music. When Hank Williams sings 'My Son calls Another Man Daddy' I am distraught. The catch in Tammy Wynette's throat during 'Stand By Your Man' reduces me to quivering jelly in the same way as a Charlie Parker solo or Hendrix's incendiary, soul-immolating version of 'Johnny B Good, Be Bad, Be Dead'. You might imagine that Mollydish, being a West Highland village, would be a repository of Gaelic and its musical culture. Mollydish, after all, is named from the Gaelic for South Beach, the curved, south-facing shore which adjoins the tumbledown, stony pier, doom to many an expensive yacht's paintwork, and kept in rocky disarray deliberately for that very reason. Mol a' Deas. The South Beach. There are daft stories about a former clan chief having an affair with an Irish princess called Molly (whoever heard of a princess called Molly?) and her galley being intercepted by a rival clan who cut off her head and sent it to the chief on a silver platter, it coming ashore here, where there had always been a landing. A nice tale for the tourists. Complete bollocks.

There is Nigel Mhor, Big Nige the English piper. He parades up and down the beach on Saturday nights sometimes, depending on the state of the tide and his blood alcohol, playing 'The Dark Island' incessantly. In the summer tourists stand, their slack-jawed camcorders gaping, as Nige, all red beard and beer muscle, dressed in a kilt of Ancient Douglas tartan (Lowland, of course) leaves Doc Marten footprints on the sand and fills up his bagpipes with alcoholic spittle until, finally, they expire in a tubercular gurgle and he is forced to accept a drink from one of his watching fans. Sometimes he is whisked away to a romantic camper van or tented tryst by some lissome female traveller, seduced by his hirsute knees and liquid skirl. But he rarely mutters more than a few guttural sweet-and-sour nothings in very bad cod-Gaelic. If he said too much his Essex wide-boy accent might become noticeable, even to a foreigner. He's a refugee from Big Bang burn-out on the currency futures market, now engaged in total immersion Scottishness with all the energy and commitment which made him half a millionaire by the time he was 28. He has a half-converted crofthouse and an old Lada Riva four-wheel-drive, and is much liked. Contrary to West Highland reputation, incomers are generally welcomed in Mollydish, even English ones, so long as they lack that receding-chin arrogance which hallmarks the Range-Rover-Vogue-quilted-waistcoat type of would-be laird. 'It's the gene pool,' Grey Donald, a retired sea captain now installed semi-permanently on a stool at the Incomer's confided to me one howling January night. 'There is a need for continual replenishment.' And with that he glanced pointedly down at his empty glass.

The Incomers on a Friday is the regular residency for the band I play in. We're called the Seven Seals, a reference not to the Revelation of St John but a bad-taste in-joke about Pete the bass player, a salmon farmer who was reported to the RSSPCA for shooting a seal with a crossbow. Seals – prone to treating fish farms as fast-food establishments – are not regarded by fish farmers as cuddly creatures one should be environmentally friendly towards. Pete once had to be talked out of throwing dynamite on to Selkie's Shore in order to deal at a stroke with about 50 pups and their mothers. However, he was later seen by a bird-watcher from Larkhall blasting off sealwards with his trusty twelve-bore, a bottle of vodka at his side. The shot-scarred body of a seal was later discovered by a horrified family of five from Scunthorpe. The RSSPCA inspector from Inverness, Mr Gillespie, had bought Pete a pint and quietly warned him that unlicensed shooting other than around his own salmon cages with explicit permission would in future be dealt with by the police. Pete had remained morosely silent until the inspector departed, then turned to the assembled eavesdroppers and announced, 'Good job he didn't hear about the other six. I got them on the shore and swapped them with they Faroese fishermen that were in for a case of vodka. Shitty stuff, though. Under fuckin' strength. That last one was only for sport.' He supped at his pint. 'They eat them in Faroe, you know. Taste like well-hung beef.' So we called the band the Seven Seals.

We're a covers group, basically. Favourites and crowd-pleasers, from Smokey Robinson to Springsteen, but quality. Songs, real songs, and with an inevitable bias towards country. Real country, Waylon and Willie and Hank and Johnny, and maybe the odd obscurity, like Jerry Reed's 'Mister Whizz' or even, if we're all really drunk, something like the Louvin Brothers 'Hoping That You're Hoping'. Pete can play pretty well, but he and Calum, drummer, obsessive collector of blues records (we do a mean version of Robert Johnson's paen to impotence, 'Stones in my Passway', which most of our Mollydish fans think is about a landslide on the Inverness road) can turn out a passable harmony whine. I sing and play guitar. Well enough to please me, and our local following, or forbearing and sozzled tourists.

Calum is a man of almost complete silence, in the normal run of things, brought to guttural Glaswegian life only by the compulsion to share his latest mail-order acquisition from the Washboard Willie or Muddy Waters back catalogue with people who appreciate such things. Nobody knows much about him, other than that he lives alone in an immaculate renovated crofthouse and smokes a great deal of dope, which can leave him either grinning and giggling like a daftie, or as slurred and comatose as a Grateful Dead fan. It was, inevitably, in the pub that he and Pete and myself discovered each other's musical bent, while the three of us were jointly floundering in a sea of whisky and heavy beer, somewhere between Christmas and Hogmanay. We'd all kept it very quiet that we had instruments, played. Drunkenly, we made the discovery that each of us was a secret dream warrior; each of us harboured adolescent fantasies in the solid form of guitar, bass and drums, and in private would indulge our memories and our trashed or trashy dreams, as favourite records played.

Pete, the only native of Mollydish, had three children and a dour Hebridean wife called Ina. We practised in one of his outhouses, Calum dampening his tiny, Charlie Watts drum kit at Ina's guttural insistence. 'You'll kill the hens and scare the children.' There we forged a workmanlike noise out of stumbling techniques, different musical loves and divergent memories. Pete was into country, pure and simple. Calum's blues obsession and my more eclectic passions were thrown into a pot which was laced with newer pop songs and a few Scottish country dance tunes for ceilidhs. We enjoy ourselves.

And there are moments. Moments when everything falls into a magical cohesion, when the emotional thrill of songs like Tom Waits's 'Jersey Girl' arrives as if newly minted into the little bar in the West Highlands, when the dream and the glory and the drink and the memories and the music all flash together and then fade away. Afterwards we pack away the gear, leaving it in the pub to collect the next day, once somebody's sober enough to drive. But I always take the red guitar home, secure in its plush case, vibrating in the night with the tunes and chords it has produced, sometimes sullen with mistakes made. Guitars remember.

The tinkle from downstairs, but this time followed by the tramp of heavy boots through the shop and the worrying creak and slight splinter of the stairs. 'Anyone at home? My God, you're not still in bed, you useless pile of dogfish scales. Hide your stash, I'm coming in.' Big Seamus, the good policeman, is in his usual bluff and hearty mood. He doesn't believe my claims to being an ex-user of the divine dope. Nearly everyone else in Mollydish under the age of 50 has a couple of cannabis plants for recreation or hospitality, or a connection in Inverness or Dingwall. He happily turns a half-shut eye to such goings-on. And I am able to indulge in safe OPD consumption: Other People's Drugs.

'Good Morning, Seamus Mhor.' I stop gazing stupidly at the red guitar and rise to welcome the vast man and his eye-poppingly tight uniform. 'A cup of tea?'

'Ah well, I wouldn't say no, now, no I would not.' He crunches into the sofa, whipping off his hat to reveal a shaved head which makes him look like Alexei Sayle on the scale of an American football player run to cheeseburger junkiedom. I rumble among pots and pans for clean mugs, and flick on the kettle, hoping there's enough water to avoid melting the element. Ah, the laziness of the lonesome male householder.

'It's cold, Seamus.'

'Cold? Ach, this is not cold. I remember when the wool was frozen stiff on the sheep, so that when one fell over it snapped off like china. God, I remember the sea being frozen 30 feet out from shore, and men fishing off the edge and catching fish by the ton. And the deer came down off the hill for warmth, and something made them run on to the shore and on to the ice, and Jesus but didn't they fall like lemmings into the sea, thrashing about and screaming like children until the cold got them. My, the men were out there with ropes, pulling them in as fast as they could, but Michael the Snapper from up the glen fell in and died of a heart-attack. He was only just 80, as well. But there was venison in every house for a long time afterwards.' Seamus lights a Capstan Full Strength and sucks like a suspect bilge pump, his lungs making liquid, crackling noises. I put a teabag in his mug and half fill it with water, then add four teaspoonfuls of white sugar and a little milk. I leave the teabag in before handing it to him. He is a man who appreciates tea you could use for preserving fence posts.

'Aye, those were the days, right enough Seamus. Thank God we don't get winters like that so often.'

'We're due one, though. Then the climbers'll be tumbling off the hills like bloody sky divers, only their only parachutes'll be their bloody heads. And I'll be picking up the pieces and mailing them off to their bloody sweethearts.' Seamus, his smoke-savaged chest notwithstanding, can walk the ankles off any superfit climber and loves the hills. Despite his apparently callous scorn for walkers, he takes each death personally, and like every other mountain lover I've ever known, would go to hell and back if there was word someone was in trouble. There is a pause. We both nod wisely at the floor, as Seamus thoughtfully stubs out his cigarette on the piece of cold toast I've inadvertently left on the arm of the sofa. At last, he decides to come to the point of his visit.

'Had a call from Inverness the morn.' Fagless, he glances up at my woodchipped, emulsioned and artistically cobwebbed ceiling, looks down, clasps his massive hands together and rhythmically rubs them, producing the sound of two lumberjacks manually sawing up a redwood. 'Aye, some Inspector laddie in the control room. Seems a poor fella from Craig Dunain got out two nights ago, stole one of the nurses' wallets. And his car. And his jacket too.' He pauses, hesitates, then swoops into a pocket for another cigarette. Leaking smoke happily, like an old kitchen range, he continues. 'A male nurse, I should say. Then I got another call, this time from Loch Whingerach, up the road there. Polis there, Jimmy MacAllister, found the car early this morning, parked in the Forestry Commission carpark, all the doors lying open.'

I look at Seamus. All I can think of is my pornography-seeking SAS officer, clearly some kind of psychopathic schizophrenic paranoid murdering weirdo. He has undoubtedly slaughtered godfearing families in their beds and very possibly eaten them, sautéd with garlic and Bisto, while reading a Thomas Harris novel. I have clearly had a very narrow escape. I cough an intended firm and decisive cough which comes out sounding tremulous and terrified. 'I had this guy in this morning. Said he was army and looked it. Said he wanted to buy dirty books for his men and ended up paying a tenner for a Biggles.' Is it too early for a drink? 'Fancy a wee nip, Seamus? I've got some Irish whiskey here, triple distilled. Doesn't do you as much harm as the cratur.' His eyebrows twitch assent. 'My guy was in hillwalking gear, though. Where would he have got that from?' Seamus takes his glass of Bushmills reverently.

'Ah well, it seems this is not just a complete doughball of a madman, if you catch my drift. An educated man. Educated enough, anyway, to use the nurse's credit card to buy himself some expensive stuff at yon poncy climbing shop.' Here Seamus pauses for a snort of contempt. All his unofficial clothes are purchased from a cavernous Inverness warehouse called Highland Industrial Supplies, a wondrous repository of such items as Dickies American Work Trousers (a pair of which, in point of fact, I am wearing myself. Of all trousers in the world, they are the most flattering to male waistflab), hobnailed, steel-toe-capped boots, thermal underwear and insulated fluorescent boiler suits. Not to mention cement mixers, compressors, scaffolding and all the general accoutrements of motorway or skyscraper construction.

'Seamus, is this guy, emm, in any way . . . dangerous?' The big policeman's eyebrows knit together in a solid band reminiscent of a very bad storm sweeping from the Atlantic. 'Well, that depends. The reason I came to you first was the books. He's a bit of a danger to books. He used to be a librarian, it seems, and one day the region had a complaint from someone, that a book had been defaced. Anyway, this chap, whose name is Freuch, a damn strange name I think you'll agree, Freuch, it sounds like a sudden vomit, he was suspended, and they found that bits had been cut out of hundreds of books. And you know this?' I know. 'It was all the dirty bits! My God, some of them, bloody hell, there couldn't have been much left!' I'm wondering what Mr Freuch could have done with *The Joy of Sex*, just as an example, but Seamus is telling me. 'The thing was, when they looked around his house, where he lived on his own, by himself of course, they found all the bits he'd cut out, pasted to the walls. Apparently some of the rooms were just wallpapered from top to bottom.' It seemed, by the sound of it, that Mr Freuch was also acquainted with the life and works of one Joe Orton, bibliopath extraordinaire.

'He wasn't violent, then?'

'Och, no, not in the least. Well, just to books. And even then, some might say the books deserved it. It was only the smut he took out, though he obviously wanted to put it to some kind of personal use, you might say.' Hmm. It crosses my mind that books ought to be innocent until proven guilty, but I say nothing. I am biased, as they're my business, and must be protected against marauding vandals such as Mr Freuch, sick though he may be. It seems I was not at risk of being sliced up; my stock was.

Seamus has his notebook out. When was Freuch in the shop? What did he look like? What is *Biggles of 266* about? Which direction did he go in? I shrug what answers I can, the morning dram blunting both memory and wakefulness. Or maybe it's sugar dumping from that Weetabix I had for breakfast. Anyway, having shambled Seamus off the premises I feel a need to slump into my one good armchair and sleep. As I get older, excitement tends to affect me like that. I wonder if politicians are the same. Obviously not, or there would be far fewer wars, disputes and confrontations. *Prime Minister, the Norwegians have just invaded the Shetland Isles, claiming the puffins are being poisoned by waste from Dounreay and starved by greedy fishermen who are murdering millions of defenceless sandeels, their staple diet . . . Oh really, Secretary of State for Plankton Affairs? God, that's so terrible I may sleep for a week. Wake me up if they go home.*

But politicians fall asleep all the time during boring, flatulent, nonsensical speeches, as televised parliament reveals. Perhaps, in their case and mine, it is neither the Weetabix nor the excitement, but the drink. I slouch down into the old 1930s armchair, which had to be de-bugged last year, and within seconds I am dreaming of Biggles, who is bombing Germany with old copies of *Hustler*, dropped from an SE5a with skilful aplomb, or aplombful skill.

The phone wakes me. It is an old 1950s Bakelite receiver with a metal dial, and its ring is like one of those black Wolseley police cars you see in Edgar Wallace Presents films, hurtling through the streets in pursuit of decent villains in pork-pie hats. Wotcher guv, it's a fair cop. It's Seamus. Could I come up to Small Trees as soon as I can? I pull on a jumper and my scarred motorbike jacket and set off, locking the door behind me against book slashers.

Small Trees is a patch of old Caledonian pine forest, naturally reseeded over the centuries, full of gnarled and stunted trees whose ancestors were evidently too gnarled and stunted for chopping down, like nearly all the rest of the Highlands' great forest was. Now Small Trees crouches above Mollydish, surrounded by towering Forestry Commission plastic Sitka in serried rows. The icy mist has cleared, but the low cloud is glowering down on the small group I come across. Seamus, Mary MacCalman the doctor and Mr Freuch. He is still wearing his expensive anorak, cords and boots. The boots, however, are swinging about two inches off the ground, and his neck is attached to one of the twisted old pines by a loop of multicoloured climbing rope. He has cut just enough for the job in hand. Lying next to his small rucksack is a top-of-the-range Swiss Army knife and the rest of the rope, coiled neatly. And *Biggles of 266*.

'Can you lift him?' Mary, the lovely Mary, who spurns we local men, most of whom would die for her in a minute, although not in a Freuch-like fashion. Instead, she socialises with us in a pleasant but distant way, occasionally vanishing off to her native Aberdeen and sometimes coming back with a man in tow. The last one had a shaved head, no visible means of support and claimed to be a sculptor. We were certain he was simply after an easy life as a doctor's wife, but it was difficult to have a personal discussion about such things with someone you knew was going to have to examine your piles. We sighed and shook our heads. She is a good doctor. Seamus and I lift the cool, but not icy Mr Freuch enough for Mary to slip his head out from the noose. His face is bloated and blackened, his tongue poking out idiotically. He is clearly dead. Mary comes to the same conclusion. 'Ach well,' says Seamus. 'Ach well.' He can't think of anything else to say. Seamus has the softest heart of any policeman I've ever met. He hates death. He hates it personally, perhaps because he can feel it creeping up on him, every time that liquid scratching comes up through his chest. Before he forces it back down again with another Capstan.

Mary does whatever doctors do with dead people. I pick up *Biggles of 266*, and flick through it. Nothing appears to be missing. It is, in fact, a good book, some say a great one. Some say it is filthy warmongering crap, unsuitable for kids. Morons. It communicates the innocence and horror and enormous thrill of the Great War, and of youth and flying and death. It was the first irreligious book I ever read on my own, a gift from my favourite uncle, wild, down-on-the-floor-with-the-weans Uncle Phil who had backslidden from the Brethren and eventually slid so far he

24

slithered right out of our lives. He always seemed so happy, so bubbly, so smiley . . . of course, he was drunk. And then he was gone. But not before giving me that one literary present. Maybe it was Mr Freuch's first book too, and that is why he bought it to die with. There is no sex in it. Nothing dirty, save the vastness, the gross waste of the death it carefully avoids dwelling on. It is, after all, a book for children. Had I a son, I would send him that book, I think.

Born Again

Fuck it, fuck it, fuck it. Oh Christ, save me, forgive me, preserve my soul, save me from the devil, from these thoughts, Christ, fuck you, save me, fuck it, fuck her, fuck me, save me. Save me.

I was converted, became a Christian, was delivered, born again, saved, sanctified, plucked as a fiery brand from hell, because I did not want the terrible vengeance which God took on the crew-cut Technicolor sinners of the Billy Graham film *Hometown, USA* to be wreaked upon me. Cancer stalked Billy Graham films, God's own judgmental or grace-endowing tumour, killing some courageous Christian as a witness to others or because *Lord, she was just so full of Light you decided to call her to Your Own Side. Heaven was where she belonged, amen.* And later there was *The Restless Song*, where 1950s teenagers, members of a church choir, were nearly but not quite seduced by the evil, throbbing – and, it was spelled out, African – rhythms of rock'n'roll. This film, shown like all the others in flickering, chattering 16mm at a badly blacked-out Bittermouth Gospel Hall, was lurid beyond the expectations of even a late 1960s Ayrshire Brethren congregation, which for such evangelistic extravaganzas turned out in geriatric force, all shining, hairless pates and naphthalene overcoats. And that was just the women.

The Restless Song had music aimed at impressing weedy, prissy, 1950s American youth with its weediness and prissiness. ('Like an angry rushing tide . . . The Restless Song.') In the movie, the big, bad beat of rock, symbolised by a totally evil transistor radio, polluted the minds and inflamed the genitals of two choir members to such an extent that, well, it was made quite clear that they had Known each other in a truly Biblical Sense, and I don't mean holding hands on the way home from the Youth Fellowship. The girl had a backstreet abortion, no less (this, like the actual sex, was not shown, although the abortionist, a cross between Eva Braun and Dame Edna Everage, was), and, courtesy of a very angry God indeed, promptly bled to death in a toilet. Unfortunately, as I was only 11 at the time, I didn't understand much, if any, of this at all, especially the wave of shock which passed around the already-tense Gospel Hall when the girl announced that she was pregnant. There was a splash of horrified tutting in the darkness, accompanied by giggles from the Sinners, a group of young tough guys and gals from the street corners of Bittermouth, bribed in by promises of free (hey, dig that hip street jive, man) 'Coke, crisps and conversation' afterwards. I thought this was a piece of comedy, news of babies in my experience always being greeted with laughter and rejoicing. Not wanting to appear childish – I'd been given special dispensation to come to this frightening adult film, as I'd just been born again courtesy of *Hometown, USA* and God was clearly working on me through the medium of celluloid – I laughed loud and long, slapping my little hairless thighs beneath my horrid C&A suit trousers. 'That was really funny, dad, wasn't it, that bit where she said she was having a baby?' We were driving home afterwards.

'No, it was not funny. It was one of the most tragic things I have ever heard in my life,' the man replied. I was confused, and slightly hurt. How could having a baby be bad? And why had the girl been lying in a pool of blood in the toilet? Had somebody shot her? It took years for me to piece together the plot of that film, which would be hailed nowadays as a kitsch masterpiece. At the end, the choir re-united, including the back-from-backsliding pregnant-getter, repentant and forgiven, but almost certainly with his willie cut off and hung out to mummify somewhere. The song they joyfully warbled has remained with me. 'Gone are the restless songs/ Happily we belong/ Red white and blue we wear/ Witnessing everywhere . . .'

I was, of course, already Of The Lord by the time I saw *The Restless Song. Hometown, USA* had hit me where it hurt, with its lingering use of the death of a mother, and children weeping and then more deaths and all the family at-risk-ness little boys are most susceptible to at 11. I wept, too. I howled. And later that night, in bed, I prayed for Jesus to come into my heart, and the man and woman, tearful and smiling, brought me my hot orange and homeopathic shock pills. It was such an important moment, I didn't even have to brush my teeth for the second time after drinking the orange juice. I remember feeling strange. The man had told me that the reason I was feeling bad was because I was scared of death and hell and if I took Jesus as my personal saviour,

I would never have to be scared again. And so I prayed along with him that little prayer, and felt a great weight of fear lifting off me. And lo, the man and the woman were pleased. The fear went. 'Now you'll have to witness,' the man said. 'Once you become a Christian, you have to tell people.' A twinge of a different fear stirred, down among the orange juice. It was a fear which would grow and grow for 17 years, like a cancer, a huge tumour of terror, or a mutant foetus, and eventually it had to be hacked out of me, bit by bleeding bit. Along with my faith. That was when I was born again. Again.

At eight, still deep in the mire of sin, I used to accompany the man on his winter post-Sunday-lunch evangelistic duties, as part of the team of 'young men' who, attired in good, solid Brethren Harris Tweed, would knock on doors in the housing schemes of Bittermouth and its surrounding villages, spreading the bad news about sin and death and damnation. For me it was a carefree jaunt in the world of adults, holding a huge bundle of small leaflets bearing headlines such as HE THOUGHT THE BUS WOULD STOP (it didn't, and ran him over before he had a chance to confess his sins and experience rebirth) or, in the case of creakily 'modern' examples, STOP THE WORLD or THE ROCK THAT DOESN'T ROLL. The man was always restrained, polite, kindly; a ring at the doorbell, and some bleary Sunday afternoon face would appear. A leaflet and a smile would be proferred, then an invitation to the gospel meeting. I would be standing nearby, clutching my bundle of Good News, small and innocent, a heart-string-tugging visual aid for The Message: Unless Ye Become as Little Child, Ye Shall Never Enter the Kingdom of Heaven. It went on, winter after winter, until at last I asked the man why I couldn't go and engage in the actual business of witnessing at the door, representing the Brethren. After all, I had a small version of his Harris Tweed coat. I knew what to say.

'You haven't professed Christ,' he said, rather awkwardly. 'You're not a Christian yet. When you're a Christian, you can witness; not before.' I couldn't believe it. Or rather, I did, and after *Hometown, USA* I was delivered, tearfully, into the Kingdom of God and solo Sunday doorknocking.

Oh Lord help me love this, like this, love you. Stop this bastard fucking bastard fucking bastard hatred of everything, the words, the words, Christ, don't let the devil, Christ . . .

In the summers, doorstep witnessing was replaced with open-air seafront services. The summer Sunday School was held next to the Bittermouth putting-green, behind a white canvas wind-break which, on gusty Firth of Clyde days, would sometimes

28

uproot itself, scattering the clutch of formally suited adults, all stiff black trilbies and funeral bonnets, into the passing throng of semi-naked, ice-cream-licking holidaymakers down from Glasgow for the day. The Sunday School, with its free sweeties, Flannel-graph Bible stories, object lessons and red-faced bonhomie from the Superintendent – whose never-to-be-joked-about name was Mr Smellie, pronounced Smiley, at least officially – usually attracted some sand-and-sewage-coated kids and their embar-rassed or drunken and guilt-ridden parents. There were prizes for any children who would come and recite a Bible verse, or sing a song, accompanied by Arnold, a tall and spotty youth who sat like a fleshy scarecrow at a tiny portable organ, scrawny limbs poking from his too-tight suit, pumping furiously at the pedals with his feet and squeezing out thin notes which the seagulls and the gritty breezes mocked perpetually. And I was a star.

Beautifully turned out by my adoring mother, like all the other little Brethren boys and girls, I was primed to perform. Not only was there a prospect of instant reward – usually boiled sweeties and an illustrated cardboard text – but there was the smiling appreciation of my parents and their friends, and sometimes surreptitious bribery from old women afterwards. If either of my two grannies happened to be present, a spot at the open-air Sunday School could become seriously lucrative.

I would climb up on the little portable platform, puff out my pigeon chest and belt them out, those choruses of instant, utterly satisfying faith. Some were triumphant assertions of fundamental Biblical infallibility:

> Romans ten and nine
> Is a favourite verse of mine
> Confessing Christ as Lord,
> I am saved by grace divine
> Now hear the words of promise
> In golden letters shine
> Romans, ten and nine!

Of course, you can't hear golden letters shining, except in the most mystical, St John-ish sort of way – but I was hardly caring much about such contradictions. Besides, there were so many alternatives. Real favourites which revealed, scientifically, the true location of heaven:

> Somewhere in outer space
> God has prepared a place

For those who trust Him and obey, hey
Jesus will come again
And though we don't know when
The countdown's getting lower every day
Ten and nine, eight and seven, six and five and four
Call upon the saviour while you may
Three and two, coming through
The clouds in bright array
The countdown's getting lower every day.

'And that Russian cosmonaut,' screamed Mr Smellie into the buffeting breeze, a tinny battery Tannoy system rendering him distinctly squawky, 'that Soviet pilot, product of an evil and godless regime, when he came down from his first orbiting of the earth, do you know what he said: I did not see God. I have been to the heavens, and I did not see God. And he laughed, brethren and sistern. He laughed. Let me tell you, when Mr Gagarin does meet his maker, what will he say to the Great Creator of heaven and earth and all within it? He will say: I see thee now, oh Lord, forgive me. But it will be TOO LATE! Let us now sing "Store Your Treasures in the Bank of Heaven". . .'

But my favourite was the cheeky, truly child-like triumphalism of one jingle, which danced along to a Sally Army adaptation of a brass-band rhumba:

One, two, three
The devil's after me
Four, five, six
He's always throwing bricks
Seven, eight, nine
He misses every time
Hallelujah, hallelujah, amen.

Nine, eight, seven
I'm on my way to heaven
Six, five, four
I'm knocking at the door
Three, two, one
The devil's on the run
Hallelujah, hallelujah, amen.

It was simple, easy, sunny summer's day stuff to please parents and relatives and the adults I was brought up with. Within the confines of the Brethren, I was a carefree child, naughty, physical, occasionally lifting the flip-up seats in the Gospel Hall just before one of our winter Sunday School teachers sat down, or belting out a chorus wrongly and without fear or guilt ('Up from the grave He arose/ With a mighty cold upon his nose'). But at 11, I was brought face to face with my sin, the dreadful evil which had infected my life from birth, and was converted, and began to live the life of the called disciple. So it was that as an 11-year-old born again believer, I fell in love with the red guitar, that dank night in Kilmarnock. But there were no red guitars, the man said, in heaven. Prayer and Bible study didn't help much, though I did take some comfort from King David. He had, without any doubt at all, played on a harp, and there was no indication in the Old Testament of its colour.

To be honest, the Bittermouth Assembly was liberal, as things went in Brethren circles. My mother and father had grown up amid the dark, satanic steel mills of central Lanarkshire, in a place where the red and grey sandstone tenements and roughcast council villas were uniformly soot-encrusted. The rotten-egg smell of pit bings; the great towering orange and black mounds of old industry, the huge, tottering, already-obsolete edifices of steel production. In the midst of it all huddled the town of Bogesbrae.

This was where the Brethren had rooted itself, in the industrial revolution's heartland, offering not just spiritual consolation and escape from the soul-breaking hardship of mine and mill, but intellectual stimulus and discipline, a social structure and an alternative to either radical politics or radical drinking. Fundamentalist, democratic, with each small gathering of saved souls responsible for its own government, the Brethren evangelised on street corners in a dourly determined way, the gospel brought outdoors to the drunks on a Bogesbrae Saturday night. The shouting, pleading man would be no stranger to the reeling refugees from pub glory; neither would his silent, neatly dressed supporters, standing behind him like a poised rugby forward line ready to chase a kick, with one or two flankers handing out tracts. On Monday morning, they'd be together in pit or foundry or furnace, where the grace of God had to be worked out by the Chosen in full, constant view of hard, cynical men. But the Brethren were often the hardest of them all, plucked as brands from the burning bowels of hell. A fiery, pulsating, all-too-familiar industrial hell. These had been real sinners. Big men with battered faces and misshapen hands, who, squeezed into Sunday suits, would preach at Bittermouth evening meetings, and come for tea to our house. Although each assembly was independent, there were informal, invisible networks through which preachers would be approved and praised. Small, badly printed magazines, united in a never-fully-stated theology, signified a tentative unity which could nevertheless explode into spiritual civil war at any moment. In some towns there were three or four different gospel halls, splintered from the original one, sometimes due to a division on belief (was sinless perfectionism possible?), practice (should Christians vote?) or personalities (I abhor thee, brother, because . . . I just do).

Women were not allowed to speak, either preaching the gospel or worshipping at the weekly 'morning meetings', simple communion services where ordinary bread would be broken and ordinary – if usually fortified – wine would be ceremoniously sipped by the universally teetotal brethren and sistern. Any male could take part in the morning meetings, by giving out a hymn from the approved *Believers' Hymn Book*, praying, reading a passage of scripture or sharing a word from the Lord. Women, who had to wear hats 'to disguise their beauty from the angels' (because, I learned, the angels had once been tempted by the charms of women to come to earth and have a wingless fling or two) sat mute, their responsibility to shush the children and ponder the roasting joint in the oven at home.

In such communities, men educated themselves or were taught by other brethren, just as the early socialists organised in small groups to educate, agitate, organise. Indeed, there had been a cross-fertilisation between religion and politics in the early twentieth century; that had faded, though, with the Brethren entrenched, largely, in a put-away-the-things-of-the-flesh-and-the-world kind of attitude, which included activities such as striking. The Brethren's model of industrial relations came from St Paul's teaching on how slaves should regard their Roman masters. It was educate, organise, pray and obey.

Bittermouth was one step and one generation on from classical industrial Brethrenism, though. That Christian drive for education and advancement took my father into lucrative chiropody and away from the steeltown environment. The assembly in Bittermouth was clearly different from the pure, driven simplicity of Bogesbrae. It had an organ, an 'American'; a pedal harmonium.

Music was important in the Brethren, but regarded with intense suspicion. On grannyvisits to the Gospel Hall in Bogesbrae, gas-heated and tin-roofed as it was, the singing was led by one old, gravel-voiced man. No piano, no organ. At Bittermouth, there was a piano and a harmonium, slightly out of tune with each other so that the effect of both played together was oddly bagpipish. And yet, in both Bogesbrae grannyhouses there were harmoniums which took up entire walls, all polished dark wood, mirrors and little crenelated spires, turrets and shelves containing bits of china. Singing hymns and choruses was a favourite social activity, but the only time a keyboard would be allowed in the Gospel Hall was for a wedding, when strong men would lift a home organ into the hall for the day, then remove it before Sunday called for the simplicity and purity of worship without distraction.

Organs and pianos had been spiritually rehabilitated by the 1960s in Bittermouth. Guitars were something else again. They reeked of dancehalls and the devil. And as for a red guitar . . . red, I knew, was the colour of the devil and hell, fiery and bright. I once heard a Glaswegian gospel speaker refer humorously to the Pope one night over tea as 'Old Redsocks'. I knew the Pope only from the frightening pictures of him in St Bartholomew's Roman Catholic Primary School, where my class from the Protestant Bittermouth Primary had once been decanted after a heating failure in our own building. The entire class was silent and terrified all day in St Bart's, where huge black-and-white nuns fluttered in the corridors and blood-dripping crucifixes adorned the walls.

But red was also the colour of the Vauxhall Cresta my father not-very-secretly coveted, the one belonging to our next-door neighbour, a dentist. Red was for fire engines, safety and rescue. Red was post boxes and telephone kiosks, and children's toys. Red was cheery and alive. We had a red aluminium tea pot. Red cola was my mother's favourite drink. So red, surely, was not all bad.

Eleven, born again, and expected to witness. To tell of my great joy in Christ, my all-consuming love for the Saviour. Oh, the pain of that, going to secondary school for the first time, playing rugby and being a Christian, doing schoolwork and being a Christian, having friends and being a Christian. 'I can't do that because . . .' Being born again brought so much shame. The mocking, the grinning . . . And so I kept it not secret, but quiet. Like some dreadful illness. Of course, it came out.

'Why can't you play football on a Sunday?'

And I would say it. 'Because I go to . . . to church.'

'You don't go to church. You go to the GOSPEL HALL!'

I would cringe, but internally know that this cringing was good, because I was witnessing, I was being a fool for Christ when I ran away from the boys with their dirty pictures. Somehow, they would see Christ in me and wow, they'd be so impressed that suddenly they'd be converted. How I longed for the most popular people in the class to be saved, so that I wouldn't be alone . . .

Long before, at primary school, having just moved to the middle-class seaside milieu of Bittermouth from grimy Lanarkshire, I'd been alone, different, outcast. And then, fuelled by the DC Thomson comics my parents allowed, along with the somewhat more uplifting *Eagle*, I lied my way into a limited acceptance. My father was a secret agent, I confided in one or two of my more gullible schoolmates. Somehow, I persuaded them it was true. A whole fantasy world was built up, with my father as a god, the master spy, and me as his secret-agent son. One boy, Stephen, became my disciple, and together we patrolled the golf-course bunkers for bombs and hid in gorse bushes, examining golfers for suspicious radio transmitters in their bags.

But I was still an outcast from the tough local Ayrshire boys, because I had been sent previously to a small private prep school in a big house outside Bogesbrae, run by a nasty, moustachioed little woman called Miss Fish, who had specially made plastic belts which the other three teachers were allowed to use, on five-year-olds. She reserved the privilege of meting out punishment with a brutal black leather taws herself. I was initially so terrified by all this I used to shit my pants to get sent home, but gradually grew, among the nice, privileged little boys, into a coper, a survivor, even a minor-league playground big shot. Then we moved to Bittermouth, where the sprawling primary school was full of large, threatening, confident, tough boys. I was the stranger, the weirdo, the soft kid from a clearly almost posh background, picked on and pushed around. So I became a secret agent.

Inevitably, I was found out. Stephen and I were being harassed by a fat playtime hoodlum called Alex.

'Fucking bastards,' he spat. (I had to ask the man what this meant, pronouncing it as 'fockin pastor', which I loosely imagined had something to do with a kind of minister who preached at the almost acceptably Christian Baptist churches. 'Those are bad words,' he said. 'Never, ever say them.' I couldn't understand why Baptist ministers were called something so awful.)

'Just don't take any notice,' I told Stephen. Alex would go away and then I would disclose his awful status as a Russian agent, whose father was the Bittermouth representative of the KGB, and that my father was shortly to kill him with a new death ray he had invented in the secret experiments he conducted behind his chiropodist's shop.

Alex did go away, but unfortunately he later cornered Stephen when he was on his own. Stephen, an innocent wee army brat from the camp along the road, an outcast too for his English accent, bragged that he, Alex, had better watch out. All was known. His father's cover was blown. A death ray would soon beam from the chiropodist's and blast him into nothingness. And his evil dad. He knew this because my father, the secret agent, had told me everything. Because I was a secret agent too. And Stephen was an assistant secret agent. Alex laughed and laughed and laughed.

One day he gathered a crowd of his chums and other extraneous classmates, and they corralled Stephen and I in the bike sheds. 'Ah ya fuckin' secret fuckin' agent' (push, jostle, spit) 'go on, then, show us yer fuckin' gun, yer radio. Go on, then, go on.' I tried to stare stonily and mysteriously beyond the crowd, to the world I longed to believe existed. But the verbal and physical buffeting continued. Stephen started to cry, as everyone laughed and made pistol-firing noises (peeeoooww!), and I tried to keep staring above and away from it all, hoping against hope that the bell would ring. Alex grabbed me, shoved me to the ground, rubbing my face in the dirt of the bike shed. 'Go on, say it, say it was all fuckin' lies, wasn't it? Just fuckin' lies. Fuckin' spy, fuckin' secret agent. Fuck off!' Thump. 'Fuck off!' Thump. 'Fuck OFF!' Scrape, grind, thump. The torture seemed to last for hours, the breathless grinding into the dirt, the price of escape the admission that I'd made it all up, that there was nothing special about me, that the man was a foot doctor who treated corns and smelliness and other foul toenail things in a shop near the harbour. I began to sob, the total confession. No secret agent would ever cry.

'Let me up, let me up . . .' and at last the blessed bell went, the jeering crowd dissipating like seagulls frightened away from the end of a sewage pipe. I staggered to my feet, aching and gulping and snot-streaked with dirty tears.

Fuck them Christ, fuck them, destroy them, the bastards, pastors, kill them, rip their arms off, their eyes out . . . no, no, stop these thoughts, stop these thoughts, let me love them, love them, forgive them . . .

I was late for the class, having desperately splashed cold water on my face to get rid of the dirt and, more important, the signs of weeping. The tears, the snot and spittle. The physical wounds were light, a reddening, a few scrapes. I walked into the sniggering world of that big classroom, face burning, to be whiplashed with icy anger by Miss MacMirrin, a ramrodded, grey woman whose entire face had been hauled into vicious immobility by the drawing of her hair back into the hardest, tightest bun imaginable. She looked like she was in the process of being mummified alive.

'Sit down, boy. I do NOT want to hear your excuses. Class!

Stop that disgusting chortling.' I stumbled to my desk. Stephen, my immediate neighbour, would not look at me.

Later, at dinner time, he turned once to face me, his face stony with contempt. 'So it was all a lie?' I looked at him, misery flooding every atom of my body. I nodded. He shouldered his schoolbag and left, running down the corridor to catch up with Alex and his band of laughing, carefree, well-adjusted truth-tellers. I followed slowly, alone in a world without consolation, without friendly death rays, without a father who was more than a chiropodist; without salvation.

At 11, I had salvation, and as I grew up, I became wiser and more wary. There were accommodations to be made with the world, and gradually I found that if you kept your Christianity reasonably quiet, if you were good at things other kids respected, like, in my case, by the age of 12 being bigger than anybody else and sometimes funny, you could get by. And I had other Brethren pals, too, by that time, including Joseph, who brought a real guitar into my life.

Joseph was not, it had to be admitted, pure-bred Brethren. His parents, Mr and Mrs Merryweather, were originally from the dangerously liberal Baptist Church, but Bittermouth's had recently closed, and the congregation had split itself more or less equally between the Gospel Hall and the Kirk, with a few tongue-speaking weirdos heading for the Elim Pentecostal Church, where, the stories went, adults frothed at the mouth, rolled about the floor and took all their clothes off. As my now-long-left-behind teacher Miss MacMirrin was a member, this was very hard to believe. Maybe there she loosened her bun, and her whole face sprang back into human form. It seemed unlikely.

Anyway, Joseph's apparently laid-back parents had bought him a cheap, nylon-stringed acoustic guitar, one devoid of redness and all it had meant to me that cold Kilmarnock night. Bereft as I was of worldly television (although Joseph was able to watch *Top of the Pops* and other intensely evil examples of fleshliness in action) and of rock records ('You'll never bring a Roy Orbison record into this house,' my father once declared, after I casually dropped the Big O's name into a tea-time conversation as being quite possibly a good singer, although I was just being smart, because I had no idea what he sounded like) I had heard the Beatles on the radio and listened to my parents' shocked horror about the Rolling Stones. At Joseph's house, I would often stay for tea on a Thursday night, there to savour the mysteries of Pan's People and the tinny beat of bad bands and worse singers. It all seemed from another planet, and nothing to do with my life.

Although I knew that the red guitar was a piece of equipment necessary to the production of those sounds on the radio and TV, it seemed quite divorced from them. Everything televisual in those days was black and white, of course, and the red guitar remained in glowing, glinting larger-than-life loveliness, a sign somehow of things I hadn't yet discovered. Mystery, suspense, yearning and joy were in the mental picture I had of the Rapier. Of course, I'd been back to the shop many a time, but it had long since disappeared, and the guitars in stock were shabby creams and cheap sprayed sunburst and poor plywood imitations of what I would later recognise as the only great guitars: American ones. Joseph's guitar was not great; it had been made in Poland and rattled under full power-chord attack. But it existed, was within my grasp, was touchable. Real.

Out There, beyond the Bittermouth Brethren, beyond even the glamorous rumours of what went on at Glasgow Baptist churches, Christianity was, it seemed, embracing the guitar. Joseph had books of hymns with guitar chords, records of country musicians singing gospel songs. He would painfully strum along with things like the Cowboy Church Sunday School's speeded-up Pinky and Perkyisms, encouraged by his parents as they dandled his little sister, Sarah, from knee to knee. Joseph was suffused with embarrassment at these performances. Although born again, he longed to strum his Cs, Fs and G7s along with the groups and singers he saw on television. He was, I now realise, a long way in front of me in the growing-up stakes. Yet he would sit there and scratch along with that awesome record:

> If you don't go to Sunday School
> You'll grow up to be bad
> You'll never know just what you missed
> And someday wish you had
> If you want to someday see the Lord
> You'd better start today
> The ones who miss the Sunday School
> Are on the downward way
> So
> Go the highways, tell 'em on the byways,
> Tell 'em, that you're their friend
> Tell 'em, the church is open, they're welcome to come in
> Talk just a little bit, sing just a little bit
> Throw 'em a smile or two
> Go heavy on the how-de-do
> For the Lord is counting on you.

Oh Christ forgive me for not witnessing (fuck you, you little bastard,
you're not a Christian or you wouldn't have words like this going through
your mind, you little cunt). Christ, stop this, stop this (fuck). Get the
devil out, away from me, oh Jesus . . .

Joseph's mum and dad would clap, his sister would squeal, and
Joseph would squirm. 'Up in Glasgow, at the Kingston Baptist
Church there, they have gospel rock bands,' he told me once.
'That's what I should be playing, not this stupid kids' stuff.' He
showed me a duplicated sheet of Christianised pop songs, with
simple guitar chords. 'She Loves You' had become 'He (i.e. God)
Loves You'; 'I Wanna Hold Your Hand' had metamorphosed into
'God Wants to Hold Your Hand', and even the salivating 'Come
On', Chuck Berry via the Stones, had been redeemed into 'Come
On (For Christ is Calling)'. This was impressive stuff.

I told the man and woman that the Merryweathers were
planning a trip to Glasgow for a gospel rally at the Kingston
Baptist Church. This was essentially a social event for believers,
offering members of different churches a chance to get together
and enjoy themselves guiltlessly under the grace of the gospel.
Music was always a big part of these things, which had been
called, as far as I was concerned, 'sworries' when I was growing
up. I was in third-year French before I realised the word had been
'soirées'. The man was flourishing in the professional classes of
Bittermouth by this time, and sluggish winds of change were
blowing through the Bittermouth Gospel Hall. The youngish,
better-off members were beginning to feel slightly ashamed of the
Brethren's slightly ridiculous image, the apparent necessity of
continually and publicly being a fool for Christ. It was a social
liability, the Gospel Hall, and there were even murmurings of a
name change, to the Bittermouth Evangelical Church. The woman
had begun gently pointing out that my education could suffer
through not having a television to watch natural-history programmes on. Anything which propounded evolution could be
switched off, she argued. I was studying biology at school and
convoluted, illogical Brethren books on creationism were being
pressed on me by elders and my concerned father. 'You just need
to look at a foot, at the wonders of the ankle and the toes. One
look, and you know only a Creator God could have designed it,'
he would say, shaking his head. He would not deny that evolution took place within a species, he said, but not from one species
to another. Monkeys could not become men. Except in the case of
some pop-music groups, like those Rolling Stones, he wondered
whether men were actually becoming monkeys, ha ha ha. 'When
you come down to it,' he would say, 'it's as if you were walking

along a deserted beach, and lying on the sand you find a watch. You pick it up, and inside you see this incredibly complex set of mechanical workings. What do you conclude from that? You conclude that somebody else has been there before you. And that somebody knows how to make this thing, because you do not.'

The long and short of it was that yes, I could go with Joseph to Glasgow. I didn't tell them, although surreptitious inter-parent phone calls to Mr and Mrs Merryweather probably had, that among the ministries represented at the rally was the Christian 'popular-music band', the Cornerstones.

And the Cornerstones changed everything. In the huge, packed Baptist Church, a preacher with a strong Ulster accent grinned a toothful, face-splitting grin, shouted a godly greeting, and prayed as if God was conducting an audition for effective interventionists in the affairs of men. He prayed for everything, from the Queen to 'each and every loyal member of our glorious armed forces'. We sang bouncy hymns, with a piano vamping furiously and somebody playing a big, inaudible, acoustic guitar. But Joseph and I were watching the huge black amplifiers, their red pilot lights shining, which stood mute behind the preacher; he conducted each hymn, his teeth flashing among the old wood and brass of the big church, the black amplifiers waiting at his back. During the prayers, you could hear a subdued, unearthly humming, and a tiny rattle from the blue spangled drum kit which inexorably drew every eye in its glorious, trashy worldliness. It was no good denying it. Drum kits could not be anything but sinful. They reeked of dancehalls and Too Much of a Good Time.

The Cornerstones came on at last. No applause, as this was a Christian event where the glory had to be given strictly to God alone. They carried their guitars, the three young men in identical blue polo necks and halfway long hair, while the drummer, also in a polo neck but somehow more rumpled than the others, slid in behind his kit. All three guitars – bass and two six-strings – were red, and they shone out from the front of that church like beacons.

They played. Nothing had prepared me for the awesome volume of it. At least 30 members of the audience left at once, including a little old lady who was weeping and wailing as if she'd just found out that Christ had come back to take his saints to heaven and inadvertently left her to a mad world where churches were taken over by hooligan rock'n'roll bands. Truth to tell, it was probably not loud at all, but few Christians had ever experienced anything like this. The bass drum pummelled our chest cavities, making our whole bodies vibrate. The guitars clanged like some huge industrial process, and the singing, absolutely indecipherable, was unearthly, raw, animalistic.

Joseph and I sat stunned, along with at least half of those remaining in the church. Joseph's mum and dad gaped with strained smiles on their faces, and I noticed Mrs Merryweather desperately crushing up paper hankies and stuffing them in her ears. I began to smile, uncontrollably, as the hairs on the back of my neck rose and a strange sensation grew in my stomach and groin. The band stopped, then played another song, announcing the swirling, echoing racket (no doubt rendered opaque by the booming acoustics of the venerable building) as 'Christ is Coming'. They were about halfway through it when the Irish preacher ran on to the platform, waving his arms at the Cornerstones, clearly upset. The group stopped playing, and in the silence, the preacher grabbed a microphone and began to pray. 'Dear God,' he intoned, like the echo of a tomb, 'we thank thee for the enthusiasm of these young men, and pray that you will bless their ministry, and give them sensitivity and grace in their endeavour to communicate thy wondrous gospel to the youth of today . . .' There was more, and then he opened his eyes, dismissed the awkwardly shuffling Cornerstones, said 'amen' and preached his sermon, which even at 12 I realised was the most ridiculous thing I'd ever heard. It was based on the story of the Good Samaritan, which, according to the Irish preacher, proved that Christ would return in the year 2000.

'How many pence did the Samaritan give to the innkeeper to look after the injured man? Brethren and sistern, he gave him TWO pence. Now, in the time of the New Testament, a penny was a day's wages, so that was a lot of money, oh yes. A lot of money. But the Bible says that a day is a thousand years in the sight of the Lord. And we can take from that that the year 2000 is the year that Christ will return to gather His saints from every part of this planet. There will be a meeting in the air, and aeroplane pilots will be taken and their aircraft will crash, mothers will be taken and their sons left, bus drivers will disappear and their passengers will scream and scream but there will be NOTHING! NOTHING! Nothing they can do. IT WILL BE TOO LATE FOR THEM!'

Joseph's parents took us out before the end. We drove to a nearby fish-and-chip shop, and as we sat in the car, snug in the hot, holy smell of vinegar and grease, Mrs Merryweather pleaded with me not to tell my parents about the Irish preacher.

'I don't know about Kingston Baptist Church,' she said fretfully. 'That man was just a little . . . more than a wee bit just not what you would call . . . and that group! That noise! No wonder he stopped them playing. You couldn't hear yourself think. And I can't get this paper tissue out of my ears, at all.'

In the end, Mrs Merryweather had to go to the doctor about the tissue jammed in her ears, and then for an operation at Kilmarnock Infirmary for the treatment of an abscessed eardrum. She became permanently deaf in one ear because of the Cornerstones. I told my parents nothing, but pleaded for a guitar, so that I could develop a modern way of witnessing for the Lord. For my 13th birthday, I got one, a plain, laminated, spruce-top Eko acoustic steel string, made in Italy, it appeared, to withstand nuclear attack. I had an instruction book by someone incredibly ugly called, Bert Weedon called *Play in a Day*. It took three weeks to learn 'Bobby Shaftoe's Gone to Sea', but after that there was no stopping me, as with God's help, and methylated spirit to harden my throbbing fingers, I learned to play hymns and choruses by the dozen.

When Joseph was 14, he left school to begin an engineering apprenticeship, and we kind of lost touch. Although we were the same age, he was a working man, and I was a mere schoolboy. At 16 he sold his guitar to buy a Triumph Tiger Cub motorcycle, and quickly backslid from belief, as motorcyclists inevitably do. Years later, I heard it whispered that the Irish preacher had been hospitalised, before making an almost complete recovery, losing his faith, falling into alcoholism and then becoming a club comedian in the north of England. I could swear I glimpsed him on an edition of *Opportunity Knocks* I saw once, silently flickering from a TV-shop window. But maybe not. When I was 15, and Bittermouth Gospel Hall was running a special youth mission in a marquee down by the shore, the Cornerstones came to play a special evangelistic rally. There were only three of them this time. They had shorter hair, and were dressed neatly but casually, with no attempt at uniformity. The blue polo necks and red guitars had long gone. So had the drummer. They sang close-harmony ditties which everyone over the age of 30 thought was wonderful, youth-orientated missionpop. Afterwards, I spoke to the lead singer, and asked him about that night in Kingston Baptist Church.

'Oh yes,' he laughed, embarrassed in recollection. 'Basically it was the same songs we do now, except the drummer was very loud, and we had electric guitars then, and big amplifiers, because we had to be louder than the drummer, Ronnie, who's now completely fallen away from the Lord.' He shook his head and pursed his lips. 'My pastor' (he was a Baptist, but the Bittermouth Assembly was loosening up, slightly) 'believes that drums are of the devil, and I think he might be right. Look at the jungle, at the cannibals, at the druids and their human sacrifices. Drums are for dancing, and you know what they say about dancing?' Actually I didn't. What was Ronnie the drummer doing now, I wondered? 'I think he's in insurance in the Greenock area,' said the singer, after some thought. 'I'm an accountant myself. What field are you planning to go into?' He just managed to avoid adding a horribly patronising 'when you grow up'.

I was 15, but I already had plans. Big ones. Holy ones. 'I want to be an evangelist,' I said, 'a musical one. I want to use rock music to communicate the gospel to young people.' The singer looked at me.

'Well,' he said. 'Steer clear of drummers. Drummers could be your downfall. Drummers and God don't mix, mark my words. That beat could lead more than your feet astray. Trust in the Lord and remember' – he gripped my shoulder fraternally – 'if your feet are on the Rock, and your name is on the Roll of those who have eternal life, then that is all the rock'n'roll anyone needs.' I smiled, shook his hand, and left. I was sure he was wrong about drummers. I loved God. But I loved the big beat too. I didn't tell him it was all his fault, or rather Ronnie the drummer's fault. After all, Ronnie was now a backslider, and I wanted to be a soul-winner. Maybe I would one day be instrumental in bringing Ronnie back from his life of sin to the Lord, and together we would find a way of playing holy drums, and he would join my band in our worldwide mission to inspire and convert the young. It was possible. With God, the Bible said, all things were possible.

> Climb, climb up Sunshine Mountain
> Heavenly breezes blow
> Climb, climb up Sunshine Mountain
> Faces all aglow
> Turn, turn your back on doubting
> Look up to the sky
> Climb, climb up Sunshine Mountain
> You and I

Stop this, Jesus, stop this. Stop these thoughts about girls and all this sweaty thinking about legs, thighs, breasts, Christ, forgive me, stop it, forgive me, fuck shit cunt fuck shit cunt fuck fuck fuck . . . STOP IT! FORGIVE ME! CLEANSE ME! Cleanse me, Jesus. Make me pure.

Animals

Question: what do you call a sheep stuck in a fence on the Isle of Lewis? Answer: a leisure centre.

Oh no, not the sheep jokes. Here, we are beyond sheep jokes. In Mollydish, sheep, each with its government subsidy attached, are gods and goddesses, virtually valueless in terms of wool and mutton, but with an invisible cash dividend adhering to them, at least on paper or in the depths of a computer's hard disc. And the ones which don't really exist out there on the hill, which only lurk as pixels or pen-strokes in an official list, are every bit as valuable. Yet the bestiality does happen.

Over the hill in Corrylocken, always a dubious and immoral place admittedly, if the remaining natives of Mollydish are to be believed in their lip-pursing, head-shaking, hiss-sucking disapproval, there was the case of the horse. A horse called, in point of fact, Roger, which seemed so crazily appropriate one could only laugh. Roger was old enough to know better, really, and tall enough to make things difficult. But for a widowed farm labourer called Aloysius Smith, the height difference was not a problem. It was lust at first sight.

No, I know it's not really funny. Poor old bastard, lonely, frustrated . . . and just unfortunate that he should one night fall off the Black and Decker Workmate at the first fence, so to speak, breaking both ankles and knocking himself out cold. The only reason the local policeman found him was because his midnight groaning frightened the living nightlights out of a passing drunk, who thought some drink demon had come for him. He had staggered into the police house, dragged out the constable and, indeed, the noise of anguish had echoed weirdly along the road. Traced to Smith's mean little stable, the noise was found to be emanating from a trouserless Aloysius, lying in agony on the stone floor while Roger's hin'end towered massively over the embarrassing scene in all its accusatory glory. He was taken to hospital, plastered and bandaged, but even there the giggles and behind-hand comments were ward-wide. He was formally charged with having illicit relations with an animal, namely Roger, who never complained once, it was claimed in the Dingwall court by a snorting legal-aid grabber. The Sheriff could hardly pass sentence for coughing away his suppressed laughter, but eventually imposed a fine and suspended jail term. Aloysius had already moved away from Corrylocken, to Glasgow some said, or Caithness. People had been perfectly civil to him on his return from hospital, hobbling on clumpy white casts and with crutches. It was just the way they kept making *kick-kock* horsey noises when his back was turned; and some of the boys shouting 'Trigger!' after him was perhaps a bit cruel. Roger was sold, probably to grace the plates of French or Belgian carnivores in the end. He was not a young horse, and Aloysius had almost certainly been his final fling.

But sheep. Now it must be said that personal attachments to sheep can develop, particularly when the rigours of lambing lead to some skittery orphan black-face being brought into the kitchen for bottle-feeding next to the Rayburn. Sometimes these delightful young things grow to be 'caddie' lambs, actually young and large and energetic sheep which shit all over the garden and expect human attention morning, noon and night. All very well and good, you might say. But sometimes things can get a little out of hand.

I was in the Incomers one Thursday night with Pete, talking about rap music and hi-energy and the new dance tracks we had just heard on *Top of the Pops*, which we both still watched religiously, as backslidden adherents. We had concluded that there is a wondrous freedom, as middle-aged music fans, reared on rock, on its secret pleasures, on its impotent rebellion against adulthood, once you admit that most modern pop music is crap. And a lot of it is crap, it really is. Once you stop trying desperately to stave off ageing by pretending to love all the talentless drivel, you cast off the burden of self-deception and can begin to live comfortably with yourself. At least, that's the conclusion we had come to after four pints of Murphy's each.

Then Fergus came in. Fergus Mandelson, 17-year-old son of white settler neo-crofters Christina and Montague, bleached-out, dessicated ex-hippies who'd made a pile in computing and then sold out their home-counties scatter-cushion lifestyle to buy a croft, sheep, goats ('only tinkers and English keep goats,' say the Mollydishians), hens and, in the loft, a veritable flock of computers. Telecrofting, Montague called it, but really all he and Christina had been looking for, I often thought, was a place they could grow plenty of grass and get stoned with impunity. They had a suspicious Gro-Tunnel behind their house and two enormous long-haired Alsatian dogs which, though generally friendly, didn't look as if they bore uniforms gladly. Why is it that computer-whizz adults are often dopeheads? It's not that they need to escape from their green or paper-white screens, because all they ever want to talk about is computers anyway. Is it because computers, once you stop using them as tools and they become ends in themselves, only use up one lobe of the brain, or one set of nerve-strands, and everything else has to be kind of damped down in case it explodes from sheer boredom, or fizzles into a blackened mess of radiation-fried cells? I know not.

Fergus wasn't thick; he wasn't Albert Einstein either. But, good for him, he hated computers, had suffered the classic allergic reaction to parental influence and become very interested in the crofting lifestyle, especially sheep. This boy had studied sheep in detail and depth. He was fascinated by the North Country Cheviot, the sheep brought in during the nineteenth century to replace the cleared crofters, and would bore anyone who'd listen on their genetically engineered qualities. He had a crew-cut and rode everywhere on a Honda Big Red all-terrain quad bike, which had a special wooden platform on the back for his sheepdog, Gandalf. The dog had been named by his mother, after the program she and Monty had written some ten years previously to control the operations of all the sewage-treatment plants in the Western Water Authority region, and which had been copyrighted worldwide, making their fortune. The puppy's early incontinence had amused Christina greatly. 'It's all a load of shit, darling,' she would trill, merrily. 'Money is shit, and in our case, it's a load of shit, ha ha ha ha . . .' They were white settlers of what Pete called the 'yoooaaawwwt' category. 'Yoooaaawwwt' was the aural equivalent of UAWWT, loosely standing for Up Against the Wall With Them.

But Fergus was all right. He had been drinking in the pub since he was 15, as per common Mollydish, not to say Highland, practice, and had developed a taste for sweet black and tans with accompanying dark rum, a combination which occasionally led to Gandalf the sheepdog having a very unsteady ride back to the crofthouse.

'How's it going, Fergus?' Pete raised his half-empty glass of Murphy's to the lad, who was ruggedly inhabiting a worn biker's jacket and a Megadeth T-shirt. Gandalf lay silently at his feet. I hate well-trained sheepdogs. They're like snakes. Hairy snakes with four legs and big, nasty mouths.

Fergus mumbled into his pint glass, the dark rum gripped tightly in his other hand. 'All right.' There was silence for three rums, three black and tans, and two more pints of Murphy's.

'How's it goin', Fergus?' It was my voice, although it seemed to be coming from somewhere else. Somewhere nearby, like the Tennents Special pump. I tried again, wondering idly if I'd accidentally developed some hitherto undiscovered skill in ventriloquism.

'All right.' Fergus had slumped slightly forward on to drooping elbows. He turned to look at Pete and me. There was no one else in the bar, and Algernon had gone upstairs to feed his parrots, Keith and Floyd. He had removed them from the bar the night a severely inebriated punter had threatened to bite their heads off, Freddie Starr style, if they didn't stop shrieking 'ARSE-nal! UP the Gunners', their only attempts at human communication. Afterwards, I was informed that the said severely inebriated person had in fact been myself, which I found hard to believe, until Algernon refused to serve me the next evening. I suffered a week's barring, until it was realised that a significant portion of winter profits was liable to disappear along with me and my permanently parched throat, not to mention the availability of cheap live music, should I be prevented from entering the Incomers. But Keith and Floyd were removed to a place of safety.

Algernon. Our landlord. Algernon Douglas. He named his parrots after his hero and role model, but actually he's about as wild and crazy as John Major on a valium drip. About 45, with baldingly long grey hair in a scrappy pony tail, an accent which sounds like the Dick Van Dyke imitation cockney in *Mary Poppins* – which he claims is genuine – and, omnipresent and horrifying, a kilt in Ancient Douglas tartan. 'Oi'm proud of me 'ayeland 'eritage,' he is wont to proclaim, chewing each word and spitting it out like half-digested cow-cud. Nobody has told him that Douglas is a Lowland clan. Actually, Big Nige sold him one of his spare kilts. He was invalided out of the Fire Service in London after falling off a burning ship into the River Thames and nearly dying of blood poisoning. 'Oi banged me nut orf the 'ull and split it awopen,' he will tell you, several times a year. 'It's not waoowter you ken,' (this is his proud attempt to integrate cultur-ally by the use of slang Scotticisms) 'it's blaaauudy virus syrup, innit?' He loves Keith Floyd and insists on providing innocent tourists with bad imitations of dishes the Cook with the Marinated Brains has demonstrated on telly. No local will eat them.

Suddenly Fergus pulled himself upright, and turned to fix Pete and me with the kind of unblinking stare it takes large quantities of rum and stout and heavy beer to perfect. 'Orf,' he said, quite out of the blue, in his almost perfect local accent, were it not for the stretched and twisted vowel sounds which signify his parenthood. 'Orf.' Pete and I remained silent, somewhat shocked. Had the power of speech been so damaged as to remove the 'fuck' from an imprecation aimed at getting us to leave, and showing at least a little dislike? No, both of us had always been on good terms with Fergus, and had done nothing to upset him or Gandalf since their arrival at the Incomers. Gandalf twitched at his master's feet and gave a small whinny of disquiet. 'It's orf,' said Fergus again. What was he saying? Piss off? 'It's a case of orf,' he shouted at last. 'She says it'll go away eventually, but Christ, I don't know . . . how did I get it, for fuck's sake. I've got to tell you, I have not been shagging any sheep. I have not. No way!' His eyes were full of drink and fear and pleading, and I stepped forward, eliciting a warning grumble from Gandalf.

'Come on Fergus, come and sit down over here and you can tell us about it.' I was slurring and stumbling, but my heart was in the right place. Roughly.

My foot wasn't, though. As my Doc Marten AirWair Commando sole connected with Gandalf's tail, he yowled like a werewolf and snapped for my inner thigh, his jaws closing with a heavy click a millimetre or so from my crotch. I staggered backwards, while Fergus shook his head.

'That's right. Might as well. Bite it off. Bite it off. It's no fucking use, no use for anything.' He looked at me as I examined my Wranglers for small tears and bloodstains, just in case I had anaesthetised myself too much to feel a castration. 'Mine, that is. Useless. Orf.' Then he shouted at Gandalf: 'Sit, you bastard. Bloody hungry bastard'll eat bloody anything. But you've bloody had your dinner, you bastard.' Dear God, what did the dog have for its meals: reconstituted genitals? Had it developed a taste for testicles?

'Hold on,' said Pete, and with a manoeuvre which, had he been sober, would have been deft, it was born of so much practice, he reached behind the bar and poured himself a fresh pint. He also whisked a Pepperami, one of those spicy, dried Italian sausage things, out from the gantry and threw it to Gandalf, who swallowed it, wrapping and all, in two chomps. I rubbed my thighs together uneasily. It took a while for the Murphy's to settle, and then I thought I'd better have one too, and then Algernon came down and started shouting the odds, shyly but loudly ('you baaastards better pay for that or . . . else . . .') so we paid up, and Fergus had another rum and sweet black and tan, all the time murmuring to himself, quietly, like a mantra he'd learned from his kaftaned parents: 'Orf. Orf.'

At last, we sat round one of Algernon's home-made antique tables, the base of a treadle sewing-machine with a bit of stained mahogany on top. Pete kept pedalling the remaining works of what had once been some housewife's pride, joy, and possibly living, much to the consternation of Gandalf, who followed the movement of the cogs and wheels and Pete's foot with a glittering and intense stare. 'Better cut that out, Pete,' I said, remembering the snap of those long jaws in the immediate vicinity of my manhood. Slowly, Fergus explained.

'I had this problem, see, sore and red and itchy and sort of scratchy and scaly, and, you know, lumpy. Down there. My dick, for God's sake.' My eyes, and Pete's, both dropped involuntarily to our own frontal zips. Fergus's words had the effect of whatever the opposite of a hard on is, at least on me. It was like coming off a motorbike after three hours fast driving in frost. My willie pulled up its undercarriage and became a negative presence. Talk of scaly, scratchy, sore dicks made every organ in my body flinch and cry, 'No, no, please no more, not me.' But Fergus wanted to tell someone. Nothing was going to stop him. 'I went to see Doctor MacCalman, Doctor Mary, and Jesus I was shitting myself, going to a woman with something like this, but I was just beside myself. And it was getting sorer and sorer, and peeing was a problem, and it was sort of like athlete's foot, only it was my fuckin' dick, man.' I looked at Pete. His mouth was hanging open, and both his hands lay motionless on the table. His Murphy's lay untouched. As for me, I was feeling distinctly queasy. This was not the kind of thing you expected to hear when out for a quiet binge. It was not the kind of thing a man did, was describe his willie in public, especially one which was certainly not likely to pass any kind of genital MOT in the near future, by the sound of things. And it was not what you expected of Fergus, with his heavy-metal T-shirt and crew-cut and his quad and his sheepdog. But then I thought, wait a minute. This is male bonding, this is Iron John, round the campfire, bear each other's burdens stuff. This is fuck-feminism-brothers-together, a problem shared is a problem solved. I felt quite emotional, and reached out to grasp Fergus's shoulder in a friendly and supportive fashion. He lurched back as though I'd tried to kiss him, and Gandalf bared his yellow teeth at me in a blast of foetid dog-breath.

'On you go, then Fergus.' I was trying to work out, drunkenly, a way of saying 'and by the way, don't worry, I'm not a poof' and eventually struck on a slaveringly lascivious comment about our good doctor's undoubted physical attributes. This fell quite flat. Mary was clearly some kind of divinity to Fergus following his recent medical experiences.

'You mustn't tell anyone, for God's sake, not a bloody soul, please . . .' Fergus looked at us imploringly, but in his heart of hearts, he surely must have known how ridiculous a request like that was. Such was his desperate need to share this great horror with someone other than the doctor, who was, after all, both a doctor and a woman, that the essence of Mollydish survival, the gossip-protection instinct, had been temporarily clouded. And there was the question of the various rums and various sweet black and tans. Pete and I nodded, our souls' deep sensitivity and understanding and ineffable drunkenness oozing sympathetically from our eyes, going some way towards disguising the spark of salivating curiosity.

Suddenly, a spasm of something that might have been under-standing flitted across Pete's face. 'Orf,' he said. 'Wait a minute. Orf, isn't that . . .'

Fergus nodded, miserably. 'Yes.' He looked away from Pete's stricken gaze as my drinking partner's jaw began to drop, moving slowly at first like a boulder gathering speed, then falling, at least to my eyes, further down his beer-stained Shetland jumper than I'd ever seen it tumble before. I looked curiously inside the gaping maw, with its blackened teeth and mottled, stained flesh, then quickly away.

'What?' I demanded. 'What is it? For God's sake, tell me.' Pete turned his slack-mouthed astonishment in my direction, clacked his jaws shut and muttered. 'Sheep. Fucking sheep.'

'NO! I have NOT!' yelled a suddenly frenzied Fergus. 'I fucking have NOT been fucking sheep.' And quite suddenly he began to weep, while beneath him Gandalf began to howl an earsplitting, bereft sheepdog howl.

'Jesus CHRIST! What's going on over there?' Algernon was clearly rattled. Such obvious male emotion expressed in a High-land bar was virtually unprecedented. Sheepdog grief added a new and disturbing dimension which, frankly, I could understand Algy not particularly liking. Fergus stumbled to his feet, gulping back the sobs while Gandalf continued his imitation of a werewolf. 'I was not. I was not. I was not . . . it was on my hands, it must have been on my hands, and I never even normally look down when I'm having a piss, but a couple of days out on the hill it was bloody windy, and it was just essential or God knows, my trousers . . .' Pete stood up, knocking over his chair, and clapped Fergus on the shoulder.

'Och, never mind, son, I wasn't meaning . . . but even if it was just a wank, Christ, what a way . . .'

'I FUCKIN' DO NOT WANK!' screamed Fergus, while Gandalf's howls grew ever more pervasive. 'Jesus, if I'd been doing that my knob would've fallen off, everybody knows THAT!'

'ALL RIGHT! That's ENOUGH!' Algy was advancing on us in agitation. 'If you bunch of perverts want to talk dirty, you can do it outside my pub. I've never heard the like in all my life. Some bloody sense of humour you bloody Jocks have got. Go on, get out of my sight.' Vanished was the normal attempt at Caledonian inflection. Algy was speaking purest English, and by the way he whipped our glasses away from the table, he was serious too. I wobbled upwards.

'Aw, come on Algy. We're just going over that video, you know, that comedy, what's it called, *The Cliff Richard Experience* . . . Fergus here knows one of the sketches off by heart.' I grinned at Fergus encouragingly. Frankly, I thought I'd done quite well. It wouldn't, after all, do for Algy to think we'd been sitting discussing masturbation and genital diseases over his beer.

'Well, I call it DISGUSTING,' shouted Algy, breathing heavily, as Gandalf reduced his yowling to a subdued whimpering. 'Now get out of this bar, and when you come back, try to keep a clean tongue in your head, or tongues in your heads. OUT!' We shambled out, Gandalf panting emotionally, Fergus sniffing, and me still none the wiser about whatever the hell orf was.

'It's a disease of the sheep's anus,' Pete told me on the phone the following afternoon, by which time I'd sobered up and responded to an English couple who'd angrily insisted on the shop being opened so they could look for 'anything you've got about birds, perferably old and illustrated'. I knew by their contemptuous flicking through the few books I had of that ilk that they were print-hunters, the book-ripping philistines who tear the often hand-coloured illustrations out of Victorian and older books, frame them up and then sell them for small and sometimes quite large fortunes. Heaven forgive me, but when they'd finished, slammed the books down and offered half the marked value for Sir Reginald Fortescue's 1879 *Reed Warblers of the Suffolk Coastline and Other Indigenous Species*, I said quietly that I thought they should fuck off back to planet Zog or England before I lost my temper. I mean, I'm not normally anti-English at all. I welcome the incomer, the so-called white settler, as long as he or she comes in peace and humility and love. But I wasn't feeling very well, and these two were complete wankers.

Wanking was what Pete was phoning me about, or rather Fergus's wanking and his sworn lack of it. The previous night we'd staggered out of the pub and felt that open-air hit of total illness which is the corollary of heavy drinking followed by exposure to the Highland outdoor atmosphere. That atmosphere is usually wet, moving quickly and uncomfortably malicious. In our collective state, everything was, in addition to the wind, tumbling around us in circles. It was bad. Somehow, we made our separate ways home without falling asleep in ditches or hedges and dying of exposure. At least, I did, and Pete had. Fergus had Gandalf to look after him, although even Gandalf couldn't drive the quad, which I had a dim memory of hearing start up with its ragged sputtering roar . . .

'What did you make of that last night, eh?' Pete was in a seventh heaven of gossiping delight, a common Mollydish condition. 'Jesus, orf. I looked it up in a Department of Agriculture health handbook. He was right, it can be transferred through broken skin. Dirty bugger, eh? I mean, he was either shagging the fucking sheep or else having a wee fantasy out by the fank, and God knows what that was about. A wank by the fank. I mean, maybe he's really into Blackfaces or Suffolks rather than Cheviots, and he just decided to use his imagination.' Just then I heard the ambulance's siren, faintly, quite a way up the hill. Stupid having a siren on in this neck of the woods, where everyone knew where an ambulance was an hour before it arrived and besides, the roads were emptier than the Beirut Holiday Inn. But then, maybe the driver from Raigmore had been jammed behind an ignorant tractor, or some magic-mushroom-munching sheep.

I was walking down to Mrs Goodwin's shop to get some milk about an hour later, having sold a copy of *Bagster's Comprehensive Helps to Bible Study* to a holidaying minister, the dog-collar stretch-marks evident around his elongated neck. Dr Mary's Toyota Hi-Lux four-wheel drive was coming along the road, slowly, and I waved, as usual, wondering what the ambulance had been called out for. Not that Mary would tell me. She adhered rigidly to a rule which forbade any discussion of health problems except your own, about which she could be brutally embarrassing if no one else was about. One of the main things which stopped me truly fancying Dr MacCalman was my piles, and the fact that she had once treated them, with her usual cool good humour. Maybe I would get over it eventually, and forget that the person who was theoretically the most fanciable woman in the vicinity had spent some seconds peering up my arse in the interests of science, to my gross and total horror. But God those piles had been sore. 'How's your bum problem?' Dr Mary had once asked me, when we'd met casually on the beach, each out for a walk. Maybe she'd just been playing the doctorly fuck-off card, because I had patted her arm in a companionable way a few times. She certainly had the desired effect, as I bade her a flushed farewell.

But there she was, at the wheel of her Hi-Lux, and white as a washed Merino fleece. She didn't see me, drove straight past without even a nod, an unheard-of occurrence in Mollydish. At Mrs Goodwin's shop, a miniature supermarket with everything from soft pornography through tinned mince to Tilly lanterns on its glinting shelves, Mr Goodwin, like his wife a retired teacher and would-be watercolourist from Sheffield, was behind the till. Mrs Goodwin – nobody knew her first name – was clearly out with the paintbrush. They took it in shifts to produce searingly lurid land- and seascapes which they displayed, clip-framed, in a back corner of the shop they had partitioned off and called the Goodwin Gallery. They sold well in the summer to tourists, and the Goodwins were always trying to get me to stock them. I had apologetically told them that visual art of such contemporary quality would unfortunately be a distraction from the main body of my stock. I had not told them that I hated the crap they produced.

'Sad about young Fergus, eh?' Mr Goodwin mumbled the words as I paid for the milk and a small jar of Nescafé, with the usual extortionate mark-up all local shops in remote areas claim is the consequence of isolation. I froze. I hoped Fergus hadn't crashed comatose into some ditch the previous night, lapsing quickly into his last snooze while Gandalf licked at the frost gathering on his chin . . .

'What happened to him, Mr Goodwin?'

'Oh, I couldn't say, couldn't say. Just heard the ambulance was up at the house, at the croft. His mother found him. Some kind of domestic accident, apparently. I don't know any more. But it's serious, all right.' Pleasurably, he licked his thin lips.

I dropped into the Incomers for a quick restorative hair of the dog, so to speak, but no one there knew any more than Mr Goodwin. In fact it was a long time before the truth came out, and I could understand why a pale and shell-shocked Dr Mary had been oblivious to my waving. Fergus had cut his dick off.

It was Christina, in fact, who told me what had happened, one night when I was up at the Mandelsons trying to fix their stereo, an ageing but ludicrously expensive in its time Linn Sondek turntable with Naim pre- and power-amps and those stupid Quad electrostatic speakers which look like radiators. It all sounded like shit, actually, even on minimalist classical music like Satie, new-age blipandblop brainmelt and the Cocteau Twins: the dope soundtrack which was all they listened to. I had soldered up the speaker connections, while Christina's husband Montague lay in bed, dead to the world, having spent 36 hours solid working on a computer program for the Sullom Voe oil terminal in Shetland, fuelled by copious supplies of herbal tea and an assortment of drugs. I hoped the tanker captains navigating their way into Europe's biggest oil terminal weren't going to suffer any serious mishaps as a result. Some of the Mandelson drugs were a little weird. Anyway, Christina had found Fergus slumped over his four-wheel motorbike, Gandalf barking and yowling. His jeans were dripping blood. She had hauled him into his bedroom and called Dr Mary, who made the awful discovery that about half poor Fergus's rhythm stick had been hacked off, and bandaged tightly with several Elastoplasts, a clean yellow duster and some masking tape.

Not tightly enough. Nothing, apparently, bleeds like chopped penis. Fergus had lost a lot of blood, but was still alive, and after he'd been stabilised, dripped and the hospital in Inverness had said they could not send the air-ambulance helicopter because the health minister was on a visit to the Highlands and had force-landed with the chopper – unfortunate term – in the middle of the Caithness Flow Country, a desperate search for the missing lump of prick began. They turned the place upside-down, but it was, in any case, too late. When I heard this sorry tale, all I could think of was the supposed practice in Thailand of wives dealing with adulterous husbands. Apparently they cut their dearly beloveds' willies off, and then tie the severed sections to ducks, which are encouraged to fly off into the sunset, presumably pursued by the bleeding husbands. The intention is to prevent any remedial surgery which, oddly enough, is quite successful in the area of lost Thai genitals, for some reason that my copy of *Strange and Amazing Facts*, found in a job lot of magazines I bought for the shop, did not go into.

Fergus had been cured, presumably, of his orf, and had recovered from what Christina referred to as 'his little accident'. He had not returned to Mollydish, understandably, as it would have been very difficult not to gaze at his zip out of curiosity, not to mention, when drunk, possibly pass a few comments like the ones which were already being made: *Pass the scissors, Algy, I want to trim my pecker. Hey, do you think I should sand it down with the*

Black and Decker or just rip it out and put a new one in? That sort of thing. It would have been hard to cope with. Some people might have managed, but not Fergus. He had gone off to be a shepherd in the remote Sutherland hills, taking Gandalf with him.

'Apparently he did it with his Swiss Army knife,' sighed Christina, who had been aged and rather shrunken by the whole episode. 'He was always very proud of it. He sharpened it on the electric sharpener in the kitchen.' I wondered if she knew about the orf. I couldn't bear to ask, despite the fact that we were both completely ripped on hash cakes. She laughed. 'Oh Christ, I know you shouldn't laugh, but then . . .' She giggled hopelessly, druggily for several minutes, and so did I. I thought of the mountains of cornflakes I'd end up eating next morning when the post-cannabis munchies took hold, and that made me laugh all the more. At last, tears running down her cheeks, she said: 'Oh God, we looked and looked for it, but we couldn't . . . it was like the parable in the Bible, the widow's mite. Searched all night, found nothing. And I didn't want to ask Fergus, son, look what happened to that, you know, that missing . . . piece? But in the end I did.' She stopped laughing. I bubbled titteringly for a minute, and then fell silent too. There was a pause. We were drinking Barley Water Lucozade, and I took a gulp.

'So what did he say?'

'He said he just threw it down on the floor, and after he'd bandaged himself up, he was going to flush it down the loo, but when he looked for it, it had disappeared.' Quite suddenly, she began to cry, great gushing sobs which shook the entire room. I picked up my soldering iron and left, floating; next morning I woke up knowing exactly what had happened to the missing piece of Fergus's plonker. I hoped he was all right up there in Sutherland, with the sheep, his beloved Cheviots. Now, at least, he was safe from woolly temptation, had that been the source of his orf. At least, I thought so. I didn't like to speculate on the rehabilitated sex life of a man with a self-mutilated dick, especially if it involved mutton on the hoof. I drank a litre of water, ate four bowls of cornflakes with drifts of white sugar, and recalled the snap of Gandalf's jaws that drunken night, the orf night, millimetres from my crotch, and the way that sleekit creature had gulped down the Pepperoni sausage, complete with wrapper.

Bloody sheepdogs. I hate them. They're like snakes. They'll eat anything.

Immersion

'You don't know where babies come out of!' Barry and Stan, who were in my class but certainly not Of the Lord, lived near us in bungalowland, on the outskirts of Bittermouth, where new building for the Glasgow commuters was ripping cheerfully into the old pine woods. They danced backwards in front of me as I trudged home. They jeered and danced and hopped and spun and skipped, and they were right. At ten, I had no idea what orifice babies appeared from, although I knew mothers 'had' them somehow. To be frank, it had never even crossed my mind.

'Of course I know,' I said scornfully. Barry and Stan stopped dead.

'Where, then? Tell us. Go on, tell us where!' I assumed what I hoped was a superior expression and walked determinedly between them. 'You don't know, ya fuckin' baby, ya wee stupid cunt, ya bastard.' Sticks and stones will break my bones, I muttered to myself, hunching my shoulders as they continued to shout after me. 'They come out women's bums!' yelled Barry. Stan laughed loudly and with an artificially adult heartiness.

'Bums!' he shouted eventually. 'Out their bums!' I broke into a trot, in a hurry to get away from these stupid, dirty-mouthed boys. I wasn't shocked. Nothing nasty done by Barry and Stan, with their well-established bad-boy reputations, would have surprised me. But babies out of bums, like giant jobbies? It was so disgusting I simply could not believe such a thing was true.

In fact, I was 17 before I had the technical whys and wherefores of reproduction and birth explained to me, and even then I didn't believe it. It all seemed so clumsy and energetic and involving items of the anatomy which had always necessitated thorough hand-washing after the slightest contact. 'Did you wash your hands?' The woman would look up from her frantic, somewhat

55

wild dishwashing or cooking or hoovering and fix me with a theatrically fierce glare. 'Touch your willie, wash your hands! How many times do I have to tell you! Soap and water!'

The woman, silenced in church by the Brethren's displeasure with those naughty angels who had been seduced by sweet-talking earthwomen back before the Bible, was not naturally quiet. She was half Irish, thin and prone to sudden explosions of emotion, sadness, humour or anger, which would just as soon die away or still into something unexpected and opposite: she could go from grief to giggles in a nanosecond, or vice versa. 'Did you see Mrs McParland's hat! That fruit! I thought we might see a bird of paradise appear any minute! Oh, it was tragic about Bill Flanagan's mother, though. So sudden!' And she'd be solemn, on the verge of tears. She had flyaway red hair, usually packed into a tenuous bun which frequently dissolved down her back like fire, and a strong superstitious streak from which Christ had not been able to rescue her. Rush out of the house and then return because you'd forgotten something, and you had to sit down and count to 20 before leaving again. Mention a recently deceased person's name and salt was hastily found so a handful could be thrown over your shoulder. Every sneeze was blessed, because of the demons which could only rush in and get your soul when you were sneezing; wood was frequently touched, and people with brown eyes much distrusted. She was intensely interested not so much in health foods but in weird health supplements. Dozens of vitamin pills went sliding down my throat, along with over-the-counter homeopathic remedies for every conceivable ailment. When I sat my O-grades, I was made to drink a glass of Sanatogen tonic wine (the added-iron version) before leaving the house, which at 15 left me reeling into exams, reeking of healthy, 36-per-cent-proof confidence. Which very quickly wore off.

Where the man was careful, quiet, unassuming and deter-mined, the woman was emotional, scatterbrained and prone to attacks of helpless giggles if amused, or blind panic if suddenly frightened. Easy to say now that these were culturally conditioned stereotypes. At the time, it was just how things were. 'Fire! Police! Ambulance! Call 999! Now!' she yelled one day in the hallway, flip-flopping at speed through from the lounge in her fluffy carpet slippers. I was, maybe, nine, proud of my telephone prowess, and duly dialled the three digits, as she came haring back, a jam tureen full of water slurping spillage everywhere. By this time I could smell scorched paper and hear the roaring of flames. 'The house is burning down! Oh, Lord help us! Don't tell your father!' Heart jumping in my chest, I gave the operator our address. We needed all three emergency services, I stressed. 'My mother's put the lounge on fire.' I replaced the receiver, and there was a huge splash and a clang as the water, quickly followed by the pot, hit whatever was ablaze. An enormous hissing ensued, and as I reached the door of the lounge, I saw the woman, head held by hands skinned in pink Woolworths rubber gloves, kneeling in what seemed like the gates of hell, surrounded by billowing smoke and steam. The sound of sirens echoed in the distance.

The fire engine, the police car and the ambulance arrived within minutes of each other. Their occupants were big, uniformed men who rang the bell and then waited politely outside for the victims of the emergency to answer the door. Bittermouth was that kind of town. I opened it on two policemen in smart checked caps, very tall, two rumpled ambulancemen clutching a stretcher and apparently eyeing me for wounds and weight, and a helmeted firemaster with a large moustache, oilskin trousers and boots. Small in the midst of their official largeness, I stared, overwhelmed with the enormity of what I had summoned.

'What is it then son? What's wrong?' said one of the policemen, in an unexpectedly high voice.

'She told me to,' I said, immediately attempting to shift the blame, even though I wasn't sure if everything was all right or if the woman had been fatally affected by poisonous gases released from the extinguished blaze, leaving her kneeling in her final moments before a God who was welcoming her home to heavenly peace.

We trudged through to the lounge, the firemaster's wellington boots leaving black marks on the new Bri-Nylon carpet which took the woman (who wasn't, as it turned out, dead) months of scrubbing with 1001 ('Cleans a big, big carpet for less than half a crown!', to remove. I took them into the lounge. The smoke and steam had cleared, and the woman had risen from her previously worshipful or penitential position. There were a few scorch marks on the mantelpiece, and a mixture of water and blackened paper everywhere. When mum saw the two policemen, the firemaster and the eager ambulancemen, she fainted. The ambulancemen pounced with an excited exhalation of air, an exultation. But within a minute she was sitting up, and within five she was boiling the kettle for everyone.

She'd been trying to get the fire going by holding a double sheet of newspaper over the grate, thus creating a draught but also running the risk of setting the paper ablaze. This she had duly done. The man was the expert at fire-lighting, and I'd seen him inadvertently let the draught-encouraging paper catch. I used to love watching the yellow flames roar up behind the sober, muttering headlines of the *Glasgow Herald* or the endless adverts of the even broader broadsheets of the *Bittermouth and Hurtford Gazette*. But if it caught when the man was watching, he simply flicked it into the grate with his foot. The woman's green fluffy carpet slippers were clearly not the right equipment for such a manoeuvre. Cradling delicate china in what seemed like gargantuan hands, the five men soothed her, while I went to answer the doorbell, which was ringing again.

I was met by two junior firemen bearing a large hosepipe, thankfully not turned on, although it dripped, slowly, from the brass collar which pointed directly at my face. Beyond them I could see a dozen neighbours, a mixture of aprons with folded arms and perjink ladies in blue rinses, craning over the fence. I looked at the firemen; one was cratered with acne, his face blue and red, scarred and pimply and hideous. They both looked at me. 'It's all right,' I said to the mouth of the hose. 'She put the fire out. And it was her that started it, not me.' They looked disappointed. Unlike the ambulancemen, they hadn't even had a fainting fit to deal with.

After it was all over, and a trail of curious neighbours reassured that all was well and that it had all been a false alarm, really, the woman shut the door and leaned limply against it, sighing. 'Mum,' I said. 'You've got a black face.' Ash, tears and the hands rubbed on her face had all been forgotten. Ignominy rushed suddenly in. She screamed, a blood-curdling, end-of-tether noise, and leapt upstairs for the bathroom. To have faced all these strange, uniformed men with a black face was a horror of embarrassment almost as bad as if the house had burned to a pile of smoking embers.

'The neighbours!' she wailed. 'The shame of it!'

By the time the man came home from work, every sign of the great emergency had gone, apart from the black marks made by the firemaster's boots and some melted Bri-Nylon around the fireplace. There was even a welcoming coal fire in the grate. I had been told not to say a word, that the woman would explain everything, but as the man sat down for his tea, nothing was said, apart from 'How did you get on at work, dear?' and his reply:

'Fine, dear, fine. A few feet to hand today. A few feet to hand. Another day, another verucca, another dollar.' He was in a good mood. Digging into veruccas always gave him some kind of inner satisfaction, perhaps reminding him in miniature of his own father's heavy labouring down the pit. Labouring which had cost both my grandfathers their lives when I was too tiny to notice.

Later, my parents closeted themselves in the lounge, and I could hear the man's steady, calm vocal rumble, and the woman's sobbing.

Before my bedtime, we had a 'Quiet Time'. This was a common procedure in the Brethren, a kind of daily mini-service for the family. My father would read a Bible passage and say a prayer. It was a time when God would be brought in to shed some divine light on any of the day's events, particularly ones involving my misbehaviour. I wondered if my poor old mother was going to be brought to the Lord for a prayerful knuckle-rapping.

The man read Isaiah 43, verse two: 'When thou passest through the waters, I will be with thee; and through the rivers, they shall not overflow thee; when thou walkest though the fire, thou shalt not be burned; neither shall the flame kindle upon thee.'

The relevance of this was allowed to lie heavily in the air, which still bore a slight aroma of toasted Bri-Nylon. God, it was clear, had saved us from incineration. Not the tureen full of water; not the fire, police and ambulance. Not my cool, calm and collected telephone call. God was the hero of the hour, it seemed.

'Oh Lord, we thank thee for delivering thy servant and this child and this habitation from the flames of accident' (so the woman wasn't getting the blame, or at least it had all been settled without bringing God into it in a strictly judgmental sense) 'and pray that thou wilt continue to preserve us in our day-to-day lives, that we may continue to be a witness, for thee, and that thy servant's son be brought to a living knowledge of thee through faith, and that thy grace should indeed burn like a fire in our hearts, but a fire of love, and that we should bear always the sense of deliverance from the fiery coals of hell . . .' And there was lots more. There always was. I was pleased the woman had not suffered too many recriminations, but I didn't come to the Lord that night; the fire did not convert me as the Billy Graham film would two years later. The fire had been real, but rescue was available at the end of a telephone line. I knew that, because I had summoned those big, eager men in their uniforms. But anyway, the woman had started it and stopped it, and I was quite happy to trust in her rather than God. For around two years, anyway, until Big Billy Graham and his mind-bending, soul-crunching movie made me recognise the depths of my sinfulness, and demanded repentance.

It was after my conversion that girls began to make a significant impact on my consciousness, or rather my body. I had no idea what was making me pant and sweat and squirm in class with a desire to sit near the luminous, freckled Katrina MacCulloch. As a Christian, it terrified me, and I ran from the dirtytalk huddles of my classmates, the whin-bush poring over some scuffed and torn copy of *Playboy*. Yet I had no idea what was going on. Months passed. Why was it so pleasurable to lie on the floor on my chest, reading *The Eagle* or watching our strictly allotted half hour of children's television? I was getting a bit beyond *Blue Peter*, but that was what we were permitted. At school, the talk was of movies like *The Sand Pebbles* ('Aw, it's great, you see somebody getting crushed to death by a ship's engine!') but the frighteningly decrepit Torvale Cinema, with its cracked colour photographs pinned up outside, was as off-limits to the born again as hell itself. 'If Christ returns,' a preacher had once thundered, 'how will you feel, rising to meet him from the seat of a picture house, or from the floor of a dancehall? The believer must have nothing to do with these fleshly pursuits.' The week *The Sand Pebbles* was being shown, I was walking past the Torvale, with its dirty cream-and-green-tiled exterior. The door opened, and a man in a black bow-tie walked out, his thinning hair slicked back, a bulging face closed around a cigar. The smell hit me: the cigar smoke, thick and heady, and something else. A musty, stale, dark aroma, wafting out of the open cinema door. The reek was exciting, terrifying, full of promise and threat. I told Satan to get behind me and walked away from *The Sand Pebbles*, Steve McQueen, the movies, the flesh and the world. Only Billy Graham films shown in gospel halls were permissible.

Biology at school began hinting at embarrassing things which might happen down one's trousers, or inside the panicky mysteries of girls' skirts. But I don't know, maybe I just wasn't listening, or I switched off. It was exciting, as many of we boys discovered to our grey-serge-bulging shame, to be shown line drawings of female genitalia. But, and this is not a word of a lie, until I was 17 I thought male and female just sort of rubbed against one another, groin to groin, with nakedness an option, and, hey presto or Thank the Lord, babies began. I was for years ashamed of what I finally realised were wet dreams, because I thought I was peeing my pyjamas. This was not a big, angst-ridden problem, though. I had, after all, religion.

My parents made no effort to tell me what was happening to my body, and I didn't ask, because I was more and more interested in evangelisation, and the second coming of Christ, and growing up to be a saint. Sex, when it finally made its presence felt, erupted like a volcano in both my jeans and our family's quiet and deliberate ignorance of such things.

Meanwhile there was the Gospel Hall, and all who sailed in

her. For over a year, the secret discussions of the eldership, the committee which basically ran the Gospel Hall, leaked back into our house in overheard complaints from the man to the woman, in asides over meals, in slammed comments as the front door opened and shut. Not that my father was an elder. However, the dozen or so ancient 'elder brothers', all decrepit, wobbly on their feet, were not tremendously big on confidentiality, and tended to discuss their discussions with all and sundry over big Brethren Sunday teas. Two, three times a week the elders would meet, and for a year they discussed lights. Not the spiritual glow which ought to have been shining forth from the lives of the saints. Oh no, they discussed fluorescent lights, hanging lamps, wall lights, ceiling clusters. All this was then carefully reviewed over meals in our house, sometimes with one of the elders present. For the man was very interested in lights. 'I work with feet,' he would say, 'and without the right light, I cannot see the boils and hard skin and veruccas I must deal with. Light is crucial. The right light is conducive to proper worship.' He listened, fascinated, as over apple tarts and cold ham that year a battle raged over the kind of internal illumination the Gospel Hall ought to have. And became a war.

The old lights were, completely, done. They dangled on corroded brass chains from the high ceiling, and for meeting after meeting, I pondered what would happen if one fell on Mrs McSmith, in her fruit-basket hat.

Among the women, hats, essential accessories to worship, had become hugely complex fashion and class statements; a hat battle broke out at one point, with bunches of grapes, flowers and wide brims competing for supremacy. Until Mrs MacTaggart, wife of the so-called Corresponding Brother, or Leading Elder, the cadaverous Edwin MacTaggart, appeared one Sunday morning in a simple brown headscarf looking like a fishwife in a Marks and Spencers suit. Headscarves appeared by the dozen the following week, and competition began on how plain they could be, how simple the knot. Finally Mr MacTaggart, inspired by male disgruntlement at the increasingly Islamic appearance of the morning congregations, led a word from the Lord on how pride in one's own humility was still, let's face it, pride. Mrs MacTaggart appeared that morning in a spectacular violet-felt stetson with dried geraniums appended, shining like a shopfront Christmas tree amid the paltry, humble pride of the other women in their grey and white headscarves. Truly shamed, they returned to their hats, but in a spirit of love and equality, a general truce was called: every hat reached an implicit level of spectacular aesthetic achievement, and no hat fell below it. Hats were shared, younger women advised on what would be acceptable, and each Sunday morning saw a female congregation whose headgear happily merged like a well-planned garden. The Lord, Mr and Mrs MacTaggart (she chaired an informal women's group where hat design was discussed and prayed over) and everyone else was happy.

Sometimes, my silent worship (we were very big on silence at Brethren morning meetings, particularly if there had been a general trend towards massive fried breakfasts, say on a cold winter's Sabbath with the central heating in the Gospel Hall turned up) was quite ruined by images of Mrs McSmith pulped by a falling lamp, her poor hat turned into fruit salad, her head a kind of over-bony vegetable soup. At last, one did fall, inevitably when there was no one in the church. 'God has acted in His mercy, to show us that Something Must Be Done,' said my father. And something was. The dangerous lights were removed, temporary table lamps were brought in which lent the church a kind of intimate, not to say sinister atmosphere, and the eldership discussed things. Bitterly, in a spirit of brotherly love. And at various teatimes, the bitterness seeped into our salads and mashed tatties.

Mr Blunkett was the problem. Victor Blunkett was a local joiner, who had, over the years, assumed responsibility for nearly every major repair and alteration to Bittermouth Gospel Hall. He now guarded this jealously, arguing that, as he was the only qualified tradesman, and the man to whom (sigh) everything practical was always left in the end, he had better just get on and install the lights, which he knew how to get cheap from a good contact in wholesale. Attempts at discussing the kind of lights were met with contemptuous splutters from Victor. He knew best. The elders had better decide if they trusted him or not. If they didn't that was fine – he would leave the eldership and the next time woodworm was discovered or a pipe burst (he was an accomplished plumber as well) they could find somebody else at 3.00 a.m. to deal with it. This threat applied not just to the structural problems at the Gospel Hall, but also to elders' homes. Victor was the only joiner-cum-plumber in town. A curmudgeonly old man, immensely tall and hugely fat, with a glistening, blob-like bald head, all the children were terrified of him. 'One of the saints,' the man would say of Victor. 'The Bible says you should respect old men in order that your days should be long on the earth.' But even he had to admit that 'not only nice people are Christians, you know'. I knew he meant Victor.

The man had a dream, a vision, but because he was not an

elder, all he could do was lobby, aided by the woman's home-baking. He had heard that in America, the Brethren assemblies had turned their halls into comfortable, carpeted places, where the lighting was welcoming and outsiders, unconverted people, felt more than at home: they felt cosseted and comfortable and lulled into a position where the gospel's dart could penetrate without pain. He was cautious about how he shared this with the various carefully chosen elders who turned up at our house for tea, though. He was already marked as being young, too well-off and soft of hand. A foot doctor, sneered the retired shipbreakers, the roadmen and joiners and butchers (that was Mr MacTaggart, but he was counted as hardened-by-life, because he wielded a bone-shearing knife with the best, and besides, everyone had an account with his shop). As a first step, dad wanted soft, atmospheric, intimate lighting. The ancient elders slurped their Nambarrie tea and picked raisins and pastry from their ill-fitting dentures, and made whooshing, sucking noises while nodding or shaking their heads. Victor, who was an elder, was meanwhile conducting a potent campaign on his own behalf.

Some elders had their own illuminatory axes to grind. Ernest Tubyard, retired shipbreaker, prayed in worship long and hard using seafaring metaphors, and lobbied for the adaptation of old ship lamps, to give a nautical flavour to the hall ('after all, was not Christ himself the great Fisher of Men?'). The Bittermouth shipbreakers had hundreds which could easily be converted to 220 volts, he argued. Actually, he had dozens himself, stored in his garden shed, but he didn't mention that. Mr MacTaggart, a close personal friend of Victor Blunkett (and it was rumoured, a fellow Freemason and secret smoker), said nothing as the debate raged from meeting to meeting. Victor repeated his threats, the man argued for design and softness (but then he would, the foot-caressing sissy), Mr McSmith said he had always liked 'these new-fangled flower-scented lightbulbs' and others murmured and muttered and said amen during impassioned debates which never reached a conclusion.

Eventually, sick of the whole affair, Victor took unilateral action. One Saturday he unlocked the hall, took in his ladders and tools and installed the lights he had purchased as bankrupt stock more than a year previously. When people arrived from the morning meeting on Sunday, they were met with a hall bathed in an eerie, livid purple glow. Above them were four massive industrial arc-lamps, meant for exterior use. The whole place seemed to shiver and tremble in the harshness of the light. It was as if God was very, very upset with everyone and had come down to cast a baleful eye on proceedings. Every colour was reduced to a painful monochrome. The starched white tablecloth on which the bread and wine sat for communion was impossible to look at, so ferociously did it shine, like the Ark of the Covenant about to smite the Philistines. After half an hour of tense, not-very-worshipful silence, someone – no one knew exactly who – sneaked out the back and switched the lights off in the middle of a prayer. When we opened our eyes after the amen, the whole room flashed and swirled in violet pulses. It took the rest of the morning for the effect to wear off.

There was an emergency elders' meeting on the Monday night. An unapologetic Victor said that everyone would quickly get used to the new lights. People were there to worship, after all, and they should be able to ignore such distractions. It was, he said, bright. That was the main thing. The new lights were bright. The elders adjourned from the back room they usually met in to the main hall. The lights were switched on, taking 15 minutes to warm from a hard greyness to their full, purpley-violet, shadow-less attack. The elders sat in silence for half an hour, then went back to their discussions, Victor loudly praising the lack of shadows, the sense of space the lights gave to the building.

But there was opposition. Mrs McSmith had been confined to bed with a migraine all week. Mr Tubyard argued forcibly that the new lights were a distraction from 'the welcoming lantern of righteousness which is the grace of Jesus'. In the end, a compromise was proposed by one of the men my father had assiduously entertained to tea, Mr Beckett the baker. Lights identical to the dangerous pendulum ones removed previously should be found, purchased and installed. The Blunkett lights must be torn out forthwith. Mr MacTaggart abstained. Only Victor voted against. He walked out of the Gospel Hall that night and never returned.

For a while there were crises in the homes of Bittermouth Gospel Hall's eldership. Plumbing was the main problem; burst pipes necessitated calls to the neighbouring town of Greyburn, where, at vast expense, the plumber would reluctantly attend, charging exorbitantly for mileage. The infamous Blunkett lights were removed and taken by a Glasgow contractor from the hall to Victor's shop. It was closed, had been shut ever since the ignominious defeat of that momentous elders' meeting, so they were dumped at the back entrance. They lay in a pile and rusted there for over a year before the cleansing department at last removed them for scrap. My father and mother held a special celebratory tea with three different kinds of home-made fruit tart, one for each of the man's tame elders. The Blunketts joined the local Church of Scotland, and Victor, it was said, became a leading light in the Royal Arch, the senior branch of the masons. He sold his joinery and plumbing business to his Greyburn competitor, and then one day, six years after the affair of the lights, he was found floating face down in the sea, washing up and down in the tide off the north Bittermouth beach, in full masonic regalia. One trouser leg was still rolled up to his knee, and he had punched a small plumber's penknife through one eye. His car had been left on the harbour, locked and with a Bible lying on the front seat, open at Matthew chapter six. After the Lord's Prayer, verse 23 says: 'But if thine eye be evil, thy whole body shall be full of darkness. If therefore the light that is in thee be darkness – how great is that darkness!'

Of course it was a major scandal, and the business with the lights was hinted at in a couple of newspaper stories. But most reports concentrated on the masonic connection. Had he been murdered for betraying the lodge's secrets? There was some lurid speculation, but the Procurator Fiscal took no action, the press interest faded, and everyone in Bittermouth Gospel Hall knew what it was all about. Victor had never forgiven the Brethren. His widow spoke sadly of long depressions, of an obssession with switching every light in the house off, of sitting in the darkness. She asked if the elders of the Gospel Hall would take the funeral. Mr MacTaggart led proceedings, and the man and his three elders kept a very low profile indeed. The funeral took place in the summer, which was just as well. The Gospel Hall's new lights, yellow and warm and old fashioned like the original ones, but safely chained in stainless steel, did not have to be switched on.

When I was 16, I was baptised, and made a full member of the church. This involved being interviewed by three of the elders, giving my testimony at a gospel service – basically describing my life of sin and degradation up until the age of 11, when Christ rescued me from the shifting sands of evil and set my feet upon solid rock, and gave me happiness and peace within – and then, in full view of an evening gospel meeting, being plunged completely into an enormous tank of water, head and all, backwards. The tank lay hidden for most of the year beneath the speaker's platform. Sometimes preachers would proclaim that they were standing not on a platform, but on a grave. This was the crucial symbolism of baptism by immersion as opposed to the ridiculous concept of sprinkling infants. The believer had to show, publicly, that he was buried with Christ. That tank was a tomb, a watery one. You had to come out of it as well, of course, as that was crucial to the symbolism: buried with Christ, rising to eternal life with Him. Wetly.

The problem was that suddenly I didn't believe in the resurrection. It hit me one day as I was mowing the lawn, a job for which I earned 50 pence a week. Round and round my head went St Paul's words: 'If Christ be not risen, we are of all men most to be pitied.' Suddenly I knew he was right. Christ was not risen, and I was a moron.

The day of my baptism drew nearer. Both grannies,frail as they were, were coming, as were uncles and aunts and cousins and all kinds of pseudo-relations also called 'uncle' and 'aunt' but actually just friends of my parents. I was adolescent in everything but lustfulness. Strange sensations shook my body, especially when girls were around, but they were uncertain, unfocused. Sex was wrong, but what was sex? How far could you go? I didn't even know what you did to instigate the activity – did you throw a six or something, like in Monopoly? The idea of a kiss fascinated me, though. What happened to your nose? What if you dribbled? I was shaving my upper lips once a week and my chin once a month, more in the hope of making something substantial grow than actually removing the flimsy fluff which slowly gathered there. And I was undergoing a major spiritual crisis, only days before my public affirmation of Christianity in a glorified sunken bathtub.

I devoured the fundamentalist literature on the resurrection, much of it aimed at proving, logically, that a man could rise from the dead. The book *Who Moved the Stone?* was emotional but pretended not to be, apparently based on irresistible logic, but flawed by the question of trusting the accounts in the New Testament, which, some drawlingly intellectual schoolmates had informed me, was stupid, as they'd all been written hundreds of years after the event. 'How could the disciples, frightened, angry, doubting, be convinced by anything but the reality of a risen Christ?' Modern psychology could answer that question easily enough: the subconscious desire to be persuaded, but then I knew nothing about that. My mind teemed with the implications of renouncing the resurrection, my baptism, the Brethren: how could I live? I knew nothing else. My heart flapped and fluttered in fear, and yet where was the logic in all this, the common sense? Deep, deep inside, I knew the core of my faith was false. That there was no proof. 'There is the evidence of the human heart, changed by the power of the risen Christ.' Then there were the old hoary chestnuts which showed the born-again human heart in all its warmongering, Jew- and Catholic-hating glory. I confided in no one, read the New Testament and prayed for an unthinking, unshakable, certain belief.

I got it. I reduced Christianity to what I considered its core: was there a God? Yes, self-evidently there was. Somebody made this, made me. How do we know God? The only way we can know God is through Him revealing himself in the form of Jesus Christ, His Son. How do we know Jesus was, in effect, God and not just some ordinary prophet with a nice line in miracles and parables? Because he rose from the dead, exactly as predicted by the Old Testament prophets hundreds of years previously.

There were serious flaws in this. Was it self-evident that somebody had made me and the world and cholera and TB and such useful animals as, for example, the tsetse fly? What about all the other religions, all the people who had never heard of Jesus? Were they condemned to hell for ignorance of something they could not possibly have heard about? (And incidentally, if they were only damned once they'd heard and rejected the gospel, did that mean that Christian missionaries were simply, through warning ignorant pagans about the One True God, condemning millions to an eternity of suffering?) Why couldn't the documents have been faked for political reasons or whatever, supposedly proving that Christ had risen? Couldn't the grief-stricken be fooled?

In the end, I chose to believe, and abandoned the doubts, or shelved them. It was easier, and I had felt my whole world slipping away from me. Besides, my grannies were coming to the baptism, and it wouldn't do to upset them. Or my parents.

On the night, the atmosphere inside the hall was charged and heavy. It was January, and the packed congregation sweated as their coats' dampness condensed; the walls dripped. There were hymns, a sermon. I changed into a white shirt, cream sports trousers, white gym shoes. I was wearing shorts under my trousers, because underwear was important in the soaking aftermath of a baptism. Once, a young woman's bra and panties had been unforgettably outlined against the white dress she had been wearing for the plunge, before three towel-clutching sistern had screened her from the locked stare of aghast and fascinated eyes. In a creaking, breathy silence I walked out on the platform to tell everyone that I had been born and brought up in a Christian home, but that at the age of 11 I had realised I was bound for hell, and that only Christ could save me. There were sighs and amens. Every eye was on me, and I could feel a tight enjoyment of the moment, of my chosen, arbitrary belief and its demonstration. That childhood desire to be a preacher, an evangelist, a performer of the gospel, suddenly returned, and I began to cry, the perfect conclusion to my testimony, this large, spindly 16-year-old, proud and intelligent and a credit to his parents, crying in the Lord, proof positive of his commitment . . . Meanwhile, the excitement had very definitely gone to my groin. I hoped against hope it was invisible. The trousers were new and rather loose fitting.

Behind me, Mr MacTaggart had emerged, dressed as always for baptisms as if he was going fishing. He was wearing giant waders and oilskins over his suit. He sploshed into the tank, the cold depths of which had been heated earlier by carefully applying several kettles-full of boiling water. I joined him. In the Name of the Father, the Son and the Holy Ghost he baptised me, he said, then threw me down backwards into the wet grave. I arose, water up my nose, gasping but alive, as the whole congregation burst into that chorus I'd blasphemously mis-sung as a child:

> Up from the grave he arose
> With a mighty cold upon his nose . . .

It was all I could hear as I staggered towards the waiting towels. Triumph O'er His Foes, I kept telling myself. Triumph O'er His Foes. The man was shaking my hand, the woman crying. Both grannies were there, and soaking wet as I was, one thrust a five-pound note into my hand. Through in the main hall, the brethren and sistern were singing, singing louder than seemed possible, and although their voices were dulled by the walls between, the whole building seemed to shake with their joy at my death and resurrection with Christ. I knew, then, that it had to be true. At that moment, it was true. A last hymn:

> Oh Christ, He is the Fountain
> The deep, sweet well of blood
> The streams on earth I've tasted
> More deep I'll drink above . . .

Six months later, sex happened.

It was the Rolling Stones' fault. But then, I expect it often was. My parents were on an early Easter holiday, and I was alone in the house with my maternal grandmother. The newspapers were full of the fact that the Stones were to tour, and were going to play at Glasgow Green's Playhouse. Tickets were only available by applying in person at the box office, and would go on sale on Wednesday morning at 11.00 a.m.

I told my granny, who had certainly heard of the Rolling Stones and knew them to be agents of Satan, that I was going on a shopping trip to the city, and at 6.00 a.m. on Wednesday I caught the early commuter express from Bittermouth to Glasgow Central. On the trip up through Ayrshire I asked myself why I was doing this. Me, a born-again, baptised believer with a desire to serve God. Of course, since we had acquired a telly I had caught glimpses of the Stones; but my record collection amounted to a few Jim Reeves albums, a record by the Cornerstones which was awful, nothing compared to that wonderful wall of aggression I remembered from the past, and a Christmas present from uncle Phil of the third, terrible LP by the Monkees. I still strummed the guitar for Youth Fellowship chorus singing, and sometimes tried to hum some radio tune along to the few chords I'd learned. But, as with my attitude to girls, I was unfocused, essentially uninterested. The Stones attracted me, perhaps, because they were so alien, so much the opposite of my entire, Gospel Hall orientated life. I knew I was doing wrong, but a big, beaty excitement was in me as the train clattered through Renfrewshire into the dawn and the sprawl of Glasgow.

When I arrived outside Green's Playhouse, soon to become the Apollo, there were police on horseback struggling to control a huge snake of people. The pavement was blocked for what seemed like miles. I joined what appeared to be the rumbustious queue's end, feeling certain there would be no ticket for me. At 8.00 a.m. the police, fearing a complete disruption of the morning rush hour, forced the theatre management to open the box office. Things moved surprisingly quickly, and in an hour I was clutching a ticket to what my parents would certainly have regarded as damnation. I half agreed with them.

Three months later, the fateful day of the concert arrived. I had just passed my driving test, and was the proud possessor of an old Morris 1000 bought for £75 by the man as a combined baptism and examination-success present. I was university-bound and safely in the bosom of the Brethren, something worth rewarding with a degree of mobility. I told my parents I was going to a youth rally in Glasgow. Which, in a manner of speaking, I was. 'I think there's a Christian rock band playing,' I said, off-handedly. 'I'm meeting some of the people from the Kilmarnock Youth Fellowship there . . .' They nodded, I should be careful, driving on the Fenwick Moor late at night.

I sat alone in what was now called the Apollo, smelling the odd aroma of Europe's biggest theatre, that damp, hamburger, earthy, sweaty, subway smell. My seat was in the very front of the circle, next to the mixing desk. If there had been a sense of expectation at my baptism, the Apollo that night was a tropical storm seconds away from bursting into lightning and deluge. I sat there, a lone believer among 3,500 wildly relaxed people, smelling the cigarette smoke and an odd herbal scent I'd never caught before, and jealous of the boys and men clutching perfumed girls and women to them, or openly kissing in the double seats the Apollo had inherited from Green's, the wonderfully named Golden Divans.

Suddenly a voice louder than any voice I'd ever heard said: 'Ladies and gentlemen . . . the Rolling Stones,' and amid the tumult, the band members walked briskly out on to the stage, from where I sat almost touchable. This was long before the great high-tech stadium performances, the musical build-ups, the grand, operatic entrances. Here was a rock'n'roll band doing a job of work. They donned their instruments like journeymen. Charlie Watts rolled a few rhythms around his tiny kit, and they were ready. Then Jagger walked on, into the screams and applause, and everything changed. Everything changed.

Keith Richards was moving forwards, lunging. Jagger, pouting in a spangled cat suit, feline and androgynous. There was the sound of tenements collapsing, of road drills, of exploding radios, all flashing up the memory of schoolboy guitarists, of the tiny, pale imitation once heard at that Cornerstones concert, now revealed in all its ersatz ineptitude. There was a rushing, tugging, whirling sensation, and I was standing up, leaning out over the balcony, far out, and screaming as those huge, pumping, perfect chords to 'Brown Sugar' ripped every Christian atom out of my heart and soul and scattered them to the ends of the universe.

Gold coast slave ship bound for . . .

It's a song about sex, about slavery, race hatred, lust and depraved, leering, male mistreatment of the opposite gender (. . . *see him whip the women, just about midnight . . .*) but for me, then, it was release. I didn't have much idea what the words were but I knew what they meant. It was the snarl of guitar and lip which caught me, the perfect crack and crash of the drums, the chest-crushing boom of Bill Wyman's caveman bass. All the hair on the back of my neck stood on end, my body shook and tingled and I was laughing, laughing and weeping at the same time. I was back in my bedroom, supping hot orange after the Billy Graham film and the prayer that had supplied spiritual rebirth.

As the concert went on, I calmed down. I was shocked at 'Starfucker', appalled but thrilled by the huge rape epic 'Midnight Rambler'. Then, as 'Gimme Shelter' ripped the audience's delirium to shreds, I was lifted up again to the heights of ecstasy which had overwhelmed me during those first six chords. It was as if I could see and understand everything, suddenly; I knew that this moment, this furious excitement, this massive, communal, physical joy, was all there was, all there ought to be, and that I wanted to be part of it for ever and ever, amen. The song ended, the Stones, as ever, refused to encore, the fire doors swept the night air into the sweat-fogged auditorium and the house lights went on. It was over.

I was partially deaf for a week, ears hissing and ringing, but as my last holidays before university rushed to a close, I woke up day after day in my parents' house and each family morning brought the inescapable, dragging certainty that I still believed. The sign of that baptism was upon me, my statement of belonging, of family as much as spiritual identity. Yet something stirred, something occasionally whirled within me from that night; something dark and uncontrollable, which smiled without reason, laughed wildly and worryingly. And I was overwhelmed with a desire to kiss a girl, to hold a body other than my own. I couldn't, however, believe that any girl would actually want to kiss or hold me.

Rebecca arrived with her family during my first term at Glasgow University. I endeavoured to neutralise any disruptive force in my general arts course of English and Biblical Studies (taught by vicious liberals who poured scorn on fundamentalism, but whom it was possible simply to fool with the provision of the answers they sought) by travelling home every weekend to worship, and by immersion too in the Christian Union, a deeply serious body of evangelical Christians who were, worryingly, Church of Scotland, Free Church and Baptist as well as Brethren. I went to their meetings, mostly interminable Bible studies and stickily uncomfortable worship sessions, with caution.

As a fully fledged member of the Bittermouth assembly, I was able at last to break bread and drink wine at the weekly communion. I had always loved the smell of those morning meetings: bakeries and the fragrant whiff of pubs passed in the early morning. Yesterday's unsliced pan loaf, on a silver platter, covered in starched white linen. Two goblets of strong wine. Years earlier, on a post-Sunday School dustbin raid, some pals and I had discovered the discarded bottles: Old Tawny British Strong Port. It was the same wine drunk by down-and-outs in the street; heavy, sweet and very powerful indeed.

Different communicants would drink the wine in contrasting ways. Old men would lift the goblet to their lips and down a mighty draught, hovering pinkly several centimetres off the ground as they shook hands with everyone after the service. The woman would delicately take a tiny sip. My first mouthful was also my first taste of any alcoholic drink, and I loved it. The fragrance, the warmth as it trickled down, the flush of face and finger. Desperately, I would try to think of what you were supposed to think of, the blood of Christ. But while the bread was easy, a simple symbol, the wine was complex. It gave you such a hit, especially at that time in the morning, and what were you meant to make of that, theologically? Wine that maketh glad the heart of man, yes, but what about all these pain-wracked prayers about the crucifixion? This stuff made you feel good. I eventually put it down to the resurrection. The alcohol must be the resurrection, the coming to life, the joy, I pondered, little realising that I was touching on the ancient John-Barleycorn-Must-Die pagan belief of death-burial-rebirth which is in the seasons and especially in the malting of barley and the production of beer or spirits from it. I knew nothing. No wonder Catholics simply said it becomes the blood. That removed the rhythmic, eternal pagan imagery, and substituted its own secret magic.

One morning I unstuck my eyes after the final prayer, stood up and stretched and turned around into the face of a girl who smiled quickly then looked away. A strange girl. She was wearing a blue doll's mini-dress and an enormous straw hat. Fine, dark hair and eyes which tended to flicker from side to side, model thin but with a slightly chubby face. Fogged from the Old Tawny communion wine, I stood and stared until the man nudged me to move into the aisle. We met later at Bible class, and she was introduced by the leaders as Rebecca Smallwood, whose family had moved into Bittermouth, and would we all make her very much at home? We certainly would.

Beneath the rigid social structures of the Brethren ran, inevitably, deep sexual undercurrents. They occasionally exploded in the form of excited, harmless kissing games at Christmas and New Year parties. One the Youth Fellowship played was called Poor Pussy. One person was chosen as 'it' and had to go around the various seated players, resting their head on the other's lap and miaowing, as a pussy undoubtedly would. The person in whose lap this miaowing was going on had to stroke the pussy's head and say 'poor pussy' three times. If they laughed or did not say the magic words, they had to kiss the pussy and were then 'it' themselves. (Sigmund! Let me run this past you a second!)

Sometimes such antics led to disaster, and the alcohol-free rearing of libido at a party like that had broken up two Bittermouth marriages. When sex reared its head in the Brethren outside of the marital bed, there were simply no patterns of understanding there to cope with it, no accepted modes of behaviour. Unplanned pregnancies and adulteries were like deaths. In fact they were worse than deaths, because their implications didn't vanish off the earth. You couldn't wash your hands and let God have his will and his wonderful way. It was real life, and the Brethren found it hard to deal with. Most adulterous couples or pregnant girls were quietly packed off to some place the name of which nobody wanted to know. Nobody asked. Sometimes they stayed, were ignored in the street, formed new friendships, new social circles, even went to new churches.

But for we unmarried youngsters, without knowledge or rules other than no sex (whatever that was) before marriage, we had to let guilt and our bodies run free, hoping that things wouldn't get out of hand, so to speak. With Rebecca, things quickly did.

It began, as many things did in Bittermouth, on the beach. A Bible-class barbecue, the dying fire, an accidental touch of fingers. 'Would you like to . . . I mean I wouldn't mind a walk . . . I can give you a lift home afterwards, I mean would you . . .'

'That'd be nice.'

Heart thumping, folded arms, then the link of hands, then, deep in the darkness, that first kiss. Dribbles, oh, yes, the dribbles. And the clash of noses. Suffused with embarrassment, I tried to wipe my mouth silently. What did you do with your tongue? What was happening in the crotch department of my Seadog flared jeans? Was this sex? Was this too far? Rebecca didn't seem to think so, anyway. Afterwards, I took her home, my lips feeling jellied and bruised, wondering if I'd put my hands in the right places, wondering if this hardness would ever go away, not even knowing it was called an erection . . . I was 28 before I could pronounce clitoris properly. So-crates. I thought it was clytorris, to rhyme with Doris. Talk about sex? No, thank you very much. And the thing was, it never seemed to matter . . . and then it did.

We became an item, a couple. She was beautiful and, amazingly, a trainee chiropodist, one year older than me. We talked of the Lord. My parents thought she was wonderful. A chiropodiste! The man was beside himself with enthusiasm, and when they were together they talked of nothing but hard skin and corns and 17 different ways of treating athlete's foot. She came of good Brethren stock, was born again, baptised and dressed well. And she fitted in. She fitted in like the shoes she had made fitted her size-five feet, those perfectly manicured feet, those beautiful toes with their superb nails which I was allowed to suck, long before toe-sucking was by royal appointment. She used to wash my feet and give me a pedicure, then a good licking before sprinkling my cuticles with talcum powder. Toe-sucking was one of the things you were allowed to do which was sexual but not sex. Rebecca was an expert at this distinction.

'Nothing below the waist,' she said, once. Then she said, 'or above the thigh.' Or breasts, I discovered, when I once inadvertently ventured in a mammary direction. And no naked flesh apart from the small of the back and shoulders, and then only on special occasions when we were alone in either her house or mine, parents far away. And no noise, no grunts, no tongues, no teeth. This was inflammation without conclusion, but for someone who knew nothing, it was pretty terrific stuff. It was all new, and it was brilliant, and at last I made the connection between willie-hardness and sex. The two were linked, no question.

Disaster struck one night at her house, an old, two-storied sandstone villa by the golf course. Her father was something to do with the fish trade, I think. He wasn't poor, and they possessed a leather sofa, the first I'd ever seen. We had been rolling about on it for about two hours; we'd got past the kissing, the toe-sucking, the ear-blowing (recently OKd by Rebecca as long as neither tongue nor teeth were employed) and there had been some wonderful shoulder-kissing and leg-squeezing. I was just about to go for the piéce de résistance, the small of the back, when an intense mixture of pleasure and pain exploded and a stain began spreading across my green canvas Littlewoods trousers. I sat up, stunned. Rebecca looked at me, and began to cry, great shuddering sobs which confirmed my belief that something awful had happened, that we had transgressed the invisible line of Brethren morality. The awful truth dawned. Fully clothed or not, we had had sex! This was it! She would now get pregnant, because the sperm (by this time I knew about sperm) would instantaneously soak through my trousers and her skirt and tights and pants and that would be it, we'd have to get married and disappear into spiritual obscurity, to somewhere like Irvine, where I would have to get a job labouring or in a bank or selling life assurance. I would never be a preacher or evangelist.

I went to the bathroom, feeling wretched and sick. I took down my trousers and examimed my distended penis, another new word I'd picked up, although I pronounced it penis as in, your pen is lying on the floor. Not that I ever said it out loud, of course, but if I had, that's how I would have said it. This was it. This was sex, the great unmentionable, the horror! The horror! I could hear Rebecca sobbing in the other room.

IMMERSION

'I'm going home,' I said, shakily. 'What if . . . you won't . . . you won't get, have a, be pregnant, will you?' But she refused to give me comfort. Either her ignorance was as deep as mine, or she saw a chance of trapping my guilt-crucified soul into something more permanent than sustained rolling on a leather settee.

'Don't go! Oh . . . I knew we shouldn't have. I knew we were going too far . . .'

Too far! So we had gone too far! I knew it! Oh, it was all over, my saintliness was soiled, and the Rolling Stones had claimed me with their sleazy thrusting and their violent, dirty music. Oh Jesus, I prayed, don't let her be pregnant, please please forgive me. Don't let her be pregnant and I promise I'll never desert you for rock'n'roll again, I'll go no further than kissing and holding hands, I'll wear swimming trunks and genital clingfilm whenever I go out with girls and prevent anything like this happening again, Oh Christ I plead with you, save me from this horror!

But the woman saved me instead.

Gospel

Oh Jesus, Christ, please . . . please . . . how can I . . . clean. Clean,
clean, clean . . .

Much later it became useful, in sexual situations where the
prevention of premature ejaculation mattered, to recall, in full
detumescent horror, that encounter with Rebecca, and how the
woman saved me. From a little ignorance, at least. It was a cold,
salutary memory, like the one a Catholic friend told me of once
when we were both blind drunk, only with him the memory was
of a priest's verbal battering, and the result was drastic: instant
and complete loss of hard-on.

I staggered in, distressed and in some shock, having little idea
what had happened to me. The woman was alone, the man being
out at some elders' meeting or other, and I gabbled out in an orgy
of self-lacerating confession, that Rebecca and I had, had . . . had
done something, and I was so sorry, but would she get pregnant
and . . . I was caught between embarrassment and a desperate
need to confess and to know, to know what had happened,
because my ignorance of bodily affairs was so abysmal and
complete. The woman was shaking me.

'Were you inside her? WERE YOU INSIDE HER when you . . .
did it? WERE YOU?' But I had no idea what she was talking
about.

'It was too cold to be outside. I mean, we went for a walk on
the beach, but we were inside her house, on the couch, I mean
her parents were out . . .' I saw something approaching panic in
my mother's eyes. Consternation.

'Was your . . . willie inside her . . . vagina?' She was blushing,
a heavy red tide of shame and anger and concern. Vagina. I knew
and understood the word, but had never really applied it to real
people. Vagina. Vesagex antiseptic cream. Regina, verucca,

angina. Vulva, Volvo, valve amplifier . . . 'Did you have your clothes off? Was your willie . . . hard?' And suddenly I knew everything. All at once the mechanics of the whole process made sense. The snippets of information, the painful attempts by my father to mention 'important facts' to me, the books left lying significantly in my room, the jokes at school, the strange sensation engendered by particular pictures. Suddenly I knew what you did. What sex actually was. It was a matter of hydraulics, of insertion, of lifting, of pushing and lubrication and pumping . . . It was so simple and so ridiculously, intimately complex. How well did you have to know somebody before you could be naked with them, before you could look at their every mole and blemish, before you could push part of your body inside theirs? How much did they have to want you or love you or fancy you before they let you do that? And had Rebecca been just as ignorant as I was, or was she manipulative in a way I found impossible to comprehend?

All that was surging through my mind as I shook my head, and her body, hyper-tense with concern and embarrassment, went slack with relief. 'Thank God,' she said. 'Thank God.' She pulled herself together. 'I'm going to make a cup of tea, and then we'll have a wee talk,' she announced, briskly. 'And not a word of this to your father.' So we talked, for the first time and maybe the last time in a clear, blunt way about sex and what happened in it and because of it. Of course, sex was only to happen after marriage, she stressed, but sometimes things got out of hand between boys and girls, everyone understood that. 'That's not to excuse you, no, not for one minute, though. And what your father would say I do not know. Mind you, I never liked that girl. Never.' Afterwards, my mind was more or less at rest on the issue of Rebecca's supposed pregnancy. However, a great pulsing boil of guilt was on the rise. I was a Christian, a would-be evangeliser and saver-of-souls. Yet I had besmirched my belief, had shamed Christ through my enslavement by the will of the flesh. I prayed tearfully, for forgiveness. If God would give me peace and forgiveness, I would commit my life to Him for His service, full-time, as a Pure Disciple. I would take my guitar, write songs of faith and sing them to sinners and follow Jesus where'er He led me. And I would never lie on top of a girl in a parentless house again. Because now I knew what it could lead to, the insertions and connections and impregnations which would for me only be permissible within holy wedlock. I glimpsed Rebecca once or twice afterwards at the Gospel Hall, but never exchanged more than a few words with her. Her parents avoided mine. Many

times since, I have fantasised about what it would have been like
if we had fucked with abandon on that couch, if we had been
guiltless and full of simple, physical joy and lust and brief,
temporary love. But no.

Four years later, I married Sharon, Saint Sharon, the lovely,
willowy daughter of Baptists, with whom I had done little more
than kiss deeply and wetly for hours on end on damp, cold park
benches. I prayed over the inevitable, near-permanent hard-on,
and ended up with a severe case of piles, which I put down to
God punishing my lusts. She was a year older than me, lit from
within with a great holiness, I thought, a light of love and affection
which came straight from heaven. My parents liked her a lot. We
had met at the Bethesda Bible College, a residential institution on
Glasgow's leafy south side. I had dropped out of university in the
face of what I piously felt were too many challenges to my faith;
besides, God was calling me in a direction where secular qualifi-
cations would be an irrelevance, and at Bethesda I had studied
practical theology, evangelism, preacher's English and basic New
Testament Greek, and accumulated an encyclopaedic knowledge
of cheap Indian restaurants. Raj Duph Singh, a student from
Kashmir, occasionally concocted wonderful curries on a gas ring
in his room, filling the bleak corridors of Bethesda with the hot
aromas of the east. The staff were ex-missionaries, some invalided
out of their soul-sapping service in places like Angola and
Somalia, with guest lectures from ministers and evangelists who
happened to be visiting or practising missionaries on furlough
from the Foreign Field, exchanging their converted cannibals for
a round of tea-meetings with special collections.

Sharon had come to the college because she had a loose idea
that she might 'go abroad' and teach. Who she would teach she
wasn't sure, but children, certainly. About Jesus. Instead, she met
me, and fell in enthusiastically with my desire to evangelise
through music. Contemporary gospel music. Youth music. The
Language of Today. 'I believe Christ has guided us together, for
His service. I'm sure He's with us, love, sure,' she would smile,
shining with pure spirituality. 'And we must watch the physical
side, of course. We mustn't let it get out of hand. We must keep
ourselves pure.' That was fine by me. We prayed together for
guidance, licked each other's ears (allowed), read the Bible and
occasionally clutched one another's knees in paroxysms of religious fellowship. Sharon and I had exchanged giggles and glances
for about a year over such uplifting delights as eschatology and
children's chorus leading when we were thrown together during
a summer 'outreach mission' to the little Fife seaside town of

Tarmoran. These annual fortnight-long endeavours were opportunities for we would-be missionaries and evangelists to put our
training into practice, sleeping in church halls on camp beds,
organising beach-meetings for rowdy and sullen vacationing children, 'gospel cafés' for 'youth' and evening open-air praise
meetings for older holidaymakers whose hearts, we felt certain,
were in search of spiritual refreshment, if only they could realise
it. It was the kind of thing I had been brought up with, and the
enthusiasm and freshness of engaging in holy warfare against the
wiles of Satan with a bunch of other young people made it seem
like fun. And the zest of suppressed sexuality between me and
Sharon added to the whole thing. 'The waiting's hard,' she would
say, her face dimpling. 'But it'll be worth it in God's eyes and in
your arms.' She cooked. Sharon was into cooking in a not very
adventurous way, and provided plenty of fried spam for the team
of young evangelists, fried spam and tatties. Her skin smelled of
grease, the whole time. Grease and purity.

It was at Tarmoran, where I returned each summer for the four
years I was at Bethesda, latterly with Sharon as my ever-present
companion, that I developed what would become my ministry in
song. Gone were the days when I had put new words to Val
Doonican's 'Memories Are Made of This':

> Jesus died on Calvary
> Jesus suffered there for me
> The cross! The pain!
> And yet He rose again
> Jesus died upon That Tree.

I had acquired a second-hand Yamaha FG180 acoustic guitar
and prided myself on my knowledge of what was erupting as
'contemporary Christian music'. All over the country, sensitive
Christian singer-songwriters were combining Dylan block chords
with 'Rock of Ages' and 'Just as I Am' to come up with winsome
guitar ditties aimed at converting Youth. Youth was all. Youth
was the hope for the future, and so the occasional Christian
heavy-metal group was encouraged by desperate church leaders
who watched their attendances drooping and drooping constantly. But solo acoustic evangelo-performers were more adap-
table, needed less equipment and could fit in with traditional
gospel meetings or propagandist rock and folk concerts organised
on neutral, non-churchy ground. I felt sure God wanted me to be
a kind of Scottish, religious version of Gerry Rafferty.

At Tarmoran we organised what was known as a Gospel Café

in the local Baptist church hall, a dreich, high-ceilinged place with badminton-court markings on the floor. Fishnets were hung from nails, wall to wall about seven feet from the floor, and every anglepoise lamp that could be scrounged was fitted with a coloured bulb and positioned in the corners and beside a little stage made of fish boxes. Candles were placed in saucers on card tables, and imitation Nescafé served for free. The reluctant Youth were dragged in with promises of 'LIVE! MODERN! MUSIC WITH A MESSAGE WHICH COULD CHANGE YOUR LIFE!' Tracts bearing out-of-date psychedelic illustrations and mottoes like 'JOIN THE JESUS REVOLUTION' were left on the tables, and the students of the Bethesda Bible College would swoop on any 'unsaved' Youth with smiles and offers of coffee and prepared questions like 'Well, have you made the wonderful discovery of the Spirit-filled life?' or 'Can I introduce you to the Four Spiritual Laws?' or even just 'Are you in love with Jesus?' if we were in particularly mystical mood.

I was writing songs which I thought would communicate with these Youth, which God had clearly guided me towards writing, had inspired, but which were, I felt, works of art in their own right. We had lectures on art from ministers who were keen to stress that evangelicalism and art were not mutually exclusive, not at all. In fact, creation by human beings, creativity, was a reflection of God's creativity. But that creativity must never become an object of idolatry, and should be handed over to God, lock, stock and barrel for Him to use for His glory. That was fine by me, I thought. Christ, looking back, it seems so fucking pathetic. All I really wanted was to be famous, to have some kind of recognition, some kind of stature as a performer and maker of things, a singer of songs, and preacher of sermons. I was a would-be hack cabaret artist, content with success of a limited, safe kind, wanking away in the world of the spirit, rather than out there in the big, bad, fleshly saga of real life, where talent was not circumscribed or limited by dogma and the need to convince or convert, where creativity could be pretentious and selfish, but was not borrowed from a jealous, petulant god.

> I'm living for the truth
> And I'm looking for the light
> And I'm trying not to go astray
> There's a peace in my heart
> Since I made a new start
> With the one who took my sins away
> He's the seeker of souls

And the speaker of truth
And the source of that living light
No matter what they say, he's the only way
And his name is Jesus Christ.

I'm wearing dark glasses when I used to be blind
Finding things I never even thought I'd find
When I die I'm going to leave my dark glasses behind
And look right at the light
See the Lord at last.

'Dark Glasses' was my first big number, so full of words they came out like an express train to a jolly little shuffle beat. In some ways, my self-and-God-penned songs of that time now appear quite . . . fresh and innocent, quite real, in the same way that black gospel music is clichéd and stupid but real, representative of a real experience. My songs were real, all right, but the experience they described was so artificial, so tiny, and so irrelevant that now they appear flimsy and silly. And blind to reality. Yet that was my reality, hard to believe though that may be. As real, but not as passionate as black gospel, with its huge, sexual underpinning, its great physical wave which moves and flows and howls with genuine emotion. There was no passion in what I was doing. It was spirituality by numbers, musically impotent because I had never, since those days back with the Cornerstones, spent any time actually listening and understanding what made pop or rock great. It was just like sex. I had no nuts-and-bolts notion of the actual workings of it all, I didn't perceive the physical, visceral power of great rock; hear the thump of its mighty engine . . . before Rebecca sex was a fragmented set of activities and bodily parts which meant nothing in reality, had never been put together. Rock music was something I played but didn't understand, and didn't listen to much because it carried unhealthy messages. I was listening mainly to third-rate crap like Larry Norman or Alwyn Wall, Christian copying of old and redundant influences. I was copying the copyists. That was my reality.

And when I die, I'm going higher than the sky
To be in the presence of the King
But before I go, I would love these people to know
The light and the power that Christ can bring

City light
Is starting to shine

In the night
It's beginning to glow
If the lives
Of the people of Jesus
Are given to him then the light will grow.

But I sang at Tarmoran and the adolescent Youth sitting guzzling the free coffee jeered and shouted and asked for Elvis songs, and I strummed my guitar and played for them, all the time looking at Sharon as she earnestly witnessed for Christ to a bunch of teenage girls and sometimes smiled encouragingly at me. After the first Gospel Café she came up and told me how the Lord had really spoken to her through my songs. 'You've been given a tremendous gift, and I am sure the Lord has witnessed through you to these Young People here tonight. Would you like a coffee?'

Later in the week, we had a beach barbecue, where I sang again, and two 13-year-old girls on holiday from Swansea broke down in tears and gave their lives to the Lord, scared shitless no doubt by my rendition of Larry Norman's despicable song about the second coming of Christ, ominously entitled 'I Wish We'd All Been Ready' and including lines about wives being snatched away by God to heaven while their husbands are left behind to cook the dinner themselves. In fact, this was a whole vein of eschatology richly mined at the Bethesda Bible College. In America, we heard, you could get special Second Coming of Christ insurance, in case the pilot of a plane disappeared towards heaven, thus condemning all his passengers to an instant flaming passage to hell. It was never clear if the pilot had the insurance or the passengers, and if you were to take out insurance against the second coming on the basis that you weren't going, why not just take the cheaper option and get born again as soon as possible? And if the pilot was the one insured, why should he care, once he was snuggled in warmly (but not too warmly) beside the Celestial Throne? But then there was also the question of not being called, not being one of the elect. If your name wasn't written in the Lamb's Book of Life, well, there wasn't a thing you could do about it, no matter how much you believed it was all true. You'd just have to sit down on earth and watch the elect get taken off to eternal happiness. Might as well insure against it.

Emotions ran high that night, as the two girls, radiant through their tears, went back to tell their parents that they were now born-again believers, and that mum and dad were bound for hell if they didn't mend their ways. The embers of the barbecue glowed, and the waves crashed on the sand, and Sharon and I went for a walk, heart-bumpingly reaching for each other's hands, and singing little worshipful songs of unstated, innocent, semi-sublimated lust.

> Lord, we thank you
> For giving us this time
> All of our lives
> Be forever thine

And I reached for her, held her close and we kissed, shyly and without great passion. 'That's enough,' she said, coyly, and she was right, it was. I could barely walk for the massive erection which was straining against my best Wranglers. We sat on the sand and she prayed for the two girls, Joyce and Marian, and I tried to think pure and spiritual thoughts. The problem was I couldn't control my mind. One minute I was interceding on a spiritual plane, the next I was sliding Sharon's knickers over her smooth, golden thighs and doing all the hydraulic engineering I'd never done with Rebecca. It was like a hallucination, coming and going, until at last we walked back to the church hall, having never done anything but kiss rather sweetly and chastely, our lips closed against dribbles, and me holding my guitar case over the spreading, sticky stain in my new jeans, feeling guilt, yes, but happy at least that Sharon wouldn't get pregnant. And that strenuous sleeping-bag prayer would ensure forgiveness.

We married in the Baptist Church linked to Bethesda, a white wedding but not an expensive one. Raj Duph Singh was best man. We didn't have a wedding cake, we had a Third World Concern lentil patty which Raj had made for us. The dress had been borrowed, and we were venturing forth into wedded bliss on the basis of my involvement with a Scottish Youth Mission evangelistic team, as singer-preacher with special responsibility for teenagers. Youth. We were provided with a room-and-kitchen tenement flat in Partick, rent and rates free. Everything else we had to raise from . . . the Lord. Or rather, His people. My parents and Sharon's, believers all, had invested in the wedding and in furniture for our new, spiritually blessed home, and cash had been quietly deposited with us 'from the Lord'. Envelopes with cash in turned up out of nowhere, and while it was hardly a lifestyle calculated to impress a building society, we felt confident God would provide. The wedding was also to be a service of dedication for our life as full-time servants of Christ, and as we both knelt in front of the Rev Martin McKendrick, a former missionary to Iran and principal of the Bethesda Bible College, he grasped our heads in his huge, knobbly hands, hands which, he had often told students, had in faith embraced lepers. I began to sweat, but his vice-like grip did not slip. I noticed that he had severely damaged Sharon's pill-box head dress, and that she had gone a shade of puce to match her apparel. Rev Martin, known to all the students as just that, Rev (pronounced with two 'v's) Martin, as if his first name had something to do with accelerating a car, began to pray, showering us with spittle which fell like sputters of rain on our bowed and immobile heads.

'Dear God and Father. Our children here before you' (at Bethesda, possibly because of the liberal Baptist influence, thees and thous had been largely abandoned for the sake of yous and . . . well, yous. God is interested in communication from us in our modern world, said Rev Martin, not irrelevant modes of speech from the days of our forefathers) 'have committed their lives to thy service' (but, unfortunately, consistency was not Rev Martin's strong point. When he'd been a missionary, he had prayed in three languages, and sometimes he lost his thees and thous and yous in a welter of half-remembered Farsi pronouns. I wish the Spirit's gifts still included tongues, he would mutter, then I would be fluent at all times) 'and we are gathered here today not only to witness their conjoining together as one flesh in your sight, but also to bless them in their joint witness for thee as your disciples. Take their lives, oh Lord, and weld them into your purpose. Bless many through them, and give them your peace and strength and support in the years ahead.'

There was a lot more. An awful lot. But the legal wedding itself was simple and straightforwardly joyful, with my mother crying, and me looking at her and wondering if she was thinking of that Rebecca night, and my father looking proud and pleased, and me proud and pleased, and wondering who it was that I'd married, and why as a committed Christian and full-time worker for God, I still found myself fancying other women. Even some who were at this, my own wedding . . .

Sharon was lovely, no doubt about it. She looked fabulous, a vision in tearful, glowing white. She was my equal in education and more than equal, it seemed, in spirituality. Yet we talked in biblical texts and rather than converse we *shared*. We prayed together and kissed and fondled. I knew her father was a banker, her mother a primary teacher, her little brother destined for university and, his father hoped, accountancy. Her dad was grinningly cadaverous, stooping and baldy and pasty, but pleasant enough when he spoke, which was rarely. I'd gone to ask permission to marry his daughter, and brashly suggested we pray together. It was Thursday night, after a long day for him at the bank, and I was only into my second extemporare paragraph of worship and thankfulness when the sound of snoring made me realise he was asleep. But who was this daughter of his, this lovely, honey-blonde creature, this godly woman, Saint Sharon? She had decided to stay at home rather than travel with the Scottish Youth Mission team, gladly accepting, after some prayer, the running of our accounts and taking bookings from our flat, which was to act as a kind of administration office. I knew she liked white Lambrusco wine, when we allowed ourselves 'for our stomach's sake, as Paul told Timothy' our weekly bottle of plonk with a special Chinese or Indian carry-out. How we could drink Lambrusco with curry I cannot understand, these days. I knew she religiously followed every jot and tittle of *Coronation Street* as much as she prayed for the world-wide cast of missionaries whose names were pinned to our kitchen wall. But she rationed TV, allowing only the news, religious programmes and *Coronation Street*, with the occasional wallow in *Prisoner: Cell Block H* if she was feeling particularly low of an evening. But who *was* she?

On our wedding night, I found out that her flesh was white and goosepimply under her clothes, and that she would not be undressed by me in the full glare of the bedroom light, Room 12 in the Nazarene Guest House, North Berwick. She was nervous and uneasy, and her kisses were distracted and dry, pecks from a trapped bird. She changed into a long, white nightdress in the bathroom down the hall, then came back to the bedroom, switched the light out and suggested we pray separately for a while. She smelled of Lux soap. I was in bed, naked, all prayed out and nursing an erection which threatened to cause a permanent groin strain. We had prepared for this moment for months. No contraception, because God was in charge of life and birth and death. If God could provide money for us, he could look after kids as well. And then I heard her sobbing.

'I have to tell you something,' she said. 'I couldn't . . . I didn't know . . . before I came to the college, I . . .' More sobbing. 'There was this boy, and things got . . . out of hand.' Out of hand? *Out of hand?* That phrase resonated coldly Rebeccawards in my own experience. 'I was a Christian then, too, and so was he, but I was just so stupid and so . . .' I listened, thunderstruck. Amazed that behind Saint Sharon's beautiful, holy exterior had hidden much more sensuality than a mere Rebecca. Then she told me about the abortion, about how her mother had taken care of everything, how her father had either not known or pretended not to know, about the horrible terraced house in Liverpool, well out of sight of prying Baptist eyes, and gradually the swollen organ between my legs shrivelled and diminished until I listened to her talk, sob, talk, sob about the past, about how God had, at the last, forgiven her, about how the guilt and stain of her action had been removed, despite the horror of killing a child, although she never thought of it that way usually, but now there was the chance to create another life and she felt so horrible, that she had deceived me, deceived all the people at the wedding . . .

And I took her in my arms and held her as she sobbed in that virginal white nightdress. I felt nothing sexual at all for her, even though it was the first time I'd slept with anyone, the first chance I'd had to hold a woman close in bed, to feel bare legs (weirdly smooth-but-stubbly: my first intimate encounter with nakedly shaved limbs) with mine. But gradually the sobbing eased, and at last she fell asleep. I did not. I tried to pray, but couldn't. Again it seemed that ideas and love and belief were betrayed and subverted by the body, by our bodies and what they wanted and by what they did and what we did to them. Sharon and the boy, whose name she had not told me, had met and joined and produced the germ of a child, and doctors or nurses had torn that out of Sharon's body, while God watched and waited to blame and forgive, and her parents sweated blood to stop anyone finding out, and no one told me until this night, this first night of marriage. I slept, in the end, having removed my arm from beneath Sharon's body. It had gone numb.

Next morning, pale and strained, Sharon asked me if I wanted to leave her. No, I said, of course not. God has forgiven you. You must forgive yourself, and I forgive you. I reached for her and gently caressed her thighs, stomach, the pubic hair I'd never felt before, so unexpectedly coarse. Her breasts were tight, large and thrusting and one was slightly bigger, to my surprise, than the other. And we made love, which was easy, easier than I'd ever have imagined, and then we prayed, and then we made love again. Then we went downstairs and had Bran Flakes and kippers with lots of tea and burnt toast. Later, after a bracing walk by the Forth, I wrote a song:

> And Jesus Won! Against Temptation's wiles he stood alone
> Untainted through the evil hour
> The only one not to be sucked down by its warm embrace
> Or bent by its demonic power
> And in His great example and his liberation sweet
> We can find a victory; temptation must retreat
> In Jesus' name, we can fight! And know we'll win!

Affleck McCaig was the leader of the Scottish Youth Mission team, a large, tweedy Englishman, called from life as executive in the family pest-control empire to Christ and His service, of patrician bearing, baldingly 50 and desperately keen to appear Youthful. 'I may not be a Youth,' he would say, chortling. 'But I understand Youth, and Youth's deepest needs. I know the Young People of today need Christ. There is a gaping hole, a gaping hole in their lives, and only Christ can fill that gaping hole, can satisfy, can bring that endless, that eternal contentment.' Affleck was the preacher, and unfortunately such unintentional double entendres as 'God will fill your gaping hole' were not uncommon. School assemblies were a common venue for the team's performances, as part of missions in towns across Scotland. No one, absolutely no one, is more cynical or more prone to recognising the sexual symbolism of the most innocent statement than the second-year male pupil. 'There is a hole in your life. Everybody has a hole. Everyone, and Jesus Christ can fill your gaping hole . . .' Talk of gaping holes automatically provoked titters, and in wilder schools where the teachers were merely tolerated, and sometimes not even that, there would be heckling.

'*I cannie get my fuckin' hole, pal* . . .' Affleck would smile, then frown, above it all but recognising the need to say something, to communicate with these Youth. He would plough on, sometimes to disastrous effect. I remember once at a prison, he determined to get on the vernacular level of the inmates, and having got it into his head that the criminal slang for burglary was the word 'screw', also used as a verb, he attempted to communicate with these actually not very tough lags.

'FEAR!' he shouted. 'Many of you will have known fear in your lives. Oh yes! You may appear tough now, hard before your friends. Now you're a hard man but – do you remember that first screw? Do you remember when you were just about to start screwing, and the tension was gripping you, and the fear of being found out, as you . . .' but the whole place was in uproarious hysteria, with even the screws wiping tears of laughter from their eyes.

At the same prison our other two members, the drama team who went under the title Sonrise (as in Son of God, rising from the dead, 'but the symbolism of the yeast in a loaf of bread is no accident – we play on that'), disgraced themselves and the whole of Scottish Youth Mission, which was prevented from doing any evangelism within the Scottish Prison Service afterwards. Priscilla Bosomworth and Evelyn Worthington-Hindmarsh were physically pronounced and mentally ethereal figures who specialised in dance-worship, which they always tried to get me to provide the music for. They would waft chiffon scarves through the air and turn beaming faces to heaven while waving their arms like football supporters. They also wore wispy hippy dresses which occasionally wafted in the draft of their movements to spectacularly revelatory effect. They were not, bodily, in the Pan's People class, however, so this rarely caused much sensual excitement.

Sonrise much preferred the emotional release of impromptu spiritual dancing. They were the only two tongue-speaking charismatics of our group, liable to let loose torrents of jumbled glossolalia during prayer meetings, much to Affleck's discomfort and my confusion. At first I thought they were having fits. At Bethesda and elsewhere, tongue-speaking had been much-discussed but never actually performed. Once I realised what was going on, I always felt rather creepy when it happened. I mean, if someone actually had God speaking through them, that was something fairly extreme, wasn't it? Except nobody could understand the tongues but Priscilla and Evelyn, who helpfully translated each other's gifted sayings for Affleck's benefit, and mine.

At the prison, a rural but very definitely not open establishment, Sonrise determined to perform one or two meaningful message-ridden sketches. One involved Death, subtly portrayed as a big black figure carrying chains and a large bullwhip and wearing a stocking mask (Priscilla) being shot by Love (Evelyn) who was armed with a starting pistol and wore diaphanous white robes. The denouement was Love's declaration in ringing tones that 'Only the Bullets of Faith can defeat Death.'

All this was duly performed, and I sang three songs, then Affleck spoke about how we all had to face death, but Christ could bring life, not just forever with Him in heaven, but here and now a renewed life of joy and happiness. Then we went for tea with the Governor; Sonrise left their props bag behind in the chapel, where we had been doing our evangelistic thing. A panic-stricken return proved that it was still there, along with the bullwhip, the stocking mask and chains, the bizarre accoutrements of a Death very closely aligned, if my innocence had allowed such a perception, with sado-masochistic sex. The gun, however, had disappeared.

Was there trouble? The Second Coming would have been less trouble. There was a general alert, we were held and questioned by police for four hours, Priscilla and Evelyn were accused of smuggling firearms into the jail for the sake of some inmate one of them had become smitten with. ('Happens all the time,' one warder told me. 'Bloody religious women visitors, just want to get their oats, and see these young, frustrated bastards ready to wank in barbed wire.' I could tell he was impressed by my air of religiosity by his tone. 'Do any thing for them. Anything. I've seen them sucking them off through the interview grilles.') But finally they let us go. A full search of the prison eventually turned up the starting gun in a toilet water tank, which finally led to Scottish Youth Mission being fined for unlicensed possession of an offensive weapon. Because as it turned out, it wasn't a starting pistol at all, it was a 9mm Beretta which Evelyn's father had stolen off an Italian prisoner at Monte Cassino. It would all have been fine had the *Sun* not got hold of the story, and splashed it across their centre pages as PRAISE THE LORD AND PASS THE AMMUNITION – BONKERS BIBLE THUMPERS ARM JAILBIRDS. That seriously affected the way God exercised his People to donate funds to Scottish Youth Mission for a while, although our income gradually recovered. Evelyn and Priscilla seemed to spend much more time speaking in tongues, though, and were reluctant to do anything but spiritual dancing to taped music which resounded with aching, self-conscious holiness, even in primary schools, where most of the little children looked at them as if they had just stepped out of a *Scooby Doo* cartoon. The Death sketch was abandoned.

Affleck had various set-pieces he used in his preaching, one or two of them truly incredible pieces of audience manipulation. One involved him rushing onstage in the middle of one of my songs or while Sonrise were doing their thing and insisting on immediate quiet. Brandishing a piece of paper, he would bellow through the microphone that he had just been contacted by the local police, and he had been asked to inform all reserve police-men or territorial army soldiers in the crowd to report immediately to their units. 'Ladies and Gentlemen,' he would say. 'There have been reports of a large explosion, possibly nuclear, in Manchester. Please do not be alarmed.' Quite often, by this stage two or three men would indeed have rushed from the room to report to their units, and people with relatives in Manchester would be sobbing – or, on one famous occasion, fainting and concussing themselves on a radiator. And then, of course, Affleck would tell the story of a great general who had offered to exchange himself with the enemy if only the fighting would stop, and the great general had done that for His people, and died for them and in exactly the same way Jesus had . . .

Sometimes there was real trouble over this, with complaints to church leaders and the police and indeed the army. But Affleck would just smile and say, 'By all means necessary. All means must be used to communicate the Greatest Story Ever Told.

Especially to the Youth.' And he would stand in front of some school assembly, attempting the act which involved holding up a £5 note, and inviting anyone, anyone to freely come and take it. (Just as salvation was being freely offered.) But on one fateful occasion, he improvised, put his hand in his trouser pocket and said, 'I'm holding something right now. Something wonderful. Something that you can have, too. If you want it . . .' The place erupted.

This went on for a long time. In Scotland, England, and Northern Ireland, where we were popular in Protestant circles. I was at home infrequently, but Sharon was always there, glowing and loving and eternally supportive. Money came in, sometimes even anonymously (though I suspected this was often from our families) and we continued to have sex, though no conception took place. I wondered increasingly if it was good sex, as described in some of the books and magazines I came across. I didn't seek them out, obviously; it just so happened that I would find myself with some free time and there they would be . . . What was good sex? Sharon didn't moan or even move around, as some fictional characters did. Things didn't last very long, but it always felt quite good to me. The problem was that I began to wonder what it might be like with someone else, just as a means of comparison. Anybody else. The women next door, virtually any remotely attractive female I saw in the street. And I still didn't really know who Sharon was. What, I asked her on one of my weekend returns from the home mission field, did she do when I wasn't there? She was washing my clothes at the time, by hand. We couldn't afford a washing-machine, although we had placed a few hints in our monthly prayer-letter that we were praying for God to supply one. I did nothing around the house. Because the Man, after all, was head of the household, was head of the Woman just as Christ was Head of the Church. And Saint Sharon seemed happy to accept this. But what did she do?

'Well, I take the calls about the Mission, and organise things for you when you're out there at the front-line, and clean up the house, and pray for you and for all the others on our prayer-list, and I go to the Baptist house groups, and the ladies' circle, and the prayer meetings, and sometimes I watch a little television . . .' She frowned, and reached to hold me by the shoulders. 'Do you think I should be doing more, my love? Should I be spending more time in prayer? Isn't the house clean enough? Are your clothes OK?' And suddenly, like a demon, I felt something bursting into my mind like the strange lusts which sent my eyes wandering after other women in the street, and this was evil, truly evil stuff which leapt unbidden, not to my lips but to somebody speaking inside me.

'WHY DON'T YOU FUCKING TALK TO ME, YOU CUNT. TELL ME ABOUT YOUR FIRST BOYFRIEND, WHAT HE WAS LIKE IN BED. TALK TO ME ABOUT LIFE AND ABOUT HANK WILLIAMS.' (I'd recently begun obsessively collecting old Hank Williams tracks, on the excuse that there was a strong spiritual thread running through his material, but actually because there was something so extreme and unsettling and indeed frightening about him. Dead at 29, and capable of writing 'A House of Gold'.) 'TALK TO ME ABOUT WHAT YOU LIKE, ABOUT WHAT YOU WANT ME TO DO TO YOU IN BED. TALK TO ME ABOUT HORROR FILMS AND CHAINSAWS AND FOOTBALL AND ROCK'N'ROLL MUSIC. TALK TO ME ABOUT OLD MEN FALL- ING DOWN METHYLATED IN THE STREETS. LET'S GET DRUNK AND TAKE DRUGS AND GET FUCKING LEGLESS AND THEN FUCK EACH OTHER'S BRAINS OUT ALL NIGHT, THEN TIE EACH OTHER UP WITH WIRE AND STIMULATE OUR GENITALS WITH ELECTRICITY . . .'

But instead we would hold hands and pray, and sing a few worship choruses together (I am Empty, Fill me Lord), and kiss and have what I decided was stolid, inactive sex, and then I would go away and convert the heathen of, for example, Dunfermline. But as time passed, the demon began to haunt my relationships with Affleck and Priscilla and Evelyn too, and sometimes with church members and ministers. Affleck would come out in front of a group of schoolkids and smile his fatuous smile, and I would be standing behind him with my battered Yamaha guitar, and he would begin to rub his hands together, getting on the Youth wavelength. 'Well, we're glad to be here, here where it's-all-happening, eh?' and inside me went the shouting: 'You old fuck-ing bastard, you stupid bastard, what the FUCK are you doing? WHAT ARE WE DOING? We're scaring these kids, the ones who can be scared, and these fat cunts and you, you old prick, it's all you can do, fuck it's all I can do. We're TELLING THEM SOME CRAP WHICH DOESN'T EVEN WORK FOR US! Because how do we know this is real, this Christ stuff. How do I know? I know because THIS IS HOW I WAS BROUGHT UP. This is wrong, wrong, wrong . . . fucking wrong.' But all the time I smiled and bowed in prayer and played haunting appeal music at the end of our Godshows, and people would sometimes come forward to be saved, while inside I screamed, 'Don't DO it! Don't fucking do it!' Knowing that a few converts would look good in the next prayer-letter Sharon and I wrote, and the money would keep rolling in.

Because that's how it worked. We had prayer partners, supporters, sponsors, who paid money every month, some of them by standing order, and on their behalf I converted people, I did the Lord's work for them. And I had to demonstrate that I – or rather we, me and Sharon – were giving good value for money. So we sent out cyclostyled prayer-letters, information on souls saved ('Praise the Lord for His Mighty Grace') and any needs ('the sink has flooded the kitchen twice, but Sharon is still smiling and our clothes are reasonably clean most of the time'). Wee joke there, they always liked that. And sometimes cheques would arrive. But no washing-machine.

Yet I did believe it all, I think. It was just that constant exposure to the clichés of fundamentalism wore them down, drew their spiritual sting until at the last you could see how weak and fatuous they had made my brand of Christianity. We were turning Christ into a commodity, one you could purchase for a quick deal involving the currency of prayer. We were reducing an eternal mystery into a quick-fix valium substitute, a piece of emotional engineering. Within me, the voice grew louder, more frequent. I was, I decided, demon possessed, and sought out an exorcism.

I'm perfectly serious. I was drifting between two worlds: one of fundamentalist certainty, where demons were real and so were angels and airline pilots who were going to be zapped away to heaven leaving aeroplanes to crash in flames; and one where flesh was flesh and people were people and where there were things to do and see, be and touch that just caused my whole being to ache with desire and frustration. I was, in point of fact, going bonkers. So I went to see an exorcist. This, so they said, very nice exorcist called Owen Cadwallader, leader of a tongue-speaking community of charismatics in Lanarkshire. He it was who acted as a kind of guru to Sonrise, giving them prophetic words as to how their ministry could improve, directions they might pursue, God's will for them. I drove out to see him using the Ford Escort estate car Sharon and I had been given from the Lord by an old lady in Mauchline. It was ancient but hardly used, and the pleasure of driving a car alone after endless periods of time stuck in a minibus with Affleck and Sonrise was intense.

Owen, or Brother Cadwallader as he preferred to be addressed, was a giant, smiling man, who was genuinely charismatic in the way that Hitler was. He had luxuriant, wavy grey hair, a crinkly smile and an inner power, a radiance which sucked you in, made you want desperately to impress Him, and inside me the voice was saying: 'This bastard's into power; watch him. The prick wants control.' I had telephoned in advance, and he had heard all about me from Evelyn and Priscilla. Would I like a tour of the community? Of course.

The Pentecost Community was really a small country house in overgrown grounds which, Brother Cadwallader informed me, he was hoping to turn into a Christian housing scheme with a school and even Christian shops. 'What a witness, eh? What a witness? A city set on a hill cannot be hid!' The community had been gifted the house in the same way Sharon and I had received the Escort. An old lady, now being looked after in a council home, 'where someone from here visits her regularly'. About five families were living together in the house, and they all appeared rather jolly, smiling in a kind of dippy way. There was much embracing, lots of hugs which even I was the recipient of, and it felt good, I had to admit. Nothing sexual, just a welcoming and touching. One young wife, plump and dark haired with a fine moustache, was introduced as 'Trish, our very own prophetess.' She laughed, then looked hard, strangely at me and burst into tears. Brother Cadwallader led her away and they spoke in whispers for a few minutes. He held her in a bear hug with his eyes closed, and came back over to me. 'Trish would like to speak with you for a moment.' My heart was pounding, painfully. This was it. These lovely, spirit-filled people had sussed out the demon.

I sat down with Trish on an old, threadbare couch. Brother Cadwallader had gone to speak to her husband, Dave, and I could hear her two young children playing in the room next door. She put her hand on mine. 'I have a vision of you and for you,' she said. 'I cannot do anything but tell you what it is. When we met I saw you with a very beautiful woman, a blonde woman all dressed in white, and you were hitting her, and hurting her, and she was lying on the ground bleeding, and you were walking away from her into the arms of another woman, even more beautiful, but not your wife.' She looked at me, tears running down her face. 'Is that you? Is it you? No, don't tell me. I know it's the truth.' I said nothing at all. I felt odd. Trish leaned over to embrace me, and I was suddenly overwhelmed with lust. Suddenly I was kissing her on the mouth, and she was responding, her mouth working hard against mine, her teeth grinding against mine, her hands pushing mine determinedly on to her large, soft breasts, while next door I could hear her children playing and shouting and the low rumble of Brother Cadwallader talking to her husband, Dave. But I was reaching under her long floral skirt and fumbling for what turned out to be silk knickers, while she was unzipping my trousers and then we were on the floor and she was pulling me into her, and it was all so wild, so natural and so utterly wrong, so completely . . . *awry*, and yet there was no alternative, none at all. She had her hands on my buttocks and was pulling me hard, harder into her, into her being, biting my ear, and I was thinking of Sharon and thinking of God and the demon and thinking I had to stop and fucking her harder and more unheedingly than I had ever done with Sharon, and then I came and I wanted desperately to be sick. Still the rumble of voices and the children playing in the next room. Trish pulled away from me. 'Stand up,' she said. I did, reaching to pull up my trousers, but she stopped me, and then her mouth was at my testicles, licking, kissing, and one hand was rubbing my backside, and it was if she wanted to be inside every crevice of my body, she wanted to consume all of me. I was hard again, and she pulled me down to the floor, smiling all the time, before climbing on top of me and then she fucked me, fucking me in a way Sharon never had, wantingly, with pleasure, like someone eating a good meal with a massive appetite. And the voices from next door rumbled on, and I wondered how much noise we were making. Although we hadn't spoken, and there was a thick carpet.

We stopped; got dressed. There was a numb moment of mutual concussion. Silence. As if on cue, Brother Cadwallader came in. 'Well, I can see Trish has been able to tell you what she saw for you, what God has given her for you.' He fixed me with a smile so lit from within it was like being hit by a searchlight. 'That is what we do here. We share, we share knowledge and we share ourselves.' And then I realised he knew what Trish and I had been doing, had expected it. 'God wants you here. God wants you to use your gifts here with us. And he wants your wife to come here and be one with us, and be part of us.' He reached for me, to give me one of his bear hugs, his holy embraces, and Trish was caressing my arm, and dimly, muffled came the sound of Dave and the children . . . For a second I could see the warmth and welcome and the hypnotic power of the Cadwallader eyes, and the powerful sexual authority of Trish, and I wavered. But then the demon shouted, screamed loud and clear.

'YOU FUCKING STUPID BASTARD, GET THE FUCK OUT OF HERE. TWO GOOD FUCKS DOESN'T BUY YOUR SOUL. THESE SCREWBALLS ARE FUCKING BAD NEWS.' I ran for the door, down the corridors of the old house to the Ford Escort, started it, revved away from the Pentecost Community like a bat away from hell or heaven. Along the M74 I went, the engine screaming, and all the time I was shouting, aloud, right out into the engine noise, 'FUCK FUCK FUCK FUCK FUCK FUCK FUCK FUCK FUCK FUCK FUCK . . .' All the way from Lesmahagow to Glasgow, non-stop. And it wasn't the demon speaking, because in the nausea, the heart-pounding heavy pulse of that rushing headlong flight, I suddenly knew, coldly and clearly and calmly, that there was no demon. Somewhere about Hamilton, passing the squint burial chamber of the Dukes of Hamilton, subsiding into old mineshafts, I knew. There was only me. Just me. It was me who was shouting 'fuck', and God wasn't striking me down with a bolt of lightning. It was me who knew that everything I'd lived for was wrong, totally, desperately, sickeningly wrong, and that I had to get away. Away, out, apart, gone. Nothing else mattered.

I had a chequebook, £30 in cash, God's money, and the car. At the Uddingston interchange I veered on to the M8 heading for Edinburgh, and kept going. Affleck, Priscilla, Evelyn, my parents, the Brethren and Jesus Christ were all behind me. I never saw Sharon again.

PART TWO

Cash

I'd once been singing at a small Pentecostal church in Greenock, doing one of the heavy-handed 'humorous' songs which was part of my religious act, an attack on spiritual cults like the Moonies. Cults were big in those days, with the memories of rock'n'roll post-drug gurus like Meher Baba and Sri Chinmoy, who for years I thought was called Three Chimneys. There's a restaurant in Skye called Three Chimneys, but that's not important right now. It never crossed my mind that Pentecostalism, with its mouth-foaming, tongue-speaking, vision-seeing, bodies-writhing-on-the-floor elements, might be considered a cult by some. After all, it was a traditional form of industrial-escapist Christianity, like a magic Brethren.

> We're the Church of the Chimpanzee
> And we don't monkey about
> We got our name from a chimp named Jane
> She'd got us all figured out
> She says we can believe what we want to
> So join our church anyway
> Your salvation is just a donation away.

It was a fairly informal Saturday night youth meeting, so people were allowing themselves to laugh. My intention was to get them relaxed and smiling, then hit them with another song about a friend who'd died of cancer, yet whose life had been a shining Christian example of hope and prayer and the power of faith. But suddenly there was a shout from the back of the tin-roofed shack, the building a remnant from the shipbuilding days when riveters and platers would flock to such places for a mystical escape to another, sweeter world. I stopped singing as a small man in out-of-date clothes too big for him stalked towards the stage, brandishing a huge floppy Bible, one of those annotated ones with red alliterative footnotes saying things like 'Oh, that the World would recognise this Immortal Truth, one where Retribution, Rejoicing, Renewal, Relationship and Reconciliation are co-mingled and expressed!' The little man, his tousled hair shivering, was reading in a loud, confident voice.

'Be ye not conformed to this world, but be ye transformed . . .' He turned to me. 'You have defiled the House of God with unspiritual song and the sound of unholy laughter. You are not of God, and your ministry is not of God, and you are a promoter of low thoughts and fleshly impulses.' Then he began to laugh hysterically. 'No God, no, do not judge us all for the sins of this man, do not send fire tonight to this place, let us learn and grow to minister for thee . . .' And in a trice he was fitting on the floor. He lay and squirmed and shook and foamed at the mouth, and I looked at him, and the 60 or so people in the hall looked at him and back at me, and I could see them thinking: Which one's the good guy? This was a Pentecostal church, for goodness' sake. They were used to this kind of thing. I wasn't, though, and I was in a cold sweat, thinking to myself, he knows, this poor wee guy. He knows about me and what I really am, what I really want. And then one of the youth leaders and a large, lumbering apprentice from the oilrig yard which was all that remained of Greenock's shipbuilding industry came and picked him up and carried him out, leaving the big floppy Bible lying on the floor where it had fallen, all kinds of leaflets and tracts spread around it like broken china on the worn red lino.

I sang my song about faith and death, and preached too solemnly, too fiercely, to try and prove that I was truly holy, that God really was with me, and that the strange little man had been wrong. When I finished, there was a rush towards me, embarrassed apologies. 'I'm so sorry, that's Jimmy, he's not well, just got out of mental hospital last week, we thought he was fine, he'd been having shock therapy, he gets carried away, he's not quite right . . .' But he had been. Exactly right. About me.

I never sang 'Church of the Chimpanzee' again, but there was a strange sequel. Three years later, as a born-again-again experimental hedonist, I bumped into the youth leader from that little church, the one who'd carried Jimmy out. He hadn't heard about my fall from grace, my spectacular backsliding, and smiled and God-blessed me and chatted about the church and how God was working in it. 'And do you know,' he said. 'That song of yours about the Church of the Chimpanzee was very useful to some of our members, because they arrived in Gourock just two weeks after you sang at our church, and they were handing out leaflets for a meeting which Jane, the guru monkey you were talking about – well, she was going to be at it. They had pictures of her. Gourock Town Hall I think it was. Of course, they didn't go, having been forewarned, so to speak. I think the council's health and safety people stopped it in the end, though. Cruelty to dumb animals.'

The world lurched. I walked away, my head nipping. I didn't dare ask myself what had really happened, or if there was a Church of the Chimpanzee, or if he was mad, as mad as poor old Jimmy, or if I was. It wouldn't have surprised me if I was. I knew the world was fairly mad, too. But not that mad, surely. I'm not making this up; it did really happen; just like that. Believe it or not.

Jimmy had been right about me. I drove that Escort along the M8 like Bunyan running from his burden of sin, except my burden was salvation and all the ancillaries which had gone with it: wife, home, clothes, holy job. Suddenly I was a blank, with no friends, no family, nothing, and it was up to me what I wrote on the empty pages of experience. Like someone who decides to tattoo themselves all over, I had lots of space to fill, and I was determined to do as much frenzied scribbling as possible. I was tumbling in the air, falling from the choking smoke of a burning building, relieved and caught in a moment which could end in smashed and bloody disaster, or . . . something else. Past the Honeywell factory, through Lanarkshire to West Lothian, grey land of levelled pit-bings and stark, grey council houses, of grazing stained black by millions of passing internal combustion engines. Harthill. Even the name redolent of dirt and decay, and the collapsing 1960s architecture of the M8's only service area promising bad coffee, cold bacon and enormous prices. On and on, mind blank, eyes recording the sights and the constant hissing, roaring soundtrack of the motorway with total clarity. A house with a bed-and-breakfast sign perched on a hillock; a cow, black and white and cud-chewing by the hard shoulder, ready to cause a major pile-up; the gigantic roundabout, with the turn-off for the north, Fife, the Highlands, and a half-glimpse of the red-leaded Forth Rail Bridge in the distance. North then? No. Unthinkingly east, not knowing why. Then Ingliston, empty and abandoned, with its miniature race track, its permanent, tawdry stalls for the Royal Highland show; the scream of jets, and the airport away to the left. No escape there. As I ran, or fell, resources from the past disappeared, too. It was a naked, poor freedom which beckoned, but I was falling under the weight of a gravity beyond my control now, driving east, east, circling the Barnton roundabout once, twice, three times, then heading for Leith, losing myself in the high tenement cityscape, the old, history-laden atmosphere of Edinburgh. A real capital, old and twisted and overwhelming, dusty and dirty and decaying and diseased. Like an infected tattoo, spreading and blurring on the skin, Edinburgh was hard to identify, fascinating, and a place I knew hardly at all. It had always possessed some vague, slightly gamey glamour Glasgow simply didn't have. There was something of the rotting mediterranean slum about it; a mystery; old streets, old buildings, old ghosts. It was a swamp, a place to sink in without trace. You could only do the same thing in Glasgow if you were able to match the hard poverty of its huge scheme-trapped populace, the accent, the look, the life. In Edinburgh, a middle-class boy could lose his way and his past more easily, because the rot of bohemianism had always been part of the capital's life.

But you can't erase either tattoos or experience. Not completely. A few days later I sent a postcard to Sharon, and another to my parents. The same message was on each, printed, unsigned: I'm fine, don't try to find me. Every two months I'd send another two postcards. I'm fine, don't try to find me. Six months after the great escape, I wrote: 'I'm fine. Don't try to find me. God bless you.' I never wrote again. Didn't try to find out anything about them. I felt nothing. My memory, emotions, seemed to have been cauterised. So why had I written those cards? There was no emotional drive to send those tiny messages. Perhaps there was a subconscious will to hurt, to remind them that the horror still lived, invisibly walked the earth, ready to blow into their lives again, the stinking bad wind of evil, of betrayal, the perfume of sin. The postcards were sent from all over the country, thanks to a lorry driver called Alex, one of my laundrette acquaintances. I had never been inside a laundrette in my life before.

I sold the Escort for £100, and the Yamaha guitar for £50, which gave me £180, a good darts score but hardly a fortune on which to base a new life. I rented a room in a damp and infested student flat just off Leith Walk, halfway between castellated Disneyburgh and the port of Leith, now being hauled upmarket, its warehouses converted into young executive flats, its pubs into wine and oyster bars. But there was still a genuinely seedy ambience to parts of the old harbour area, places where cars could be sold for cash, where others could change colour and number plates. I liked the collision in Leith between decay and development. There was something elemental about it; something I found myself in sympathy with. I spent three months shedding all traces of religion from my appearance. I bought Oxfam and Sue Ryder clothes, grew my hair, had my left ear pierced. I fancied a tattoo, and one hungover morning I woke to find that I had one, blue and bleeding on my right wrist. God Is Love, it said. At first I drank vodka in the scaly room, a damp, sordid place unmentionably stained by decades of studenthood. I bought cheap Macbrayne of Leith vodka from Sheraz's shop next to the closemouth, and the perfumed, oily clarity of the spirit dulled and then erased thought and memory. Mr Sheraz was landlord, supplier of drink and occasionally food. He was quiet, nervous even, and completely uninterested in what went on in his flat. As long as the rent was paid on time. He even let me have tick, although this privilege was not accorded to Usborne and Smith, my flatmates. Whenever they entered the shop Mr Sheraz grew visibly frightened. 'The devils! The devils!' he whispered once to me. 'Bad, evil, bad people. Students!' And he shook his head, eyes wobbling in their sockets as if they were loose. He thought I was some kind of grown up, I suppose. He didn't know about me, the devil, and God.

My flatmates were fully fledged goths, all black fishnets, leather and nose rings. They were, I gathered after several weeks, engaged in some kind of engineering course at Napier, and were, as far as I could tell, male and female. One of them had muttered, in response to my polite enquiry about what he or she was studying, 'Nape-yer. Jineering.' That was the end of the conversation. They had separate rooms, but seemed to alternate which one they jointly slept in. Both were painted in red gloss paint and great bleeding lumps of sheet-metal music would come thudding out of one or the other when they were in residence. There was no telephone. They didn't have to take messages for me, or I for them. We rarely spoke, other than to grunt non-committal city swamp noises at each other as we passed in the hall. The flat's kitchen was typhoid formica courtesy of some DIY store many years ago. None of us was going to be first with the Flash and Fairy Liquid, while some cupboards were simply never opened. Usborne and Smith was on the scrawled label on the door frame. I never asked their first names.

At first I just grew dirty. I had no idea how to wash clothes, apart from in the bath using Vosene shampoo, which I imagined would at least kill any germs I accrued. At uni and Bethesda, all my washing had gone into a black bag which was regularly fired motherwards, and later there had been Sharon. Finally, as the various pieces of apparel I'd acquired from charity shops were beginning to walk around on their own, I ventured into a laundrette, clutching a bin bag full of body odour, and timidly asked one of the attendants what to do. She was about 38, wire-thin, with short blond-streaked hair and a prematurely aged face etched in humour and resignation out of which peeped pure teenage mischief when she smiled. Dressed in a pink check nylon housecoat, smoking a cheap Berkeley King Size cigarette, she looked at me with a grim pity.

'What age are you son? No' just a teenager any more, and you don't know how to wash your ain claithes. Poor bastard. Listen, just watch me and you'll learn. Ah'll learn you. But only the once, mind. After this you'll pay for a service wash.'

Her name was Mairhi ('my dad's a teuchter frae Stornoway. Old bugger died of the drink when he was 42 and left me and mam on the social. Teuchters! All he did was sing Gaelic songs and get smashed') and we would pass the time of day together quite often, me learning from her, filling up the blanks. From her I learned to smoke, inhaling, in the end without gagging on the dirty, jaggy swirl of the Berkeleys. I was teaching myself to drink more than the chemical dullness of vodka. In pubs from the West End to the very pits of Leith I tried pints of Guinness, Murphy's, real ales and fake ales, 70 shilling, 80 shilling, pounds and pounds and pints and pints. I learned to cope with room-heaving hangovers, remembered to drink water before I went to bed, how doner kebabs always made you sick after more than six pints. And Mairhi took me to a wee pub I'd never been to before, a clean, quiet place called the Gallions, near her council flat, and taught me about halves of beer and halves of whisky, and I learned about the different effects of whisky on top of stout, that sweet burn, and how a dram could lift you out of the leaden, sleepy torpor of beery bloatedness. And then we went back to Mairhi's tiny flat, which turned out to be immaculate, bare, but immaculate, with a huge 26-inch telly and a video recorder. She rolled a cigarette which seemed abnormally big, out of lots of green Rizla papers. I couldn't work it out, because she normally smoked Berkeleys, and I'd bought a packet out of the pub machine before we left. But I was drunk. 'George, my boy, got this stuff,' she said. George was her son, 18 years old and in Glenochil for stealing cars. Fifteen cars, to be exact. 'A bit of black. It's the business for seeing you through the week. Better than the drink. And cheaper. Weird, though, eh? Your wee boy being your connection?' She snorted, cynically. Mairhi never went to see George. He could have a bed when he got out, she said, for one week. Then he was on his own. She'd had enough. It was time she got something for herself. And her own dope. She ought to be able to manage that . . .

So we smoked half the joint, and I threw up in the bathroom, copiously but neatly; accurately. Indeed, joyfully. It was the first time in my life I'd ever heaved vomit into a toilet bowl with a smile on my face. We had a cup of tea and smoked the rest of it, and Mairhi put on a video called, I think, *Thailand Nights*. In the darkness of the room, as the video flickered and bodies writhed, she ran her fingers, hard, brittle fingers underneath my T-shirt, one of the grimy, grey T-shirts she and I would watch swirling around and around in the big washers of the laundrette, and I learned about sex for its own sake. 'This is for me,' she said at one point, sitting astride me on the cheap, rough carpet, pumping her thin body up and down. 'This is for me, I'm taking, bastard, and I'm just having a good time, and fuck you, son, maybe you'll learn something.' She did. And I did.

I was making money. Not a lot, but some. Enough to get by on. The broo? God had been my employer, and there had been no question of paying income tax in the normal sense. The Inland Revenue even had a system to deal with it, evolved to cope with Catholic priests, who were allowed simply to say how much they'd earned in any one year, and were believed because they were priests. As a full-time singing evangelist, I was believed because I believed. So Sharon and I had prayed at the end of each fiscal year, and counted up the money God had given us, and waited for a vision of how much we should pass on in tax. We tithed, of course, giving ten percent back to God. In the end we decided not to declare the tithe as income. It was a deductable expense, surely.

My ungodly occupation had begun by accident, in desperation, during my trawling through charity shops in search, initially, of clothing. I became obsessed with the hunt for second-hand bargains, fascinated by the possibility that I might turn up something valuable among the cast-off shrouds of the dead. Of course I had no idea about antiques, really, but I had a feeling that if something valuable came up, suddenly appeared in my rummaging hands, I'd know. And so I haunted car-boot sales and jumble-sales, queuing up early to get in among the vicious, highly competitive ladies with their string shopping-bags and head-scarves. Markets, church sales, house clearances, skips . . . you name it, I'd be there, raking around, looking for diamonds and gold amid the crap and the belongings of the buried. You had to have a strong stomach. Sometimes lice lurked in silk linings, and rat droppings in undisturbed cardboard boxes of shoes. Once I bought a huge black overcoat for 50 pence at a jumble-sale in Dalkeith. In the lining of the inside pocket something crinkled.

On the bus back to Edinburgh I crinkled the smooth, satiny cloth up and down, wondering and hoping. At the flat, some delicate ripping with a blunt table knife exposed an ancient, white £5 note, folded in four and dating back to to 1937. All next day, a Sunday, I carried it in my back jeans pocket, occasionally taking it out, unfolding it and just looking at it, wondering about its story: A mother, sewing the cash in for her son, to be used only in an emergency; then he went off to war and never returned, lost on one of the Murmansk convoys. Or maybe this had been a black marketeer's coat, and the fiver his stash against some desperate strait or other. He'd been killed and the note never discovered. Or more likely, it had just been forgotten about. Well, it had been left for me in the end. Some old man, crumpled and grey and dying in a bed, maybe silent and dribbling from stroke, and all he wanted to do was say to someone, remember that black overcoat? There's five pounds in the lining. But there was nobody to tell.

On the Monday, I sold the note for £25 to a dealer in the New Town. That afternoon I was in a temporary Scout fund-raising shop in Musselburgh, and came across a bundle of 12 Hardy's Anglers' Guides, dating consecutively from 1914 through to 1926. They were old. They looked attractive, even to me who had not the slightest interest in fishing. And I got the lot for a pound. They were pretty heavily thumbed, but otherwise in good condition. I took them to a book dealer in the West End. None too neat and tidy himself, he looked at my scruffy, second-hand appearance and asked how much I wanted for them. I had no idea, but reckless abandon took over. 'A hundred,' I said, thinking I could always claim to have been joking. But he didn't bat an eyelid, although his pupils did contract somewhat.

'I'll give you eighty.'

My jaw began falling floorwards; snapping my teeth back together, I swallowed, ready simply to nod acceptance, when a voice told the dealer firmly: '90.' It was my voice. I walked out of there with nine tenners, brown crumpled ones smelling of male sweat, and my life as a finder-and-seller of books and collectable junk had begun. Later, of course, when I discovered *Miller's Antiques Price Guide* and began perusing it in local libraries across Scotland, until I could afford to start buying my own selection (you need every year you can get, because the listings and example pictures are different in each edition), I realised that each of the Hardy's Guides had been worth about £50. Each. But them's the breaks. Besides, I still felt sometimes that I had God, a disappointed and generally pissed-off but amused God, watching over me and playing nasty little tricks to punish me for my evil doing. At other times, I just didn't think about religion at all; that part of my life seemed to have happened to somebody else. Then again, pressure on, tension increasing, and I'd be babbling to heaven, rationalising the superstitious nonsense: I hadn't stopped believing in Him, you see. Just in the tottering, poisonous, corrupt system of knowing Him. At least, that's what I told Him when I prayed, which was quite often. 'Listen, God,' I would say. 'I'm prepared to give you the benefit of the doubt, if you'll just help me wheedle a good price out of Benny the Bonk for these vintage *Playboy* magazines.' And sometimes He was in a good mood and helped out. Sometimes He wasn't. Asking God for help flogging copies of *Playboy* was probably a bit over the top. Although I'm sure that Hugh Heffner would have sold some Bibles for Him, if He'd asked. As a special favour. One day I came across a 1941 edition of Agatha Christie's *Evil Under the Sun*, missing dust-jacket, but well-preserved. It was in a box of crappy war-printed cheap editions, things like George Sava's anti-Nazi propaganda. Thank you, God. I sold it to Peter Findlay at the Merchiston Book Company for £200. Two weeks later I saw it priced in his window at £550. Ha ha ha, God. Very funny.

Mairhi and I slept together once or twice a week, and although the dope always made me randy as hell, I really didn't enjoy the after-effects of it. I was left lazy and woolly, and found myself smiling foolishly sometimes when I should have been bargaining, snake-like and vicious with the granny at the charity stall selling a John Le Carré first edition. 'A pound! You must be joking, dear.'

'You'll be moving on, soon, sonny,' Mairhi said, as we reclined, semi-naked against her leatherette settee and watched one of her truly astounding selection of porn videos. George the criminal offspring had been out of Glenochil for exactly the week Mairhi had agreed to let him stay in her house, before his addiction to car theft saw him total a Porsche 911 Targa and end up first in the Western General Hospital, then in Saughton. He was growing up, the boy. Learning.

'Where do you get all these, Mairhi?' She was rubbing the inside of my thigh as truly ridiculous things happened on the screen involving a fresh salmon, a catering jar of mayonnaise and three clearly very hungry women.

'Och, I just picked them up. The way you pick up your books and your wee knick-knacks, around. At places . . . street corners. You know down next to the Café Royal, in those alleys? Well, there's boys come round there wi' bags, and they sell these just like it was ice-cream or something. I mean, what's a woman on her own to do, eh?' I put out my Berkeley and kissed her thin, lined face, with its humour and wisdom and strength and generosity.

'You've got me, Mairhi.' One of her hands reached for my testicles and squeezed.

'I have now.' She let go. She was wearing nothing but a pair of silk knickers and suddenly I wanted her, was inflamed with a shocking, total lustfulness reminiscent of the prophetess-fucking at Owen Cadwallader's. I moved on to her, and she began to laugh, not loud, gurgling, until she was helplessly amused.

'Aye, boy,' she said, as I sat, arms folded, a lopsided erection drooping dangerously towards the overflowing ashtray. 'Men love to be fucked. They love to be played with. God, the number of men who love to be tied up and handcuffed and shite like that. Aye, and don't look at me that way, it's not that I've done it. At least not very often. Though I've got a pair of handcuffs in the bedroom there if you fancy a wee shot. But you check out the videos, the stuff going the rounds. Most of it has men in chains, tied up, in cages, and some of it's just disgusting. That's it. Big strong men, and they want to be fucked. And yet they're the ones with the power, the ones walking around raping and hurting and destroying. Why is that? You're the smart one, aren't you?'

'Not as smart as you, Mairhi.' I scrambled up from the floor, and dressed as the fishy, fleshy scenes on the video continued. Mairhi was still sitting on the floor, watching, her thin legs stuck straight in front of her, an ashtray balanced on her crotch. I leaned down and kissed her on the forehead, brushing back the short, streaked hair. 'I'll see you.'

'No you won't.' She turned her head towards me, smiled. 'Thank you, God bless and goodnight.' And that was that. Except that even now, when I come across second-hand porn videos, I occasionally buy anything I don't recognise and which seems liable to appeal to Mairhi (not too hard, a bit funny, nothing nasty) and send it to her at the address she's probably long since moved out of. I'm stupid that way. Sentimental. I watch it first, of course. I hope the laundrette threw up another pupil.

I'd never told Mairhi about my past. I was just some bit of damaged goods passing through the laundrette, getting cleaned up, sorted out. Learning. What had I given her? Nothing but a wee bit of a good time, maybe, some drinks, a laugh. Companionship. Contact. Flesh on flesh, word on word. And it had been good. Maybe, in fact, that was all there was, needed to be. A recognition of need. A touching and giving and learning.

I'd been in Edinburgh nearly a year. It was like living in a real-life theme park, a kind of *trompe l'œil* city, some nights, when the castle blazed in its floodlighting above Princes Street, when the old buildings of the Old Town and the less old ones of the New Town reeked of history and mischief and power and lies. The festival had been insane, a great tide of colour and weirdness and hair and youth and funny clothes and sex which swept in on the summer flood then ebbed away, leaving the walls and lamp-posts scabbed with old posters. 'You should find an actress,' Mairhi suggested to me. 'Everybody gets to fuck an actor or an actress during the festival.' But I lurked in the half-shadows of bars like the Eagle in Leith, places where actors were likely to be jostled and spat upon, and let the culture and the available new flesh pass me by.

Edinburgh could be a violent place, and away from the pitted gloss and gap-toothed glamour of the city centre, there stretched the foulness of the big schemes, the hard drugs and the spectre of AIDS, just being talked about as I left, mostly with a kind of nervous laugh. I could hear God laughing. Oh yes, a beautiful trick, for me to become HIV positive from Mairhi. That would certainly complete the learning process. There was fearful talk of blood-to-blood contact, and I recalled Mairhi's particular love of fucking during her period ('brilliant sensation, son, brilliant . . . come on, don't worry about the mess. I've got rubber sheets on the bed underneath the flannelette . . .'). Fearfully, I had the test. Brusquely friendly nurses, a heartstopping wait for the result . . . negative. Thank God. I could hear Him laughing His ironic laugh. Within a year, Edinburgh would be named AIDS capital of Europe, an Auschwitz floodlit and well-stocked with new flesh and good restaurants. And in the concrete housing schemes, shared needles would continue to dull the hell of existence, bringing the ultimate communion, the conjoining of lovers and strangers and parents and children in disease and death. And what was God doing? Laughing, or shaking his head? A year out of Disneyburgh I had another test. Still negative. And I hoped, wondered, even prayed for Mairhi.

By this time I had a savings account with Girobank, the Post Office's wonderfully anonymous, centralised invention, enabling access to cash, the only form of money I used, much more frequently than a traditional bank and less personal. I also had a decrepit Volkswagen camper-van, handy both for sleeping in during scavenging trips, and for transporting anything large, only as far as a dealer. Quick turnover was the key to what I did. I was what is called in the second-hand book trade a runner: I only bought what I knew I could sell, and then usually only one or two items, or a bundle of books. Sometimes it was frustrating, when the chance to clear a house came up. But I was doing all right. Once in a while, I even bought a piece of new clothing, as in unused. I purchased a pair of eight-eyelet Doc Martens, industrial socks and a blue pea-jacket from a marine suppliers. I was still in the disgusting off-Leith Walk flat with the engineering goths. One bright, hot summer's day, I took my second-hand Globetrotter suitcase, packed it with what clothes I wanted to keep, half a dozen unread paperback thrillers (I made it a point of principle never to keep books for myself. Sometimes I read them, but then I always sold them on. Books are for collectors to collect, readers to read, and dealers to sell. They're not furniture, unless you've the heart of a librarian), went out to the VW and left Edinburgh in the sunshine, picking the fleas from underneath its metaphorical fur coat. I couldn't face another festival. The old capital city wouldn't have needed its knickers on the day I left, as it flapped its slightly moth-eaten mink around its body for refreshment in the heat. The streets shimmered, and white Scottish bodies glared blindingly as the big old stone of Edinburgh reflected the distinctive arthritic rattle of the VW's air-cooled, flat-four engine. I manoeuvred through the traffic of Corstorphine, past the zoo, the VW chattering amid the leafy, prosperous suburb to the Maybury roundabout where I'd taken the turn-off to Leith 12 months previously. Then I'd been like some automaton, blindly, blankly following some unknown urge. Maybe the devil's. Maybe my deserted God's, maybe mine. Now I knew where to go, what to do, although I wasn't entirely sure why. I signalled left and took the M8 for Glasgow.

Scotland's second city is so big, scattered, and downright brutal in appearance compared to compact and bijou Edinburgh. Bit by broken-and-repaired-and-renewed-bit it loomed up at the Clyde end of the M8. At last I was cruising along the elevated, Los Angeles-on-Irn-Bru motorway which takes you into – and out the other side of, should you desire – the old heart of the city this overblown road and its moronic designers tried to rip out. Glasgow leered drunkenly around me like some old, much-loved drunken relative: you're pleased to see them, but you know renewing your relationship is going to lead to complications, embarrassment, pain. No point in revisiting the holy haunts of the past. I slid off the M8 before the Kingston Bridge catapulted me south of the Clyde, and at the first traffic lights since Corstorphine, turned right onto Great Western Road. Away from the reinforced concrete hell of the M8, I was suddenly in the West End. Everything bigger, wider, more regular than the sudden medieval twists you found in old Edinburgh. And glinting, glittering in tawdriness where Edinburgh, away from the Disney-esque tourist traps, gloried in its genteel dirt. Glasgow, big, brassy, loud and business like, dresses for success. All the women look like film stars, would-bes, wannabes and fully fledged Madonnaesque sirens. In Edinburgh, women look like lawyers or aspire to.

In Byres Road, the very heart of pseudo-bohemian Glasgow, in the shadow of the Victorian gothic university of Gilmorehill, I checked out the advertisement cards in various newsagents. It was summer, and student demand for living space was at its lowest. I leased a ground-floor flat in Ruthven Street, one of the tenement canyons off Byres Road, right in the epicentre of the West End. It was owned by an anonymous expatriate, and looked after by an estate agent. A lady with blue hair and artificially pink cheeks showed me round, leafing nervously through the refer-ences I'd forged using notepaper filched from Updikes of Stock-bridge and James Thin and Co. I was, I'd written, a book and antiquity dealer of the highest reputation. 'We've had students, of course, in the past, and frankly, the trouble was, on occasion, a bit overwhailming. Would you be using the property for bezzniss?' I assured her that I had storage elsewhere in the city, which of course I didn't. I didn't see the need to explain to her that runners need little more than the vehicle they operate in. And sometimes just a bus ticket and a plastic bag. She pursed her lips and looked doubtfully at me. 'I suppuwse you can afford a depowsit?' I nodded. The place would do. It was big and empty and echoingly-appointed with the basics of rented existence. Nearby there was a complete selection of carry-out restaurants, and the great souk of Asian food known as Gibson Street was barely a mile away. The pubs within walking distance ranged from the blithely grim to the severely selective. You could mix with lawyers, media and moneyed drunks at the Ubiquitous Chip, with its iniquitously expensive restaurant underneath the bar; have a free-and-easy pint in the cavernous and sometimes semi-gay Tennent's; obtain various noxious substances at certain other howffs and, in my state of unfashionability, get turned away by the trendy doorman at Chimmy Chunga's. People were super-ficially friendly, but it didn't go deeper than the price of a pint. The West End of Glasgow is a place for transients, and yet I felt strangely visible all the time. I knew Glasgow, and elements of Glasgow knew me. Hadn't I evangelised on the streets, sung to drunks in Sauchiehall Street? And Glasgow, because of that surface friendliness, that easy, instant familiarity, was a place where every-one asked questions of you. I had begun drifting around junkshops and jumble sales, Paddy's Market and the Barras, and still couldn't get used to the almost instant first-name status I assumed. I was known, recognised for what I was: a dealer, a runner. The shops knew me too, but they were more reticent, unless they tried flattery and friendship in order to try and screw me.

After a while I grew nervous of the space in the flat. Glasgow was making me more and more edgy, as I lived in constant expectation of meeting Sharon or some ex-sinner I had been instrumental in converting from a life of fun to an existence of fundamentalism. I even missed the gormless engineering Goths from Leith Walk. And Mairhi. The laundrette in Byres Road was busy and hectic and, besides, I knew how to wash clothes now. I had no excuse to ask for help, even if I'd wanted to. The attendants looked like spare-time veteran female Sumo wrestlers. I advertised in a local newsagent for people to sub-let the two spare bedrooms, hoping for an intelligent, beautiful divorcee or three. Instead I got Mick and Keith.

Their real names were Graham Merchison and Paul Grant, but they had changed their names for the sake, they told me, laughing in that classically Glaswegian ironic-but-fuck-it-we-mean-it way, of rock'n'roll. 'Spirit of fuckin' rock, man,' said Graham (Mick). 'That's where we draw our fuckin' aesthetic from, know what ah mean?'

'Aye, right enough,' nodded Paul (Keith), shaggy, craggy and doom-laden compared to his friend's front-man chutzpah. Mick sang and Keith played the guitar, inevitably. They'd both been to university, but dropped out after two years ('no fuckin' vibe, man'). They were getting a band together, writing songs, and needed somewhere to stay. Could we do a rent-book scam for the DHSS? They'd handle it, get the book, set the rent at double what I was actually charging them, and claim that from the broo. Then I could pay them back half of what the DHSS would pay me directly for their accommodation. Mick smiled appealingly at me, practising his charisma like a facial athlete. Keith looked mean and chewed gum. What the hell. They appealed to something in me, that strange flame which had been kindled so long ago by the Cornerstones. This really was rock'n'roll, struggling along below the bottom rung. Primitive, glinting, longing for the glamour. They were 20 years old, and full of a kind of yearning, simple confidence I'd never known myself. I wanted a part of it, so I did the deal with them and illegally with the DHSS.

'No practising here, though.' I felt like my father. 'Not with electric instruments. Acoustic guitars, fine. And no parties unless you sort it out with me first.'

'Great, man. Aye, that's great. Fuckin' great.' Four days later,

Mick's father, resplendent in yellow Pringle sweater, failed hair transplant and Volvo estate, helped them move from their previous bedsit. Mr Merchison was desperately trying to be the liberal, man-to-man, give-'em-a-long-leash parent, and it was clear that Mick at least had a healthy middle-class background. Mick Snr, a landscape garden contractor from Bishopbriggs ('here's my card if you ever . . . well here's my card') regarded me with nodding wariness, but hey, you had to let the lad do his own thing, even if his live-in landlord looked like a drug dealer. I had, it must be admitted, acquired an Edinburgh pallor which matched my unshaven chin and pre-grunge clothes. One day I met Keith's mother, a bejewelled Jewish lady from Newton Mearns who arrived at the door with a bag of washing, and she looked at me with hastily disguised panic. She invited herself in, and I made her a cup of tea, attempting to reassure her that I was not running a homosexual vice ring. What did I do? Oh, buying and selling. Bric-a-brac. Books. A spark of interest. What kind of things? I had just come back from a trip to Stirling, where I had, miraculously, picked up a Flight, Barr and Barr tea cup and saucer, dirty but undamaged, for a fiver in what was supposed to be an antiques emporium but was actually a junk shop with *Lovejoy* pretensions. The coming of *Lovejoy* and the *Antiques Roadshow* on television had made everyone a would-be divvy, but it was still possible to dig out gems. And this cup and saucer was a small chipped diamond. I knew I could sell it in town for at least £50. I fetched it from my bedroom and showed it to Mrs Keith.

'I'll give you £40 for it,' she said. Sixty, I replied. We agreed on £50. It turned out she ran an interior decoration and informal antiques-finding service for the upmarket south-side community she lived in.

'Please keep in touch,' she said, handing me her card, discreet, modern but etched in gold leaf. 'I feel sure we can do more business.' She touched me on the arm, leaving an aroma of overwhelming femininity and wealth. Givenchy, as I was later to discover. But there was no caress. Her hand on my elbow was like someone gingerly patting a possibly verminous cat. Actually she wasn't bad-looking, early forties, lacquered and rigorously dieted. I was nearly 30 and incipiently fat. Too much beer. Too much horrible fried food. I decided it was time to shape up. I did one press-up that night, which hurt like hell.

One day the doorbell rang, and there was Sharon's dad. Christ. Sharon's fucking father. Sharon's. It had to happen, I supposed. Maybe it was what I'd wanted, to settle up, sort out the past, at least partially. To have it catch up with me. He still looked like death warmed up, blinking a watery, nervous smile. Someone from the church had seen me in the street, he said. He'd gone into Tennent's cavernous depths and asked for me. Maybe someone had thought he fancied me, who knows? Nobody there knew me by name, of course, Byres Road being like an airport concourse. Transience is a fact of life, a prevailing wind sweeping people up and away all the time. Then he'd come back every evening for a week, and haunted the supermarket, and wandered up and down . . . He told me all of this on the doorstep, gabbling it out nervously. I looked at him. I didn't have a phone. The estate agency, which operated its lettings side from a nameless office high above Hope Street in the City Centre, knew my name. Who else knew me, and where I stayed? A number of book and antique dealers. The DHSS. Sharon's dad stuttered into silence. I beckoned him inside.

'Private detective, was it?' He licked his lips, nodded. Oh my. Tracked down by a private dick. And prayer. No doubt they'd been praying, if not for me then about me, that they would find me, as there was obviously some pressing reason for this searching out. Probably, they had just been hoping I was dead.

'Your parents . . .'

'I don't want to hear about my parents.' But I did. As soon as he said the words, I wanted to know that they weren't dead. And then like bad alcohol, clutching at the guts, the thought, Christ, they'll be so ashamed of me, it would be better for us all if I was dead or they were. Or all of us. But they weren't. They had, unbelievably, moved to New Zealand, where my father had relatives. Aunty Gay had often written in the course of my childhood, praising the wonderful climate and the traditional values and the worshipping church of New Zealand. Now my dad, retired from his foot-repair business, had fled in shame the country I had defiled for him. I sighed with relief, but felt a stirring of sorrow, just a quivering echo of past joys. It passed quickly.

'I'm here to see you because Sharon asked me to find you. She . . . she doesn't want to see you.' He sighed. I was smoking a Berkeley, and all of a sudden he dived into his jacket pocket and brought out a packet of Benson and Hedges. I was astonished.

'I thought the body was the temple of the Holy Spirit,' I said, drawing on my cut-price, rasping tobacco. I couldn't resist the cheap jibe.

'We all have our secrets,' he said, and I thought back immediately to Sharon's big secret, her teenage Christian fucking and abortion. Yes, we all did have secrets. Except me. My life was an open, second-hand, not very valuable book.

'Everyone has to make compromises.' Sharon's dad blew a cloud of smoke into the centre of the anonymous room, furnished with only a cheap plastic sofa and some matching chairs. The anaglypta walls were painted off-white. A dusty spherical paper lampshade hung crookedly from the badly replastered ceiling. 'You would have been happier, you might even have been happy, if you'd been less . . . committed. If you'd just had a normal job, hadn't taken your faith to such extremes.' God Almighty. I'd barely spoken a word to this guy before or during my marriage to his daughter. Now he was trying to sell me a non-fundamentalist fundamentalism.

'Is Sharon OK?'

He sat back, stubbed out his fag. 'Yes, yes. She's fine.' He paused. 'She's living with your former associate Mr McCaig.' Mister McCaig. Mister McCaig? Who was he . . . not Affleck McCaig? No, surely not . . . Affleck, the gospel preacher with his foot perpetually in his mouth? Affleck the abnormal evangelist? Affleck? He was married with something like 18 children, for goodness' sake. 'He left his wife . . . he had been seeing Sharon to try and . . . comfort her over your disappearance. And things just . . . happened.' He was lighting another cigarette. 'These things do happen, I suppose. They claim God is still with them.' He coughed, spatteringly. I just gaped at him. 'Mr McCaig' (he obviously couldn't bring himself to use Affleck's first name) 'is working as a double-glazing salesman. Sharon is expecting a child in four months' time. Which is why she asked me to come and see you. She would like you to agree to a divorce, obviously. For the sake of their child. And also, they are still, they feel, believers, and they are seeking the forgiveness of their church.' He blew a long funnel of smoke at the ceiling. 'Of course, it is a Church of Scotland they are attending. A touch more liberal than what you were used to. And indeed myself.' He coughed again, this time a liquid, retching cough which came from his boots. I wondered why I'd never noticed the smell of tobacco smoke in their house when I was courting Sharon. 'I always smoke in the garden hut, you know. Out there in the damp, all weathers. Very bad for the chest.' He hacked again, lugubriously, and took another suck at his Bensons. And I began to laugh. I laughed until I ached, until I began to feel nauseous, until eventually I had to rush to the foosty toilet to be sick. I laughed as the vomit hit the pan, and I lay on the toilet floor and breathlessly giggled. By the time I returned to the sitting room, I was still exploding with badly suppressed hysteria every few seconds. 'So,' said Sharon's dad. 'You'll agree to a divorce?' It was too much, I doubled over, braying like a donkey, nodding like one of those dogs you used to see in the back windows of cars. What God had joined together, let no man put asunder. But My God, when you start putting things asunder, they certainly sunder. He was desperately trying to remain businesslike, and calm in the face of my hysteria. 'Are you all right?' Wheezing giggles, but I nodded. 'I'll . . . I'll tell Sharon, and she'll get her lawyer to send you the papers. There will be . . . no expense for you.' He looked around the flat with distaste. 'Your parents, you know. Before they left for New Zealand . . .' Instantly I was cold and angry and scared of what he might say. I was sweaty, gasping, furious.

'I DON'T WANT TO KNOW!' I shouted far more loudly than I needed to. 'YES, YOUR BLOODY DAUGHTER CAN HAVE A BLOODY DIVORCE. AT LEAST THIS TIME SHE'S HAVING THE FUCKING KID . . .' He got up, his face set, the graveyard pallor worse than ever. He said nothing. As he reached the outside door, it flew open, and Mick burst in, closely followed by Keith. Keith had a guitar case in his hand, an old, battered cream one with the word Fender faintly discernible on the side.

'Hey, man, wait'll you see what Keith got. Only three hundred, nicked of course, dodgy but fuck . . .' Mick caught sight of Sharon's dad, and went straight into Bishopbriggs politeness mode. 'Oh, sorry. I didn't realise you had someone with you.' Sharon's dad barged past, inasmuch as anyone whose mode of movement was a funereal shuffle could barge, and slammed the door behind him, softly. 'Who was that, man?'

'No one,' I replied, going back into the sitting-room to see if he'd left his fags behind. But he hadn't.

In Keith's guitar case was, strangely enough, a guitar. When he opened it I felt my heart skip a beat. He and Mick were like wee boys on Christmas morning, although obviously Keith had to be cool. 'It's OK, I guess,' he said, but he couldn't keep still. He was fidgeting about like someone who'd been doing some speed. And maybe they had, because that was what they were into. Some time after moving in, they'd offered me some sulphate, to be sniffed up through a rolled-up tenner. I pretended I thought they were offering to pay for some of the electricity they had managed to avoid contributing to for the past six weeks, took the tenner, unrolled it and said, 'Thanks, lads.' There was an embarrassed silence. 'And next time you can afford to buy sulph, pay the electricity first.' I was sounding more and more like my father, or theirs, or somebody's. The only time I'd tried amphetamine, I'd had a complete panic attack. Palpitations, dry throat, a tingling and trembling, no sleep for two days and then a furious hunger.

Mairhi had said it was good to take during sex, and so we'd tried it, or rather I tried it, she was clearly quite used to it. Never again.

The guitar was an old cherry sunburst Fender Telecaster, with a sweat-marinaded rosewood neck. Battered and bruised, it reeked of rock'n'roll romance. It was pretty damn close to the red guitar of my old, old childhood dreams, except for the fact that it wasn't all red, and it wasn't a Watkins Rapier. Keith picked it up, played the chords to 'Brown Sugar' – D-A . . . God, I was back at Green's Playhouse, that night, that sexual night before it became the Apollo, that night of change so long ago . . . was it that long ago? When the balcony flexed and jumped with my whole world, and my neck prickled with joy and fear?

'Give us a shot then.' Astonished, Keith hesitated, then handed me the guitar, heavy for its size, so much heavier than the Yamaha acoustic which was the last one I'd played, back in the godly days. I wondered if Sharon had sold it. I hit an E chord, then a B major. 'I thought love was only true in fairy tales,' I crooned, off the top of my head. 'Meant for someone else, but not for me . . .' I had once tried singing 'I'm a Believer', the song Neil Diamond wrote for the Monkees, as a religious anthem. It never worked, though. It was too good a pop song for that. It had sex oozing from every bar. 'Then I saw her face, now I'm a Believer' had become 'Then I saw His face' which was somewhat open to misinterpretation.

'I didn't know you could play, man,' said Mick, who had immediately began ooh-ing and aah-ing in a voice which sounded like Stevie Wonder crossed with Joe Cocker. A typical Glaswegian black-Clyde-soul voice, rough but sweet. He sounded good, actually.

'I can't. I used to . . . have you got an amp here?' By my house rules they shouldn't have had, and of course they did. I'd heard them strumming quietly through it occasionally, and I didn't really mind as long as I wasn't going to have my sleep destroyed by power chords at 3.00 a.m. They brought through a Fender Champ, a small valve practice amp which sat only about a foot high. But turned up full, it approximated what I remembered about the Cornerstones, and that in-concert rush of the real Stones, the real Keith's windmilling chords. I plugged in the Rapier . . . the Telecaster, oblivious to Mick and Keith, and it clicked and buzzed as the loose, cheap jack plug went into the socket. I tapped the wood of the guitar, and heard a kind of distant, harmonic ringing, like angry church bells. Then I hit an E major and felt the roar, that huge, tuneful house-falling-down distorted noise, hit me. I let it sustain on for seconds until all that was left was the buzz of the too-loud amplifier. Then I switched it off and handed the guitar back to Keith. He nodded, played a few fast, complicated runs which rattled and buzzed because the amp was off. He was just showing me that he was the guitar player around here, thank you very much. I was a decade older than him, and I could leave the fast fingering to more flexible digits.

'Just revisiting my youth, chaps,' I said, slightly embarrassed. 'Maybe I'll get a guitar, actually, practise up a few country songs.' There was a groan from the two would-be rock'n'roll gods.

'Fuckin' country,' said Mick. 'British Legion club music. Gerry Ford on the wireless. Mums and dads. Dolly Parton.'

There was more to it than that, of course. The real Mick and Keith knew that, as many a Stones record attested. 'Faraway Eyes'. 'Country Honk'. But I just smiled, and left the junior Mick 'n' Keef to it. When they plugged the guitar back into the amp and switched it on, I didn't object. I sat in the kitchen, smoking and thinking about Sharon and my mum and dad, and Sharon having a kid, while Keith hammered out some slow, bluesy chords and Mick sang, convincingly:

> Well the blind man
> Stood on the road and cried
> Yes the blind man
> Stood on the road and he cried, Lord
> He cried, Lord, Lord yes he cried.

Did they know it was a gospel song, a gospel blues about the blind man Christ healed with the spittle he rubbed in the dust to form mud, and placed on the man's eyes? I doubted it, somehow. But Mick could sing, all right. Maybe they did have a chance of making it.

I found a not-too-bad Hornby 4-4-0 clockwork train and tender, unearthed it from a breadbox of mechanical shite at Paddy's Market, that place where genuine poverty trades whatever scant objects it can spare, and dealers buy and sell to other dealers. I swapped the Hornby – a bargain, financially, and not to my benefit – for a Yamaha acoustic guitar, brand new, not as good as my old FG180, shiny and slightly brittle-sounding. It was the only real object I owned, apart from an increasing collection of *Miller's Guides* and the trusty, rusty VW camper. Keith and Mick's influence. The infection of youth. It was odd, considering all the stuff which passed through my hands, usually doing nothing more than sitting in the VW for a few hours until I found a buyer.

My margins weren't great, because I was selling to shops, mostly. I'd been doing a little work for Keith's mum, Ruth, finding and supplying a dozen ship models for a job she was working on, some yacht-mad couple who'd just built a gigantic kit house out near Fenwick. That hadn't been easy, and I'd had to buy at quite high prices, often from shops who were more used to buying from me. It had done my reputation some good, though. I'd been very tempted to keep one tinplate Bing model of the *Queen Mary*, but eventually I let Ruth have it for £500, having bought it for £300. Not really much of a mark-up, but what the hell. She lived on her own in what externally was a fairly typical Wimpey four-bedroom in Newton Mearns. Inside it was welcomingly tasteful, with some pleasing outlandish touches. Money. It reeked of tasteful money. New notes straight from the Cashline machine. Her husband, she said, had run off with a secretary, but had been forced to pay heavily for the privilege. She smiled. I liked her smile. It was tough, guarded but with a filament of joy running through it, ready, maybe, to be lit if the right switch was thrown. However, ours was a business relationship. There was no physical spark. Just cash.

Cash. I bought things. I had the guitar, and then I got a small, portable music centre, with built-in five-inch television, which I rarely watched. *Lovejoy* and the *Antiques Roadshow*, certainly. Prices for whatever was on those two programmes soared in the week following, so it paid to pay attention. Soap operas I avoided. The divorce papers came through from Sharon, and I signed them thinking of her weakness for *Coronation Street*. I was surprised at a certain sense of . . . yes, it was loss. Not of her. I never really knew her. But of the child she was having. Or the idea of a child. Then the ludicrous fact that it was Affleck's kid hit me, and I had to laugh. If there was a God, He certainly had a sense of humour. The Divine Comedy. Would they breed an evangelist out of guilt, rear their offspring to compensate for their sin in loving one another? Love. Now there was a thing. I had discovered an odd, but lucrative market for vintage theology, and was able to sell obscure works of Calvinist mind-fuck for big dollops of cash to the Gospel Truth Bookshop in Hope Street. C.H. Spurgeon commentaries, the works of John Calvin . . . big, brutish, black volumes of po-faced dogma. I always felt a relief in getting rid of them. Most of them I picked up in Fife, funnily enough, in places like Pittenweem or Anstruther. I made every effort to avoid Tarmoran, if I could. Maybe Calvinism had been a hobby for the fishermen of the East Neuk in the past. One night I was in Dunfermline, following in the wake of a church sale of work

119

which had turned up some J.N. Darby books. He'd been one of the Plymouth Brethren's founders, before splitting with the rest over sinless perfectionism and exclusivity from the world. I'd got talking to the minister of the church, and he invited me back to his house, where he said he had some more books I might be interested in. He lived alone in a big, echoing manse, stuffed with heavy dark furniture. In his study-cum-living-room, the only room which looked regularly used, I pored over some dull tomes from his university days. They were useless in my small-turnover, high-value trade, though if I'd had a shop . . . my eye caught some pictures on the wall, strange, highly coloured, childish drawings with scrawled hieroglyphics and what looked like bits of paper attached. What were they?

'Zombie paintings,' said the minister, who was about 50, small and with slicked-back, Brylcreemed hair, and smiling, though with something fixed about his grin which I put down simply to his job. Oh. Zombie paintings.

'I used to be a missionary in Haiti,' he said, in a jolly fashion, as if he was talking about Kirkcaldy. 'Those are voodoo pictures, supposed to be done by the zombies. You know. The soulless bodies the witch-doctors have cursed or drugged or both. They remind me of some very happy times out there.' And he sighed. I didn't like the way he was looking at me at all, and left in a hurry. That night I parked the van in a caravan-site at Ely and dreamed, fitfully, of zombies. It had been a mistake having toasted cheese last thing before I went to bed.

Back at Ruthven Street, I listened over and over to some Hank Williams tapes, learning chords and words. I loved the really extreme songs, like 'Message to My Mother' or the shattering 'Angel of Death'. But 'Jambalaya' was fine by me too, and 'Setting the Woods on Fire', so hard-edged, but laughing. Sweet but tough. Soon I could churn out a fair old version of 'Cincinatti Lou', the Merle Travis song, and was pleased with myself. One day I sat down and tried to remember one or two of my born-again self-written songs, and nothing came back to me of them at all. It was if that part of my life had been washed away, clean, white as snow. Sharon was gone, her and Affleck neatly wrapped together and posted to domestic bliss. I wondered what had happened to Affleck's wife and kids. Maybe I should go and see them, maybe there would be a neatly symmetrical sexual explosion . . . it was an interesting fantasy, but perhaps not. I sat in my room, which had nothing in it but a bed, some of the paperbacks I hadn't yet read, a copy of *Melody Maker* which, for unfathomable reasons, I'd started buying every so often, the music centre and the guitar and the country-music tapes; from the other room I could hear Keith and Mick singing one of their own new, self-penned pop ditties.

> I'll never leave her
> Now that we know
> The truth is our love
> Will grow
>
> Like fire
> Wild, wild, wild fire.

They were improving. No doubt about it.

Ghosts

Most village antique and bric-a-brac shops are sort of generalised, mushy places full of cheap shite but with the occasional jewel, either deliberately placed by a knowledgeable, cynical owner or ignored by an idiot dilletante. Worms, to all appearance, was no different. There it hunched at Number Seven, The Street: just a window and a door and a litter of temptingly inexpensive bits and pieces, leading to an inner sanctum comprising one or two medium-to-large lumps of expensive furniture and a locked cupboard with stealable goodies in it. And unlike many other dealers, inspired and not-so-inspired amateurs that they are, I know how much everything is worth. I veer towards knowledge-able cynicism. Once I had kept nothing, owned nothing, but when I came to Mollydish, all the bits and pieces I bought just kind of silted up into the shop and the flat above, until I had to recognise that I'd become a hoarder. That's what happens when you settle down, I suppose. And the joy, the thrill of discovery, fades.

West coast winter: glitteringly clear, a breathless sky of pale, icy blue, and even a tinge of warmth in the sun. Mornings like this, you're tempted to think of a nice God and His wondrous creation. All I have to do, though, to deflate such incipient regression towards spirituality is remember the summer. The Midge.

The midge. *Culicoides impunctatus*. To any atheist, proof negative of God's non-existence. Well, no, not quite. Proof, rather, of God's essentially vindictive nature. Or perhaps, to the convinced Christian, proof of the fallen nature of creation. To the pessimist, proof that we are, in fact, in summer in the West Highlands, in hell. The Scottish Biting Midge. Worse than the sand flies of Mexico's desert. More insatiable than the vampire bat. In fact, as bats are the only animal in the universe, other than ultra-wee parasitic microbes, which prey on the midge, the fluttering, whirring shapes in the eaves of Number Seven are to be loved, cherished, adored and encouraged. Words cannot express how much I hate midges. My bats make no noticeable impression on the biting, bloodsucking bile-inducers. They are the ruination of perfect summer evenings, those still hours when a hot sun has been beating down on an astonished landscape, on average once or twice every decade, and having frenziedly run about the unscathed beaches, sailed a boat, gone fishing, swimming and allowed the virginal white of one's torso to be exposed to ultra-violet light, you face the cooling of the evening with the prospect of a quiet, relaxed bottle or two of Macallan at the back door . . .

More people smoke heavily in the Highlands of Scotland than anywhere else in the country. It is sheer self-defence, an utter necessity on those summer evenings, if you insist on staying out of doors to enjoy – I use the word loosely – a Spielbergian sunset. Gauloise, untipped Gauloise, chain-smoked, is one solution. I tried a pipe, but the overheating effect on my tongue left me trying to rub Ambre Solaire on it, admittedly after copious amounts of whisky had proved unable to soothe my fevered organ. There are various herbal ointments, all of which leave you smelling like a health-food shop, significantly poorer and still with *Culicoides* sinking her (because only the females suck blood, wouldn't you just know it) pincers into your welcoming flesh. DDT works, but it gives you cancer. Smoke works, but it gives you cancer. Alcohol can enable you to ignore them, but then you wake up the next morning all red and blotchy, your face blossoming with hundreds of lumpy Brian Clough impersonators, your arms itching, your ankles dying, pleading to be scratched to the very bone. And it gives you cancer.

Foreign tourists come prepared, or just don't come between May and August. I've seen German camper-vans disgorge their inhabitants as if they were alien space creatures come to check us earthlings out for general edibility. Plastic helmets, bee-keeping smocks, gauze veils – you name it, they wear it. And quite right too. We Scots would rather get cancer. It's the image, you see. Macho as fuck.

Research teams appear, on and off, for ill-fated projects which aim to draw the bitch's sting. Somebody once suggested simply draining every bog in Scotland, the place where the horrors breed, and while away each winter doing their knitting and genetically mutating in order to defuse the latest chemical attempt on their lives. One recent group of bitten scientists was searching for parasitic mites which might kill the midges. Oh yeah? I can just imagine what would happen. Wipe out the midges, and then the mites would take over, and soon we'd find ourselves crawling with things too small even to see, all day, even in winter. They would burrow underneath our skin, set up permanent home, until finally erupting in great swarms simultaneously from every part of our anatomies, leaving nothing but ruptured, swollen, bleeding shells, eyeless on the buzzing, seething ground.

Another crowd of midgeophiles have been researching the sex life of the midge, trying to isolate the pheromones, the smells which the females use to attract males. The thinking is that if they have the midge attractant, they can bait traps and lure the evil nasties to their death. Sex and death. I like that.

But it's winter, morning, cold and midgeless. I breathe in, feeling my carbonised lungs contract with the impact of fresh air. I'm smoking again. I give up every month, and sometimes last a week. There is the beginning of an attractive, throaty rumble in my voice, which might sound sexy if I was ever on the radio, which I'm not. Or maybe it's cancer. To the shore, to the shore, to see if . . . nothing, really. Just to see the waves coming in, and to check out the beach for interesting bounty, if no one else has got there first. I light a cigarette to kill the cold. Too much fresh air can be risky.

Walking makes you think. I once read that walking is a return to babyhood, to the immense satisfaction we all once gained from being able to stagger, and that it both relaxes and helps your brain to function. I ponder the shop, and whether I should buy it. Mrs Tooth, the ancient Englishwoman who owns the building, lives in Stafford and rents me the place at an absurdly low rate, perversely because I'm not an English incomer and she perceives herself as having a kind of holy duty to keep Mollydish at least partially Scottish. This is in memory of her late husband, Arthur, who was from Mollydish but got the hell out as soon as he was 16. He bought the shop and flat for sentimental reasons involving being born there, probably in a dangerous bloody mess of newspapers in my sitting-room, but never came back. Mrs Tooth, whom I have never met, telephones every week to tell me this. Every week. Her daughter has contacted me twice since we first did the hurried deal which secured me Number Seven; offering to sell 'because mother's really not fit, we think she would benefit from the cash'. But I can't make the leap into permanence it would involve. The dealer in me knows I should, must, do it. But once I own property, my fate is sealed. Whatever that fate may be.

Along the kelp line I go, crunching and popping the hoar-frosted seaweed, searching for sea-treasure. This morning is the stillness following a vicious gale, and who knows what might be lying on the high-tide mark? A few bales of cannabis, perhaps, from the smugglers who run into the west coast of Scotland as if it was the Florida Keys? Nice if you can find it and get it out without being seen, but there's the rub. Sometimes the Customs men are watching, hidden in the dunes and waiting for you to pick it up and take it home. They'll let you take it in, they'll even wait a few days for you to telephone the police. And then they'll break your door down with big fire axes. I've never come across any sea-borne drugs myself, although Big Malcie, the creeler from Vornie just up the coast, reputedly has. Or does. Every month, so they say, picking up sealed plastic packs from the buoys which mark his lobster pots. And not just dope, either. Bright, white, sparkling Ajax substitute too. Colombian marching powder. You don't ask too many questions about Malcie, though. He has friends from Glasgow with scar tissue where their faces should be. And sometimes it's nice to be able to get a lobster, for a special occasion.

There's no wind, just a lapping rhythm from the washed-out waves and hardly a tingle of movement in the cold air. Up ahead I can see a familiar figure stooping steadily towards me on the kelp line. Scrannin' Willie has been here first. I should have noticed that the kelp wasn't quite as crackly as it would have been without someone else's searching footprints. I stop and wait for Willie to reach me. He's indeterminately old, with a full head of blazing white hair and a Dostoevskian beard. He is clutching a plastic bag, and in it will be his trophies, which will go to join the piles and piles of treasures and rubbish which take up most of the space in his one-room cottage. Willie has been a scranner, a searcher-out of beach-bounty, and a hoarder of it, all his life. I came to it quite late, and these days search and hoard for a living. Willie does it because he can't help it. And he has nothing else but the telly.

He stops in front of me, fixes me with a vast, unwavering blue gaze. 'And what about this recession?' he begins. 'What about the Tories? Is monetarism the answer?' I shoogle my head and make clicking noises with my tongue.

'Aye, Willie, I couldn't say. Just couldn't say. Hell of a situation the country's in, right enough.'

'Japanese are in trouble too. Laying people off in Tokyo. And here, at Nissan. In England. Laying people off all over the place. Nobody's immune. Bad leadership. Bad leadership for years.' I nod, shuffle a bit on the kelp, which crackles like static electricity in the still brightness. 'Fifty years ago. Fifty years ago today was the wreck. The *Perseus*. From Piraeus carrying pineapples. Fifty years ago today.' He holds up his plastic bag. 'Just picked up some floats.' Sure enough, his bag is bulging with round shapes, the plastic net floats from trawls which people like Malcie use to mark creels and arcane rendezvous points. They are worthless unless you are going to use them yourself. I know for a fact that Willie has hundreds, if not thousands, lying in his garden, and Matilda the district nurse, bless her gossiping chumminess, has told me there are hundreds more inside the house. 'Fifty years ago. Pineapples as far as the eye could see. Ate them for months, or until they went bad. Weeks. Pineapples. Kept coming ashore, tide after tide. German submarines. Torpedo. Third day, bodies with the pineapples. Pineapples and men, all mixed up. All along here.' His gaze never wavers. 'Maynard Keynes. Lot to answer for. And Magellan. Found pineapples first, his fleet. In 1519. Walter Raleigh, he thought pineapples were the princesses of fruits. Princesses and men, washed up, lying together, all inside each other.' Then he walks past me as if I was a large piece of driftwood, the kelp-crackle marking his footsteps.

Scrannin' Willie: always walking and walking and walking, beachcombing and stooping up and down the dunes in his old yellow anorak, plastic bags neatly folded in his capacious pockets, ready to receive their load. When he isn't walking he is watching television, and mentally recording everything he sees and hears, though without system or order. So you could meet him and be faced with a torrent of information about war in Angola, a congressional crisis in America, Hindu riots in Bombay. Then in the midst of it he will recall some local incident in glowing detail, like the *Perseus* and its pineapples. He is always right, too. If he says it was 50 years ago today that the ship had been sunk, then it is 50 years ago today. Every so often some oral historian will go and see him, well warned about Willie's ways, and the array of everything from old magazines to a sea-battered dummy torpedo from some forgotten test-firing. In search of some memory of Mollydish's past, some incident or other like the wreck of the *Perseus* or any glimmer Willie retains about the clearances his grandfather would have been part of. Social historians love the clearances, when the landowners evicted the crofters who had, in many cases, once been their clan family members, and turned the land over to the Great White Cheviot. The sheep ripped the land to shreds, and now most of the Mollydish hinterland is trees. Not so much a clearance as a shrouding. But there is no pushing the right buttons with Willie. He isn't like a computer, where you can hit the search key and retrieve the information you want. With Willie, you have to take what he gives you, be it long discourses on Beirut, sheep dip, Australian Republicanism, the mysterious disappearance of Jean Macindoe's baby in 1964, and, just possibly, the answer to the question you asked him half an hour ago.

Willie is a database without any satisfactory mode of access. He stores visual and audio images, material, factual material, and like a computer, has no imagination. He remembers things, he finds things, he keeps things. No one is sitting at his keyboard. He has no family. He gets his meals on wheels, the district nurse checks up on him every week, and he has had a succession of home helps, all of whom gave up in the face of the piled up sea-bounty. When things get too difficult, too disruptive for we normal people, quite soon now, he will get a lift in an ambulance to Craig Dunain hospital at Inverness, where, after a while, he may, like many of their elderly people, walk out on to the A82, barefoot in his pyjamas, looking for the beach, the pineapples, the memories, and be crushed, snapped like kelp beneath the wheels of a fish lorry.

Maybe then he will become a ghost, lurking in the twilight shadows before dawn, or on midge-ridden evenings at dusk. I've never seen a ghost in Mollydish, although my flat had once, long ago and briefly, been the Catholic chapel and had, so Matilda told me, been exorcised in 1953 by a unique combination of ministers from the Church of Scotland, the Free Church and the Catholic priest, due to a persistent poltergeist which had kept interrupting the cleaning woman – Matilda's mother – during her dusting. 'Brushes would move across the floor as if there was someone trying to help her, so help me . . . I'm telling you the God's honest truth, I am so.' It sounded like a useful kind of poltergeist to have around, but perhaps a Catholic chapel was not the place for him or her. So he or she was banished forever by the combined forces of ecumenical Christianity. Knowing the normal hell-bent-on-disagreement attitudes of Highland kirk and priest, I found this story strangely touching. Those days were over. Now there was no church of any description in Mollydish, with the former kirk converted into holiday flats which stood expensively empty for most of the year and expensively full during the midge season. Faith had shrivelled in the village, just as Gaelic had, and worshippers had to creep out on a Sunday to churches in the neighbouring communities, oddly furtive, like Muslims sneaking out of Rome to a country mosque. Sometimes I sat in the dark in the flat, wondering if the unknown poltergeist would start washing up, or doing some of my much-neglected housework. But there was no helpful shiver from the mop or the dishcloth.

The best ghost story ever happened to me in Mollydish. Not the experience of the ghost; I've never seen one, and the various chilling vibrations I've encountered have had rational explanations. Most of them. The ones not involving religion, that is. But the story happened to me; I was part of it, the catalyst, the recipient of its full frisson. It's so good, I don't tell it. I never have. It's too scary for Mollydish, really. And for me.

Anthony Bathgate was from Bolton, an inveterate reader of *Exchange and Mart*, that weekly solace for the terminally interested. Anthony was a freelance mechanic, interested in electronics, interested in old cars, interested in railway memorabilia, about 45 and a recent widower. The departure of his wife had removed the one force which prevented him becoming wholly absorbed in the mechanical mysteries of life and *Exchange and Mart*. Stooped, small, smiling and bald, he drifted into mild eccentricity, a very English one, with Mamod steam models on the kitchen table and dozens of Airfix kits awaiting construction. One week, he was leafing through *Exchange and Mart*, poring over every page, the advertisements for old records, transvestite clubs, rubber underwear and infallible business opportunities, when he found himself at the property-for-sale section. As fate would have it, his eye fell on the Scotland and Scottish isles column, where enterprising rural estate agents and solicitors place remote, hard-to-get-rid-of properties in the hope that English urban dwellers will be astonished at their cheapness and head north in search of the good life offered, usually in the middle of a midge-infested Caithness bog.

What caught Anthony's eye, though, was Laurel Cottage, The Walk, Mollydish. Two bedrooms, outhouses, large garage with inspection pit. £20,000. Glorious sea views, outstanding natural environment in West Highlands. He left the steam models and the Airfix kits and drove up overnight in an immaculate Rover 3500, the P6 model that looks like a sharpened slug, got the keys, from an Inverness solicitor, arrived in Mollydish on a pre-midge spring day of Hollywood glory, looked around for half an hour, had half a pint of Burtons at the Incomers, heard the English accents and drove straight back to Inverness, where he made a written intimation of interest in the Scottish legal way. They wouldn't take the £15,000 in cash he'd brought with him in £50 notes, the policy on his wife cashed in and kept under his Bolton bed for safety. Anthony was a very traditional, if slightly odd man. He slept in an Inverness bed and breakfast, deposited the cash with another Inverness lawyer, and bought Laurel Cottage.

Then he drove back to Bolton to clear out his council house and prepare for the biggest change his life had ever seen.

Three weeks later, he arrived at Laurel Cottage in the middle of the night, in a 35-cwt van laden with all his earthly goods, apart from the Rover, which was being delivered to Inverness by Motorail. Everything was silent, and Laurel Cottage was in pitch darkness as he got down from the cab, feeling exhausted. He unlocked the door, and felt for the lightswitch. The house had been lived in, he knew, until fairly recently, when the occupant had died, and he'd bought it with whatever furniture it contained. He had little memory though of what there was.

Of course, the electricity was off. He was not a nervous man, Anthony; he was an *Exchange and Mart* reader, a man with an interest in technical things. Not a man of imagination. So he simply shrugged, lit the first of a series of matches, and began looking for a couch, a sofa, or even a bed he could crash out on. He went from room to room, but found nothing. There was no bed, no couch. Only bare, slightly dusty floorboards, two wardrobes, a kitchen table and, in one of the bedrooms, a large rug, rolled up and standing against the wall. I have said that Anthony was not a nervous man. He was also very tired, and so, with that kind of drugged desperation fatigue brings, he decided to unroll the rug, wrap it around himself and sleep on the floor. It was a reasonably warm night, and there was more space than in the van's cab, which was crammed solid with all his Bolton bits and pieces. And he fell asleep.

He was wakened, in the unfamiliar darkness, with the rough, dusty rug heavy around him, by the sound of a door banging shut. Then came footsteps, heavy, measured footsteps that were nevertheless familiar with the house. Whoever it was knew where he – and it was a man walking, of that there was no doubt – was going. The footsteps came closer and closer, right past Anthony's head, and then they stopped.

Well, I said that Anthony was not a nervous or an imaginative man, but he was, to put it mildly, a little perturbed by this. He decided someone must have seen his van outside and come to check that all was well, that he wasn't some New Age traveller or gypsy or homeless single mother attempting to squat. It must be some concerned neighbour. But he was in a difficult position, almost pinned to the floor by the heavy rug. He struggled up, coughing from the dust the rug contained.

'Hallo! Hallo there. No need to, eh, worry, there's no problem. I've just bought the house, just moving in. I'm your new neighbour, just up from Bolton. Bathgate's the name. Anthony.

Anthony with a 'th', specially for lispers, eh, ha ha!' But there was no reply. He lit a match, but there was no one there, and no marks on the floor to show where the visitors had walked. No footprints except his own. Every door in the house was securely shut; he had to open them to get to the front door, the only outside entrance. It was as he had left it. Securely locked.

I met him in the morning, as I wended my half-hungover, half-drunk way home from Alistair Mhor's, where I had been discussing the effect of high-fat fish feed on the texture of farmed salmon flesh until approximately 4.00 a.m. Which was quite a feat, considering I knew nothing about the subject. But the bottle of Springbank seemed to know a good deal about it. I'd dozed off on the sofa, and was heading home for a proper sleep, when I came across Anthony, leaning against his dew-drenched van, and looking at the sea. His view, as advertised. I was delighted to be the first in the village to meet the much-mooted new occupant of Laurel Cottage, and would have shaken his hand had I not fallen over in my smiling eagerness. I introduced myself, and he told me what had happened the previous night. Of course, I invited him back to the flat to get warm. He had spent the rest of the night in his van, cramped and cold and, if not nervous, because that wasn't his nature, uncertain. And unhappy.

I made him a cup of tea, and he told me his story. It wasn't that I lost interest, but when he began to prattle on about the Airfix models – I suppose they were some kind of comfort to him – I fell asleep in my ridiculously deep art-deco chair, while he sat, knees together, hunched on the sofa. He was small and looked older than he was. It was as if leaving the city had shrunk him. Anthony with a 'th'. When I woke up, at noon, he had gone, and so had his van. Maybe he'd discovered some imagination.

All very well, but hardly much of a ghost story. Some footsteps in the night? Heard it a million times. But that's not the tale. After all, I said the story happened to me.

It was two days later, and I was being spoken to by Matilda. Had I seen the man who'd bought Laurel Cottage? Yes I had. Where was he? I didn't know. He'd disappeared. He was called Anthony Bathgate. With two 'th's.

'Well, God spare us,' said Matilda. 'God spare us, but he's maybe better away from that house.' She inhaled through her teeth, making a simultaneous 'tch tch tch' noise you only ever hear in the Highlands. 'That house – did you know Alfred?' Alfred, the previous occupant, I'd only seen once or twice, a big, heavy-set man in late middle age who had died suddenly of a stroke. He was a former road labourer who had retired on invalidity, and who never spoke, at least not to me. 'Alfred was a very odd creature,' said Matilda. 'Very, God save us, strange, especially later, after his daughter died. She went into the sea, quite young, maybe 17, and very beautiful. A little touched, though. No one was very surprised, if you know what I mean. My what a lovely corpse they made of her, I remember that well. Her mother died giving birth to her – that was before there was a district nurse here. It wouldn't happen now, God save us. It was Alfred brought her up. After she died, he went peculiar. Cleared all the furniture, or nearly all of it, out the house, and he would walk about it at all hours of the night. But the worst things was, he would never sleep in a bed. He slept on the floor, all rolled up in an old rug. The very rug they'd used to haul his daughter up from the seashore. Now what do you think of that, Mr bookseller, eh? Put that in one of your Strange-But-Trues!'

I swallowed. My throat felt parched, airless, as if I'd not been breathing for a while. Maybe I hadn't. It was another mild spring day, but suddenly I shivered, a big tremulous palsy. 'God save us, somebody just walked over your grave!' grinned Matilda. 'Well, must be about my business. We'll see if your Mr 'th' turns up.'

But he never did. His Rover P6 did, though, delivered by Motorail, apparently, to Inverness, then driven by some delighted adolescent Nigel Mansell to Mollydish. It was deposited outside Laurel Cottage, and the keys were posted through the letterbox. It was sand gold, immaculate. Two years later, it was still there, pitted with salt-accelerated rust, its tyres flat, its hubcaps long turned into frisbees by the local sprogs. One winter night, a big wind took down Laurel Cottage's chimney stack, sending it through the slate roof, and as the months passed, the little house crumbled and died, exposed and open to the unforgiving weather. There was speculation, of course, and whispers about Alfred and his funny ways. Somebody, it was rumoured, had shown interest in building a timber-framed kit holiday home on the site. But it came to nothing. No one ever saw the place advertised for sale, in *Exchange and Mart* or anywhere else.

The council towed the car away. Maybe they sold it, or scrapped it, I don't know. If it had been an older Rover, a 100 or something, I might have been interested in finding a buyer. But the P6 is a common beast, and besides, I didn't like to go too near Laurel Cottage, or mess around with anything associated with it. Ghosts? Who knows? The story was enough to frighten me.

The house has been pulled down, now, made safe. It was caved in on itself by a man with a JCB. He didn't go inside, didn't remove anything. So if it hasn't rotted, the rug should still be there, underneath the rubble. But there's no floor for invisible feet to walk across, measured and heavy. Just a heap of stones.

I said it was my story. I am the one person who ties it together, who knows what happened to Anthony with a 'th' that night, and why. I'm in it. I sometimes wonder about poor old Anthony, the incomer who lasted one night, who gazed at his view, had a cup of tea, then left. Someday, maybe I'll tell Matilda what happened to Anthony. But not just yet. For the moment, I'll keep it to myself.

There was one occasion, not long after my arrival in Mollydish, when I really thought I'd seen a ghost. It was an autumn twilight, lingering, all shadowy yellows and blues, with the midges chilled to death for another year and the first swirls of mist lying in the hollows. I was walking, walking for walking's sake, worrying about the build-up of tar in my lungs and hoping fresh air might counteract the carcinogenic nasties. That was before I knew better, realised that too much fresh air just made it all worse. And there, in the pine-scented ancient grove called Small Trees, was the figure, rendered a luminous grey by the fading light, digging. Tall, spindly, scarecrowish, with shaggy hair under a ragged seaman's cap, only the wrecked denim jacket and wellington boots indicated some kind of modernity. The pinched, grey face had a look of the long-dead about it. He could have been any age. The eyes were like holes drilled in a gravestone. Nervously, I wished the digger good evening, but was ignored. Slowly, steadily, it continued its task, had reached a depth of about three feet in a patch of mossy clearing among the twisted trees. I walked on, feeling a distinct chill, and calling childishly on the protection of the Holy Spirit against ghoulies.

The Incomers offered reassurances of a more tangible, not to say drinkable kind, and after half an hour's conversational dithering with Grey Donald, I raised the question of the digging figure. Grey Donald didn't smile, but his eyes twinkled in the depths of the concrete scowl he nearly always bore. His sea-scarred face cracked into a grin at least twice a year, usually when someone fell over in the bar, preferably breaking a limb. 'Scare you, did he? No ghost, him, son, no need to worry!' I laughed. Ghost? Don't be daft, Donald! 'Aye, that's Ross. Still digging, still searching. That's two years he's been at it now, ever since he came back from Glasgow.' And Donald sucked in a great lungful of bar atmosphere, shaking his head from side to side before expelling the mixture of beer fumes, fag reek, air and toilet niff in the form of a few puffing 'aye, aye, aye' expressions.

A half of whisky and an illegal quarter pint of beer, a measure called a pony, extracted the tale. Ross McNulty, former fisherman, dopehead and occasional smuggler, acquaintance of Malcie, although that bit was glossed over rather. Malcie had that effect. Anyway, Ross had been the victim, maybe scapegoat, of one of the Customs and Excise service's periodic raids, the operations the bastards mount every few years with the help of informants to try and prove to the public they're doing something about dope smuggling on the west coast. When everybody knows that for every shipment stopped, 20 get through. Anyway, Operation Dogfish, it was called, Donald thought.

The customs had been tipped off about a shipment of hash, cannabis oil and opium – I thought Donald's knowledge of drugs a bit peculiar, until I remembered his seafaring years and probable exposure to every form of vice available in the world's ports – being brought ashore one winter's night just up the coast, but according to Donald, Ross and his big-shot pals from Glasgow who were masterminding the operation had also been tipped off that they were about to get busted, after most of the stuff had been landed and some of it consumed by the celebrating smugglers. It was inconceivable that this hadn't involved Malcie, I pondered into my black beer. Or maybe it hadn't. Maybe Malcie had been bypassed by Ross and some other bunch of Glaswegian hoodlums, and had exacted a small revenge. Ross had taken three kilos of hash and buried it, somewhere around Mollydish, before heading back to his mother's croft ripped to fuck and straight into the arms of the revenue men. The Glasgow big boys had vanished, taking most of the shipment with them, but leaving half a kilo of hash and some cannabis oil – a class-A drug and bad news in the sheriff courts – in Ross's mother's coal bunker. Ross kept his mouth shut and got eight years, reduced to five on remission. He was probaby surviving on a pay-off from the arseholes he'd protected.

'So the boy came back, and you saw him yourself, grey and shrunk and a shadow of his former self. Hitting the wacky baccy in the Barlinnie, too, I think. Anyway, he wasn't back a week before he was out digging, mostly in the evenings, just as it was getting dark.' Grey Donald drained first his whisky glass, then the chaser, then primly, carefully passed wind at both ends, shifting on his stool to fart. 'Looking for his three kilos, you see. Only he knows where he buried it. The thing is, you see, he can't remember where. Terrible thing, the drugs, you know. Just terrible.' And he picked up his whisky glass, raising it to his face for an examination. He seemed surprised to find it empty.

Rock

Truth Drug's first gig was in a deliberately down-at-heel west end bar called the Lame Duck, aimed at street-credible students and other dingy would-be bohemians who prided themselves on not drinking in trendy, themed wine-bars or cool, arty, interior-designed palaces of chic where you could only get yellow foreign beers in bottles with bits of fruit stuck down the neck. At the Lame Duck they had reasonable Murphys and fair Guinness, and it was one of the few places in Glasgow you could get Raven Ale from Orkney. Even better was the special bottled Orkney brew, called Skullsplitter after some Viking chieftain. It did.

Truth Drug was Keith, Mick, a keyboard player called, or so he insisted, Zam, an elongated corpse called Mark Fiddich on bass and Bob Bonzo Charlesworth on drums. They had been rehearsing for months in a damp-ridden, bricked-up railway arch in Whiteinch, near the abandoned grain silos of what had once been the Clyde's docks. Thousands of starlings fluttered in the area, genetically impelled to swarm in search of grain long gone. Once or twice I had been convinced, against my better judgment, to pick up some gear for them in the VW and drop them off at the so-called Railtrack Studio Complex. It was basically a semi-insulated brick box built inside the railway arch. No trains ran above it. Grass grew where trains had once run, and if I arrived after dark to load some heavy, worn amplifiers into the skinny arms of Truth Drug, I would sometimes see human shapes up on the old track bed, their heads bobbing above the parapet to look down on the activity. Who were they? Kids finding some privacy to fuck or score or smoke, or drink or freebase or do whatever they had to do to get through the days and nights of nothingness? Or old down-and-outs, sucking the last solace out of a blue Superlager tin? I never made the effort to find out. But I wondered why they bothered to climb up, up the embankments then along the disused railway line, to this desolate spot near the river. Maybe they just liked the view, from being above other people, up high, up there where the air was clear . . . everybody likes a view.

Once I took Keith's mum, Ruth, out to Maryhill Park, an odd enclave of big houses on the edge of the Summerston sprawl, a kind of tatty remnant of what had once been an exclusive, mercantile community on the edge of Glasgow. An old lady had died, leaving her seven-bedroom mansion of mould to be cleared, and I was involved in sub-contracting its clearance – for a price – to an acquaintance, the kind of rough-and-tumble, dip, strip and re-sell dealer who had access to muscle power and big furniture vans. But I got first look, that was the agreement, and Ruth, who had been delivering some of Keith's washing to the flat, had asked in a haze of perfume if she could come. Why not? I spread a couple of clean – well, relatively clean – towels on the front seat of the camper, and she climbed in with little sign of distaste.

'What is that perfume?' I asked. The van had assumed a sophisticated aroma which lasted until the engine became hot, and the bizarre Volkswagen heating system spread hot oil fumes throughout the cab.

'Givenchy. Do you like it?' She turned, smiled, and as ever I felt seedy and shabby and down at heel. But there was something in the smile I hadn't noticed before. A warmth, maybe an interest.

The house was a disappointment. It bore all the signs of having been ransacked by the old lady's immediate family before we got there. Her son had got hold of me through someone I half-knew amid the bustling roar of a Byres Road bar called Losers I frequented for purely professional reasons. BBC types, academics, third-rate actors in adverts and other potential purchasers of 'interesting' items schmoozed around there, in an ambience which pretended to be traditional and unpretentious, but had been created from scratch out of a gap site. When busy, the clientele, mostly people who wanted to sell things – drugs, furniture, ideas – to the BBC types, or the dull and desperate who thought they were being touched with some of the aerosoled glamour, oozed desperate bonhomie and punted fatuous plans which mostly came to nothing. The owner, Andrew MacClintock, was an absolute cynic. The name, Losers, was his deadly accurate assessment of his customers; they thought it was *très amusant*, and Andrew laughed his graveyard chortle. He had bought some stuff from me, including some of the valueless shit which passed for bar decorations, and I would mingle with the crowd, have a drink with Andrew and be introduced to people he knew might be looking for, say, a Larkin first edition, some obscure erotica (which I generally steered clear of, as you could find yourself involved with some dubiously heavy and violent characters in that sphere, most of them serving policemen) or a Tereszcuk lamp base. In other words, I schmoozed and punted and preyed on the losers, sold my chunks of china and metal and paper and card while they dealt in ideas and people and programmes and tried to get off with each other. Maybe they were arseholes, but at least they didn't have my overheads.

Actually, all I really had to look after was the flat and the van, and, reluctantly, a small lock-up in an unconverted mews. Quick turnover was the key, I kept reminding myself. But I was getting hankerings for something else, something more settled, solid. A house of my own. A shop, maybe, with my name above the door. A woman. Stuff, things were piling up. Like silt around a boat too long in one place.

Ruth and I found a few small treasures in the house at Maryhill Park. There was a Clutha glass vase, tiny and bubbly green, which indicated that there might have been some interesting art-nouveau furniture where there were now glaring, dustless gaps along the walls. Fuck. A small washstand, Victorian, which Ruth offered me £30 for. And in a cupboard, a pile of old fishing tackle, musty and smelly, but worth £100 profit to me if I took it to Edinburgh.

Afterwards, Ruth was in an odd mood. She was wearing some delicate, beaten-gold jewellery and looked, in the orange street-lights, fine-spun and alien, something from another world, not really suitable for transportation in my beaten and patched VW. Her make-up, perfect, the expensive Givenchy smell, mixed with soft leather from one of those perfectly cut, timeless leather jackets, straight edges and seams, no rounded, bollocky, fashion-able touches. It all made my heart beat a little faster than normal. It was winter, dull, glowering and a day for the old tenements, the ones without the power-washed walls, the grey and black cliffs of people. Grey and black from the grime of working factories which had nearly all closed. The Albion Railway works, the yards . . . left as shells or bought up by developers keen to create rabbit-warren flat complexes in their venerable sandstone shells, rented out to moneyed transients with sentimental streaks, a vision of their lifestyle taken from movies on New York loft-life or brownstone bohemianism. 'Let's walk,' she said.

I shook my head. 'Not here.' It was not a pleasant place to stroll around after dark. In fact nowhere in Maryhill was, but I thought

I'd show her the aqueduct, where the Forth and Clyde canal
crosses Maryhill Road. I parked the van on a yellow line, under a
streetlight, and checked all the locks. Then I set the alarm. When
you're carrying valuables, you have to be careful, especially in
Glasgow. We stood under the bridge, hearing the rumbling echo
of buses and cars as they passed, leaving the warbling of invisible
pigeons, weirdly loud when the traffic noise faded. We stood and
watched water drip down and then Ruth grabbed my hand and
said, 'Let's climb up.'

Her expensive leather jacket was perfect for her, for a girl half
her age, for anyone. That was what good clothes were about, I
suddenly realised. Mohair, green, under it, and she had on stretch
jodhpurs and the kind of black leather sports shoes which were
to trainers what an Aston Martin is to a Mini. I heard her jewellery
give a whispering jingle as she pulled me towards a worn path
which wound upwards through frosty, overgrown grass.
Upwards. She climbed easily and quickly, aerobically conditioned,
no doubt, leaving me, smoke-slowed and panting, struggling in
her wake. Givenchy wafted in the dank Maryhill air. On the
towpath she nearly scared a night-sighted cyclist straight into the
black ripple of the water, as she appeared like an ambush from
nowhere. This was *Taggart* territory, where verbally challenged,
hard-nut detectives found mangled bodies and said things like,
'It's no' the first. And it willnie be the last. Ah ken that's the
situation, Sergeant Fuckbrain.'

In the dim light our breaths clouded, and we looked over the
aqueduct to the street below, and down towards Glasgow's
centre, which muttered and groaned and glowed fitfully in the
distance.

'I used to go hillwalking,' said Ruth suddenly. 'When I was
younger. Keith's father was keen on Munro-bagging, and he
would drag me along. I hated it. And then, after a while, I began
to enjoy being up high. Not the getting there. The being that high
up, and the seeing for so far. You felt as if you had knowledge
and power that no one else had, seeing, breathing in the clean
air. Then you go down and it's all hard drinking and red sweaty
faces in the bar, and then you go home and all you have is the
memory of it, locked away somewhere. You work, and make
money, and get married and have children and houses and cars
and the high places fade from you. Until you end up looking for
little heights, little climbs so you can see, at least something.' She
laughed, put her hand on mine, on the cold stone of the bridge.
'Were you ever married?'

'Yes. But I left.' I paused. Better say something else. 'Ehhm . . .

no children. That part of my life is sort of . . . lopped off. But it's just like an amputation, you get twinges sometimes from the limb which has gone, and when you're least expecting it.'

'But you're young. Keith thinks of you as a kind of older brother, I think. If we cleaned you up a bit, I'm sure you could find yourself a suitable wife.' She patted my typically unkempt clothes, laughing.

'You know, since I left, I've always . . . and this isn't a pick-up line . . . I've always found myself with older women. Or really just one, in fact, if truth be told. I'm not really . . . I don't . . .' but I was embarrassed, and I didn't really know what I'd been going to say, other than it was a pick-up line, a very clumsy and possibly offensive one at that. But Ruth just laughed again. That tough, wholehearted laugh. Nothing sleekit in it; nothing putting me down.

'You must masturbate a lot.' It was my turn to laugh, nervously, after a shocked couple of heartbeats.

'Not really. No more than . . . than . . .' Christ, what a conversation '. . . normal. The fantasies clutter the mind. I've started playing the guitar again, and I suppose the searching for treasures, the handling of things like that Clutha vase, the sensual . . . och, you know. Old books, too, the smell, the texture of the paper, the fact that sometimes the pages have been cut, physically by someone, with a knife, but then they stop and the book hasn't been cut and hasn't been read . . . Sometimes that, all that . . . it's better than sex.' Which was a particularly stupid thing to say, and possibly also a continuation of the pick-up line. Because it wasn't true. I was sweating, despite the cold.

'Really.' We climbed slowly down to the van. When we got to the flat, she asked if I would come with her over to her house to look at a papier-mâché tray she'd bought. I said that would be fine. I'd been at the house once or twice before, dropping things off. Ruth possessed some lovely objects, and one or two daft and outrageous ones. The papier-mâché tray was lovely. Ruth had some books, too, which were good to hold, and smell and ruffle through. A complete Border edition of Scott. But none of it was better than the sex. What was I? A bit of slightly shop-soiled rough? I didn't care.

At the Lame Duck, Truth Drug – the name had been Mick's idea, 'sort of dangerous but honest, uncompromising but slightly decadent, man' – were jammed into a corner next to the bar, using only a vocal public-address system. I had asked Ruth if she wanted to go, but Keith had specifically asked her to stay away, she said, and that was fine. 'Maybe one day, when they're at the

Theatre Royal,' she joked. I was wearing a jacket she'd bought for me, an ordinary leather flying jacket, except like hers it had been cut crisply so that it looked classically right and very expensive. I knew it had been very expensive, too. It made me feel good, I had to admit. I was shaving at least every second day. And I'd abandoned my commitment to laundrette evenings, caving in to the concept of the service wash. Having effortless access to clean clothes was a luxury I was growing to depend on. People commented that I was looking well, healthier, but I wasn't really. My clothes were.

Loud. Clearer, less distorted than my precious memory of the Cornerstones and that mythic blast of the other Stones, but loud, with the kick-drum pounding into your chest so it was hard to swallow. And they were rough, rough as hell, ragged and untogether. But Mick was Mr Charisma, all smiling pout and flickering legs, those Jagger and Bowie and Prince moves, stolen from the telly and worked out in front of wardrobe mirrors, now cramped by the tiny venue and the tables and the press of a boozy, beery crowd. Keith was the counterpoint, smoking, moody and silent, windmilling his sunburst guitar. It was melodic rock topped by Mick's soul-steeped voice, all vibrato mannerisms from Motown and Stax, but thrilling too. There were moments of sheer . . . joy about their set, and the songs seemed to work, have light and shade. But the swelling, pounding sense of hurt, the shivering inflammation and rage and change I'd felt at the Kingston Baptist Church and at the Apollo . . . those things were not provoked in me. Maybe the days for that had gone. The lyrics were full of complex passions and self-important posturing, but, well, that was rock'n'roll.

'We want to do a song now for our LANDLORD!' Mick was shouting gleefully. The bar was packed, mostly because the live-music night was free entertainment. The crowd cheered ironically. Most of them were students, and they knew what landlords were like. 'Hey, our landlord, man, he's OK, except he keeps us awake singing fucking Hank Williams songs. And he's here tonight, so this is our REVENGE!' And they launched into a tongue-in-cheek, slow-raunch, power-chorded version of 'My Bucket's Got a Hole in it', with Mick doing exaggerated, soulful imitations of a sandpapery Al Green, complete with little 'ha-has'. Keith and Mick were both hardcore Green fans, and at various times I would hear the *Spotlight on Al Green* compilation leaking smoochily from their bedrooms, employed as an aid to seducing the string of young, heavily cheekboned women who visited Ruthven Street, usually just once or twice. 'My Bucket's Got a Hole in it' became a ferociously sensual cry of frustration, deflated by the ironic antics of Mick's voice, and his body. He ended the set singing from the bar counter, lying full length while a female fan dripped Green Chartreuse into his mouth between verses. It was brilliant. Hank, that tortured, drug-racked and alcohol-soused undiagnosed spina bifida victim, songwriting genius, womaniser, devoutly religious hell-raiser, would have loved it. Especially the bit with the Green Chartreuse.

The next day I went to Virgin Records and spent £200 on cassettes. I bought a Williams boxed set for the sake of a few tracks which I didn't have on other albums. I bought a three-tape Hendrix set, because Truth Drug had rekindled my desire for that rush, that enormous, ecstatic guitar howl. A Johnny Cash double compilation, the Louvin Brothers, some hard blues, Muddy Waters and Howling Wolf. I was astonished at the ease with which you could spend money on music, old music at that. But I didn't stop to let myself feel uneasy about it. I was still on a high from the gig at the Lame Duck, and I wanted to try and keep that feeling. Maybe I was being daft, trying to hang on to the moment, that emotional rock'n'roll punch which is a combination of sound and circumstance. But it was worth a try. At the last moment, I added a copy of the Stones compilation *Made in the Shade* to my pile of goodies. It was time for that buzzing, rattling, gut-kicking riff which starts 'Brown Sugar' to be a permanent part of my life. Permanence. What was happening to me?

When I got back to the flat, Mick and Keith were sitting in the lounge with a man of about 35, small, very fat, hunched and clearly of Italian origin. He was wearing gold-framed Aviator shades. 'Hey man,' said Mick, excitedly. 'This is our manager, man. His name's . . .' Mick paused, and choked back a giggle. 'His name's Ventura Venissimo, and he says we're gonna get a deal, man!' I looked at Ventura Venissimo. He looked at me, jowls wobbling; not smiling.

'Yes, it is my real name,' he said, acidly, in an accent which was educated bourgeois Glasgow brought determinedly down-market for effect. 'Why the fuck do I have to explain this every fucking hour of every fucking day? I'm fucking Italian, a fucking fat Italian, and fat fucking Italians have fucking names like Ventura and Venissimo. My middle name's Alberto, if you're interested, though fuck knows why you should be.'

'Listen pal,' I said, feeling irritation dry my throat annoyingly. 'This is my house or at least it's my lease, and as long as you're here, sitting on my sofa, bits of which I sub-let to the half-arsed Glaswegian Wham over there, don't be offensive. Or you can fuck off to your fucking Rolls Royce, which I notice must be parked elsewhere. I don't see any sign of it outside.' Ventura glowered at me, and then let loose a smile of such overpowering, practised charm that it was impossible to remain angry. He stretched his chubby hands out, all innocence.

'Hey,' he grinned, 'hey, don't get mad, baby. I'm in the rock'n'roll vibe, hard as fuck, noise people up, make things happen kind of mode. That's just me, get used to it, that's the life, babe. That's the life in Tunesville.' Good grief. I wondered if Ventura was quite sane. And what Ruth would make of him. *Manager?*

'So,' I pondered, feeling very old. 'Are you two signing a contract with Phil Spector here? Or have you already?' I sounded recriminatory, I knew. Fatherly in the worst do-you-lads-know-what-you're-doing sense, with my Virgin bags clutched tightly in my hands. And I was only eight years older than Mick and Keith. Well, ten. Though I was involved with the exceedingly well-preserved Ruth, which was a factor. Or was it? Keith didn't know anything about that. We'd been very careful to keep our liaison a secret from him.

'Just because you're screwing my mother,' said Keith, in his usual moody manner, mumbling, but distinctly, 'doesn't mean you have to act like some fucking Dutch uncle.' I had never really understood what a Dutch uncle was, but this was an interesting development. Our secret was unsafe. I played it casual. There was a silence, embarrassed on Mick's part, frankly, amusedly curious on Ventura's.

'Do you mind?' I said, as if I was asking for a space on the settee.

'Nope,' replied Keith. 'She's happy. Or at least happier, or anyway she says she is. She didn't tell me, by the way. I found out from my Aunt Rachel, who lives three houses down from us. I mean her. She's had toyboys before' – this said in a careless, yawning way – 'not that you're exactly a boy. Or anywhere near it. But I'm not unhappy.'

'So why fucking mention it then, you prick?' said Ventura, to whom I suddenly felt rather grateful, although this was hardly the kind of managerial cosseting you expected, even from an overweight rock'n'roll hard-nut like Mr Venissimo. 'And as for your question, Mr Landlord, as you seem to have some kind of family connection with Mr Grant, however slight, I don't believe in contracts. I believe in trust. My word *is* my bond. I believe in the spirit of rock'n'fuckin'roll, and uplift. UP-LIFTING MUSIC, man, to change things, make things better, like a jewel? A diamond. In the RUST!' He was both grinning cynically and passionate at the same time. Maybe bluntness was best.

'Are you on anything, Ventura?'

He laughed. 'Just life, man. Fuckin' LIFE!' I shrugged, and took my tapes through to my bedroom. It was definitely one of those Hank Williams moments. I spun one of the new tapes forward till a song I'd never heard before, called 'Kaw-Liga'. It turned out to be a totally bizarre tale about a cigar-store indian. Surrealism with a funny native-American chanting feel. Suddenly there was a knock at the door.

'Yes?' Ventura's head appeared.

'The most crappy song he ever wrote,' he said.'"Setting the Woods on Fire" is my favourite, definitely. The first fuckin' rock'n'roller. All spirit and fire and guts.' His head withdrew. Ventura Venissimo was clearly a man of taste. If not manners.

Later, I found out that he was also shrewd, experienced in a small-time way as a promoter of minor gigs and blessed or cursed with a personality which could veer in the blink of an eye from kindness, concern and absolute generosity to a kind of considered, sneering obnoxiousness, which could leave unsuspecting victims paralysed with horror and confusion. If you gave him as good as you got, though, he lightened up immediately. 'I just get bored easily,' he told me one day, in a moment when lucidity slipped out between the hard-as-fuck, mini-Meatloaf image and the Mediterranean Godfather, take-my-house, eetza-yours-my-brother approach, which I liked to think was probably the real Ventura. Or hoped so, anyway. I liked him, he was fun, he seemed honest. Mostly. Oh hell, what did I really know? At least he was passionate, a believer in things. And he loved Truth Drug. Or rather, he loved Mick and Keith. The rest of the band were sacked immediately at his insistence.

'I'm not a poof,' he once informed me, apropos of nothing. 'I'm not trying to get at Mick and Keith's arses, if that's what you thought.' I hadn't thought he was, I told him, although in fact it had occurred to me.

'So what about women then, Ventura?'

'What about women? Do you mean who am I fucking? The answer is nobody. I'm waiting until I'm rich and famous, or rather the boys are, and then I'm going to have my wicked way with hundreds of beautiful women who'll flock to me because of my wealth and power.' But he was smiling that searchlight smile. 'Fell in love once, fucked and got fucked, and that's it until I have enough control to make sure I don't get hurt,' he said. 'Besides, I don't have time, or the energy. It's all very well for you, with your mature occasional companion. Too fuckin' adult for belief, that is. Still, let her spend her money on you, that's what I say. Live and let fuck.' He was still smiling. I couldn't hit him. I wasn't big on hitting, anyway. I smiled back.

I'd told Ruth about Ventura, and, practical as ever, she had contacted a client in the Italian community, somebody who had once been big in ice-cream and was now enormous in cappuccino machines. He had never heard of the Venissimo family, or indeed any family by that name. 'Sounds fake to me,' Signor Cappuccino had told her. 'There's no such Italian name, at least, not one that I've heard. What Venissimo does mean, but, and this isn't how you would actually translate it, but it's like someone trying to say "I came very much so." From the Latin. You know, veni, vidi, vici; I came, I saw, I conquered. Maybe it's a sort of sexual message, but you know the Italian word for that kind of coming is quite different . . .'

'By this time he had his hand on my knee,' grimaced Ruth, 'so I made my excuses and left. But it looks like your Ventura is not just all that he makes himself out to be. Venissimo, indeed.'

'He's not my Ventura,' I said. 'He's your Keith's Ventura. And Mick's.' I'd been finding my domestic arrangements a little odd. I was living with the son of the woman I was not living with but having sex with. Was very comfortable with, in fact, even if she was on hormone replacement therapy, which had been malignantly suggested to me by Ventura, in one of his grossly offensive states. Bastard. Ruth wasn't old enough for that, not nearly, but it annoyed me because the age thing was a niggle. What was it with older women? Christ, I wasn't that young myself. Ventura had never met Ruth, of course. But she was only 39, or so she said; far too young for HRT; had married young, given birth to Keith at 22 ('Jesus, I thought I was going to be torn apart. He was like Alien bursting out of John Hurt in the movie'), which wasn't all that young, really. And I realised I was getting old. I had begun to take some exercise, which sat badly with the smoking, something Ruth put up with, a pained expression sometimes flitting across her face, always perfectly made-up except in bed, when the removal of all the powder and gloss was part of her undressing, and something I found arousing. Curiously, she always looked younger in bed. But maybe that's because it was dark.

Truth Drug spent long days and sometimes whole nights rehearsing in the suppurating surroundings of Railtrack, breaking in a new band, and preparing for a series of what Ventura called 'showcase gigs'. One night he knocked on my bedroom door, when I was sitting with my Yamaha guitar, crooning to myself Hendrix's 'Little Wing', lost to the world. Applause brought me back to earth, from the heaven where Hendrix and I sat together over a barrel of Murphys, him with his trademark white Fender Stratocaster, me with a red one, and we duetted, with me matching him note for note . . .

'Nice,' nodded Ventura. 'Ever write your own stuff?'

'No. Once, a long time ago.' I put the guitar down. His appearance in my private reverie had rattled me. 'Something I can do for you?'

'Well, yes, there is, actually.' He slid into the room. 'Read this.' He held out a typewritten A4 sheet. At the top it said 'Truth Drug, The Venue, Glasgow'. Then it continued:

You don't enter the Venue, you sneak in hiding your face, in case somebody thinks you actually like heavy metal. This is a refuge for hair and dandruff and big guitars hiding small willies. But you can hire it for pennies and tonight, new Glasgow rock/soul contenders Truth Drug are parading their wares for everybody that isn't anybody. The guest list is longer than the telephone directory.

My feet stick to the floor. The beer comes in plastic glasses, but that doesn't stop someone trying to slash someone else with one. Must be from Edinburgh, or something. No one in Glasgow's that stupid. Or maybe he's a scout for a record company. I spy one or two of those runny-nosed creatures.

I'm sipping warm slops when out comes this guy, recognisable anywhere, Ventura Venissimo, well-known pop person and promoter, and a man with his ears in the right place: on both sides of his head! But somebody who sometimes has an inkling for qualipop, or has in the past. Word is he's put his balls where his ears are, and is managing something called Truth Drug. Good name, but can they cut it? Glasgow is awash with talent, and while that means the A&R men and women are zipping up and down on the shuttle whenever sheep bleat down a microphone, it also means a lot of crap is getting stage time. But Ventura's a guarantee of . . . at least two-and-a-half minutes of interest.

Listen folks, actually it's more like 20 minutes. Because surprise, surprise, Truth Drug are dead good. Rough and young and needing some match practice, but they cut the mustard, no dice, no doubt, take no prisoners, natch. Wait, you'll love this! The lead singer's called Mick, and the guitarist is Keith, and though they're both about 17, they've got all the angles worked out. And this guy Mick can sing, like a sort of Stevie Wonder with eyes. Testosterone shoots out of him like from a hose, too, if the little girlies screaming at the front are anything to go by. And the songs, their own songs, are hot properties. 'Wild' is just that, a ballad big on balls. 'Darkness in your Heart' is Conraddian melodrama via Iggy Pop and Al Green, and 'Goodness (You Don't Know What That Means)' could be a minor classic.

They encored with a great cover of the Rolf Harris song 'My Bucket's Got a Hole in it', and I went home wondering how long it would take for Truth Drug to become a habit. Catch them while the street price is still affordable.

'Ventura, what the fuck is this?'

He grinned that flashbulb grin. 'What do you think it is? It's a review of the Truth Drug gig at the Venue.'

I looked at him. His smile didn't waver. 'How can I put this, Ventura? I realise it's a review. But the gig isn't until next Monday night. This is Wednesday. And besides, you can't review a band you're the manager of. That's . . .'

'Corrupt. I believe the word you're looking for is corrupt. But listen, what do you think of the writing? Pretty good, eh, with all those little puns and alliteration and kind of Tom Wolfe New Journalism type of things? You know, all that me me me me me guff, rather than talking about the band. God, those poor sods who call themselves rock journalists. I mean, how can anyone take that seriously? Rock journalists. They're all wankers who want to hang out with talent and glamour, or who wish it was them up there actually DOING IT! when fuck, all they're any good for is promoting. The only reason we tolerate them is because we want them to help us. Until we've made it. Then they can just go fuck themselves. Rock journalists are only useful for maybe two months, to get a band signed, then before the first hit, then fuck 'em. Wank is what rock journalism is, basically. Temporarily useful wank from my point of view. I mean, these guys want to write like Tom Wolfe or Hunter S. Thompson, because they think it's easy and because it's a chance for them to vomit on about themselves, as if they're important! Bastards. Fans with typewriters? Wankers with word processors.'

'I see you put in plenty about yourself, though, Ventura. You're certainly playing the Dr Goebbels on this one. Except how the hell are you going to get it published?'

He just looked at me with the laser charm at full strength. 'Oh no,' I said. 'You can't be serious. You must be fucking crazy.'

145

'Why not? It's just a deal. Maybe a slightly dodgy deal, but you're no stranger to that, I hear. Buy it cheap, keep it as short a time as possible, sell it for as much as you can get in the time. This is just a wee bit of business. Put your name at the bottom. Go on! Hell, they'll even pay you for it.'

'Who will?'

'Well, I thought of *Melody Maker* or *NME*, but the easiest would probably be *Music Press*, because they're short of a stringer up here since the prick got busted a fortnight ago. Raid on the toilets at the Majimbo Club and someone slipped an eight-ounce bag of Bolivian Creamola Foam powder into his pocket. Not me, before you ask. A happy accident.'

I thought about it. What the hell, no one in the world of rock'n'roll knew who I was. And if it helped Truth Drug, then why not? And I could even retain some integrity if I rewrote the thing, at least a bit. It gave me a weird feeling, actually the thought of having something printed as being by me. Out there, in the world of glitz and glamour and rock and rigid role-playing. Well away from my previous field of communication, where I had been a performer, on the side of the angels, a doer and a maker, albeit at God's direction. Now I could be a critic, or rather, pretend to be one. In fact, that made it OK, the pretending. And since I'd been reading the music papers occasionally, I had some idea of the rip-off, third-rate 'new journalism' which passed for criticism in them. Trust Ventura to know all about that. 'Of course,' said Ventura, 'they might not print it. But if not, we'll just keep on with the other gigs and with other papers.'

I typed up my version of the review that Saturday at Ruth's house, on her portable electric typewriter. We had been shopping that afternoon, and had queued for nearly 40 minutes to get a table at the Café Gandolfi, where I fitted in, almost, these days. Ruth had made me buy some stupidly baggy trousers which reminded me of the kind my father had once worn on holidays: big, creamy cotton things. She kept dropping hints about a haircut, but I liked it long. Although I compromised and washed it every second day. In Head and Shoulders. When it came down to it, I didn't change much in Ventura's review. Just got rid of the breathless colloquialisms like 'natch' and tidied up the grammar. It wasn't that I could write, but I could copy. I'd picked out four reviews from *Melody Maker* and *NME*, not the really arseholish ones which quoted Jacques Derrida and licked Barthes's bum, but the enthusiastically cynical, youthful pieces which had jagged lumps of speed-fuelled American journalese poking out, and sometimes a really God-like tone of knowledge. Ventura's review was as good, if not better than, any of them, and hit all the right bases, it seemed. So I stuck my name at the end, and sent it off to The Reviews Editor, *Music Press*, Vidwell Street, London WC3. Ruth, a realist, thought the whole idea was slightly laughable, but on the whole quite viable. She was under no illusions about the intrinsic merits of journalism. Until I returned from the off-licence with a bottle of Rioja, pleased with myself and having posted the review off. It was, she pointed out, only Saturday night. The gig wasn't until Monday. Fortunately there was no collection of the post until Monday morning, and hopefully *Music Press* wouldn't spot the postmark, so long as it took the usual two days for first-class mail to reach London. And it would take a pretty sussed editor even to know that there had been a Truth Drug gig at any time in history, let alone that it was on Monday night. We drank the Rioja and laughed about it. Adults. All this rock stuff, it was probably just something which Keith would look back on when he was grown up and think, well, we tried that, and it was fun. Ruth lit candles and I sat in her beautifully appointed lounge, with its Peter Howson graduation-show painting, picked up for pennies, and listened to Erik Satie on the Pink Triangle stereo. She lay down with her head in my lap, on my new cream cotton baggy trousers that she had chosen, with her hair tickling my chest through the new Next shirt we'd bought together in the afternoon. And suddenly my blood ran cold. Was this it, then? Was this all?

Thirty-five people turned up at the Venue for Truth Drug's first gig as a Ventura Venissimo act, disciplined, and rehearsed by him, with his musicians replacing Mark and Zam, only Bonzo the drummer retained – 'and on a session basis only,' Ventura had told me. 'The band is Mick and Keith. Easier that way. They write the songs, they look the part, and there's only two. Fewer arseholes. You can just rent the arseholes and ditch them if you have to. Lease an arsehole, that's my motto!' Quite. Bonzo certainly was an arsehole, but I was told that this was an occupational hazard with drummers. Something to do with having a brain which could direct each of four limbs to do something entirely different from the other three, simultaneously. So to speak.

One of the 35 was Ruth. She and I sneaked in five minutes before the band were due to start, and then had to wait an hour-and-a-half, drinking bad beer out of glass glasses (the review was wrong) and trying to stop our feet sticking permanently to the swampy carpet around the bar. Horribly loud heavy-metal music played through a PA system which looked capable of killing pigeons at a hundred yards, while Ventura stalked about, fucking this and fucking that, waiting for influential people who were on the guest list to turn up. 'It's Monday night, Ventura,' I said. 'What do you expect?'

'I expect people to do what they say they will,' he retorted, through clenched teeth. 'When I say I'll do something I do it. I fucking do what I promise. I fucking deliver. Cunts. Journalists. Cunts. Who's this?' But of course, he knew.

I introduced him to Ruth, who smiled her own version of the football-floodlight grin. He returned it, and then some. I felt as if I ought to be putting on a pair of shades. It was like looking at tropical sun through a magnifying glass. The ludicrously expensive Ray Ban Wayfarers which Ruth had bought me, for example. 'Once you've worn them, you won't be able to wear any other sunglasses,' she'd told me. But I'd never had the gall to wear them in public. It was just so naff.

'I'm looking after your son, Mrs Grant,' he assured her. 'He's going to be a big star. You ought to be very proud of him.'

'Where does the name Venissimo come from?' asked Ruth, sweetly. 'It's very unusual.'

Ventura remained calm and charming. 'Oh, it's Italian. My family are very big in espresso and cappuccino machines. My middle name is Alberto, and as for Ventura . . . it's all bit of a Latin cliché, I'm afraid.'

Ruth nodded. 'Really.' I watched this exchange, impressed. No one was going to rip off Keith in a hurry. Not with Ruth around. Although I didn't think there was any harm in Ventura. He rushed off to greet someone he said was 'not a real A&R man, only a scout, a bloody local loser who gets tip-off fees from the record company in London.' And suddenly, without any announcement (oh shit, that review) the band were on stage.

They were nervous, but they were tight, a lot more so than at the Lame Duck. One or two of the songs had been restructured, with middle eights and repeated choruses, and Mick's more outrageous vocal pyrotechnics reigned in. It was good, but the carefree fire of that last gig wasn't there. It was good though. 'Goodness (You Don't Know What That Means)' could, I suddenly felt, be a minor classic. Great title. They encored with the cover of Hank's 'My Bucket's Got a Hole in it', smoochified, bizarrely good, and I went home wondering how long it would take for Truth Drug to become a habit. People should catch them while the street price was still affordable, I thought. Which was a coincidence, as that's what appeared in *Music Press* the following Thursday, under my name. I'd realised it was a joke, Ventura's joke about Rolf Harris writing 'My Bucket's Got a Hole in it.' But it was a bit much really. Almost blasphemous. I felt strongly about Hank.

I was making money, doing very well, in fact, but mainly now through Ruth and her voluminous contacts. If an interior designer for a pub or a bijou residence wanted something specific, I would find it for them, and there was no longer any need for the dash from house clearance to dealer, from jumble sale to small-time crook. I still used the VW, though, and dressed down for my acquisition trips. It didn't pay to appear prosperous. I was spending more and more time at Ruth's, and one night, arriving at Ruthven Street unexpectedly, I found my bed occupied by Ventura. 'Fuck' was his first word when I switched the lights on and he jerked upright, his glassless eyes screwed tight against the glare. He looked like a wee boy. Tousled. 'Look, I'm sorry . . . is it OK? I had a few beers with the lads, and I didn't want to drive, and we've got a gig in Dunfermline tomorrow. Early start. Besides, you bastard, you've got a bed with a body in it over in Newton Mearns. Fucking . . . *journalist.*' He was waking up. I collected some clothes, switched the light off and drove back to Ruth's house, letting myself in with the key she'd given me. When I crawled into her Givenchy sheets she didn't even wake up. Just turned over and put an arm round me with a comfortable sort of groaning snore. As if I was a fixture.

Journalist. Rock journalist. 'Scumcunt of the fucking earth' in Venturaspeak. But *Music Press* not only printed the Truth Drug piece, they wrote to me within ten days asking me to telephone them, urgently. 'You will receive our cheque at the usual monthly accounting,' said the letter primly. 'We would appreciate a call as we may have more work available in your area.' Ruthven Street did not have a telephone. It was something I had just avoided, had made a point of not needing. Actually it would have been useful, but I hated that feeling of being perpetually available; open to the world's invasion. It was a lack which drove Ruth crazy, but I had remained resolute. My obdurate anti-Alexander Graham Bell stance also sent Mick and Keith daft, and Ventura almost berserk with rage. But it was my lease, and I wouldn't have it. Messages could be left for me at Losers, where Andy ran an informal answering service. But I hadn't been in there for ages.

I went to Losers so I could call *Music Press*. Andy poured me a Murphy's, and I realised it was my first for weeks. I'd been seduced by red wine and sophisticated women. Or one at least.

'I've got some people who're looking for books,' said Andy. 'Any DC Thomson annuals, comics from the 1940s and 50s. Must be immaculate. And I want a chronometer. One of those you get in a box. I'll pay up to a grand.'

I felt a little spark of interest. *Dandy* and *Beano* books would make a change from bloody wall-hangings and ship models. A trip to Dundee, perhaps. But some little malcontent within me was saying, hey, *be* scum. See if you can con these paper people into printing some crap you've actually written yourself. I dialled the *Music Press* number. The reviews editor was a wide-boy cockney called Chaz Thwaite, which caused me some confusion at first. I thought he was telling me to just wait. 'OK, I'll wait.' But we communicated in the end. I went to Dundee, picked up a totally perfect collection of *Topper*, *Beano* and *Dandy* books from a former employee of the DC Thomson comic empire, hung out in two or three thoroughly disreputable bars around the docks, asking about chronometers, until someone either stole one to order or really did, as he claimed, sell it to me on behalf of an aged friend of his mother's. Got drunk on Murphy's and Irish whiskey, Paddy's I think, and slept in the van for the first time in nearly a year. Then I drove painfully back to Glasgow and proceeded to go completely crazy for three months, as a late-developing, all-sneering, no-dancing scumbag rock journalist. Fuck antiques, tell Lovejoy the news . . .

Music Press had asked me to go to a gig by the curiously named Edinburgh group Rip Strip and Fuck It. They were, it seemed, a kind of Caledonian Iggy and the Stooges, complete with reputation for arty self-mutilation on stage, according to Chaz. It sounded very Edinburgh. 'You seem to know the scene,' drawled Chaz. 'Check it out.' Unfortunately, I had never heard of Iggy and the Stooges. I bought the *NME Encyclopedia of Rock* and some tapes, and updated my education. From Hank and Hendrix to Iggy and Raw Power wasn't that much of a jump. It was extreme, but not that much further out on the edge than the Hank Williams who had written 'Wealth Won't Save Your Soul'. I ransacked the music press for clues, for a style, an approach that would be apt in this case. Boredom and seen-it-all superiority seemed the correct pose. And Rip Strip and Fuck It's gig at Strutz, a hell-hole in the bowels of the Barrowland Ballroom, made it easy:

Rip Strip and Fuck It
Strutz, Glasgow

When the manager ('I hate that word') tackles you before the gig and informs you that he 'despises the first song, it's awful', you know this is no ordinary band. [What a cop-out opening.

This is no ordinary band, and I don't have a clue about them, actually.] No ordinary name, either. Though they're prone to dropping the 'Fuck It' in search ... of what? Certainly not street cred/gull/ability. [Actually, the manager had told me that they had definitely and for good dropped the 'Fuck It', but I realised, as a good dealer, that the name was the main appeal of the band, at least to Chaz, so I kind of . . . got round that. And hey, that cred/gull/ability stuff! Wow, that it was once possible to write like that outside of school magazines!] Last year's gloriously good/unbelievably bad (both in patches) mini-album *A Month in Bohemia is Worth Two in the Bush* was no preparation for a rather tame, unrehearsed and well, well dodgy set at Strutz. Where were the broken bottles stabbed into innocent chests [which I knew Iggy had famously done]? Where was the raw howling guitar? Abandoned, we are informed, in the search for being 'taken seriously'. Well, not the guitar. That was submerged in a turgid, bass-heavy sound. But the performance never managed to escape its rather obvious origins. Those are, in very large doses, Iggy Pop (microphone inside mouth/lying on back/tortured screams, etc.) [I'd seen the pictures in the *Encyclopedia of Rock*] much Velvet Underground [cross referenced in the *E of R* from Pop, Iggy. I had also never consciously listened to a Velvet Underground song, although I remembered Lou Reed from 'Walk on the Wild Side' which I'd heard as a Christian innocent. I'd thought it must be something to do with professional racing cyclists, as these were the only men I had ever heard of who shaved their legs. In order to improve their aerodynamics] and dollops of the Cramps [again ref. from the *E of R* section on Iggy. The picture looked kind of similar]. Despite the absence of tunes, tightness or genuine tension, items like 'Rich Rich' and 'Open Your Mouth' gave the truly evil/demented/wasted/tall Carl Q. Ling a chance to intimidate. Sort of. But, again, it was all too inward, too resigned. Guitarist Dunc has some brilliant notions which never really came to anything [at least, I certainly had no idea what he was trying to do], and though the whole thing did have moments of both danger [of completely falling asleep if it hadn't been so bloody noisy] and farce [every other part] in the true Stooges tradition [whatever that was] there was never enough of either.

Buy the album, masochism fans. You might just like it.

But I thought the whole event and indeed the entire concert of Rip Strip and FI was utter shite. I also had no idea what they were aiming at. But I wrote the review anyway. It was the first time I came across the idea of just writing for money and publication about a subject you didn't care about at all. The essence, in fact, of rock journalism. What the process did was get you into gigs for nothing, often some free drink and free LPs you could sell to second-hand record shops. It was a form of dealing. I had bought a second-hand Olympia typewriter, and would write my unoriginal, pretentious, cynical, superior reviews hesitantly, using two fingers, prodding my third-hand opinions on to paper in the late mornings, while Mick and Keith slept off their all-night rehearsals and boozing and toking. Ventura didn't do drugs. He was a two-beer-and-pissed character, or at least pretended to be. It was very hard to see through his cast-iron Latin hard-nose pose, but then we were all lying, all acting. He enjoyed thinking of himself as some sort of Svengali. Turning me into a rock journalist, for God's sake! I never found out where he lived, although Mick and Keith had a telephone number with a Bearsden code. Apparently an answering machine was permanently on. He never turned up in my bed again, either, the little shite. Notes, businesslike and short ('Call me') piled up from Ruth. She arrived to see me when I didn't. I was always really welcoming, kiss kiss, just a bit busy at the moment, dear. But she was brittle, angry and suspicious. She knew something was up. I didn't know what was happening, except I wanted to pursue this rock'n'roll writing lark, had to, somehow. It had infected me, hooked me, like a drug, hooked this old-enough-to-know-better adult boy. And I was running back to seed, careless, away from Ruth's immaculate, tender, tough supervision. It was a wonder some of the clubs let me in. I even wore trainers sometimes, and these places had bouncers who were shoe fetishists, trained to repulse anyone with grey shoes or rubber soles. Trainers – this was years before they became *de rigueur* for dancing – were for jogging or street football, not ligging. As time blurred into a trough of all-night booze-soaked gigs, hanging out with glamorous, stupid strangers who patronised and flattered, I rarely saw Mick and Keith. If we met, it was in a spatter of morose, monosyllabic hangovers. Once Keith muttered: 'I have to go to get my own washing now, you bastard', but I ignored him. Ruth had stopped leaving messages. I felt a dull guilt, but nothing overwhelming.

For three months I became a ligger, a hanger-on to the coat tails of rock'n'roll in Glasgow. There wasn't a night-club I didn't blag my way into, a gig I didn't claim to be reviewing. In actual fact, the only shows I did write about were local ones, apart from having to trek to Irvine, of all places, to see The Smiths in a huge games hall called the Magnum Centre ('How long can a boy wear a thorn in his side before he gets it surgically removed?') but I played the *Music Press* card as hard as I could. I met various band managers, disc jockeys, manic enthusiasts, middle-aged loser cokehead managers who had lost their bands and their way, sad, feel-you-up gays who wanted to get close to young, pretty boy bands by offering to do publicity, manage, be an agent or just be a doormat for them. And one or two other rock journalists, who were all much younger and cooler and more knowledgeable about music than I was. They also seemed to really care about certain bands. 'Oh yeah,' said one, a heavily built, permanently flushed boy with spiky hair and an appliqué scowl, dressed in new, unscarred leather biker wear. 'You're the Truth Drug guy.' And he laughed, unpleasantly. 'That fucking Ventura. How much did the fat bastard pay you?'

I shrugged. 'I really like them.'

'Oh yes. And I hear you have a nice wee *ménage à trois* with Mick and Keith. One up the arse, one in the mouth, eh?' I looked at him. He was bigger, harder-looking than I was. And besides, I was all grown up, mature; an adult. He was grinning. I chuckled. He laughed. Then I hit him in the face with an almost-full bottle of Grolsch.

It didn't break, thank God, and by some fluke I hit him square on his fleshy nose. It didn't break either, but it bled profusely, scattering HIV-conscious cool cats in all directions. I spilt about half of the beer, and left it on the bar for some punter to finish; I left my victim crouched foetally on the dancefloor, his girlfriend caught between comforting him and screaming abuse at me. I was stumbling out into the taxi-riven night before the stewards knew what had happened, shock and alcohol sending the streets into a fairground whirl. I was losing it. Christ, I had never hit anyone since school, and even then I was such a fucking do-gooder born-again I couldn't quite remember doing it there. But why was it slipping away from me, this half-life I'd constructed since Edinburgh? Or why was I throwing it away? What was driving me? I walked down to the Clyde Walkway, the dosser-strewn attempt to make Glasgow's old hag river some kind of scenic centrepiece, and staggered among the Lanliq bottles, the hairspray containers, the empty milk bottles. Milk was used unsuccessfully to remove the poison from the hairspray, render it drinkable, I hazily remembered. Beneath the *Daily Record* building I stopped, gazed out to a massive wooden pile about six feet from the river's edge. I could jump on to that, I thought. I could do it. But I would fall, probably, and the murky currents of the Clyde would suck me down into darkness and death. Maybe I should try the leap.

Risk it. But at Off the Record, a journalists' pub where my fake hackdom was made visibly risible by the presence of real hard-men reporters in raincoats – or maybe they were just posing too, going through their Clark Kent routines – I had a large Laphroaig, and got a taxi back to Ruthven Street. No one was in.

I teamed up, briefly, with an attractively wasted girl who dressed in black at all times and was prone to wearing shades after dark. She was unemployed, but wanted to set up an agency representing Scottish bands. I suppose for her, fucking a journalist was in the line of duty. It certainly seemed that way. It happened five or six times, in all, incredibly late at night or early in the morning, after gigs, with us both sweaty and grimy and smoky and more drunk each time, in order to get through the dutiful, grisly and gristley pleasure of the essential coupling. Condoms. I had them. She refused to permit them. 'Do you think I'm a risk, then? A slag? Is that what you're saying?' Of course not darling. You're fucking Mary Poppins, what do you think? Unsafe sex. Why not? Drink, for the first time in my life, became an issue. Because I was in clubs three, four nights a week which were open until 4.00 a.m. I was drinking more. And the prices were vast. Money, when it eventually started coming through from *Music Press*, was a joke. A very cheap one indeed.

I started getting really pissed at gigs, bored nearly all the time, trying to carry out shouted conversations during the interminable wait for bands to come on stage. I grew slightly deaf. Abusive. And petty. If anything or anyone annoyed me at a show, I would take my revenge. Single-handedly, I destroyed the hopes of a young and innocent band called Skip and the Reflections, because their manager walked away from the swaying, stuttering drunk that was me, *Music Press* big shot:

> This is music without guts, without flavour, without anything save a fashionably insipid regurgitating of cliché ... Skip and his boys use forms of music clinically, cynically; performing without any discernible intensity or spirit. Talk about the passion! This set possessed all the cutting edge of used Andrex.

The poor lead singer, I heard later, had gone around his home suburb of Bishopbriggs and bought every copy of *Music Press* he could find, in case his parents or friends saw the review. Almost certainly untrue. I heard this and laughed. It was hangover writing, boorish and bitter and pathetic. But I'd grown addicted to the notion of perpetual clubbing, to the idea of some great passion, some perfect moment happening at the next gig, the next club, after the next drink. I was getting short of cash. I was getting old. I was on the verge of being an ageing joke on the scene. But I was desperate to keep moving, to keep partying, to keep behaving like the adolescent I'd never been. And I had an excuse. I was, after all, a rock journalist.

Then Chaz asked me to review another Truth Drug gig. This time it was on a Friday night, in a much plusher venue known as Maestro's, a proper night-club. I'd been dimly aware, as I pursued my accelerating bender, that Mick and Keith were becoming local heroes, that there was a real buzz about Truth Drug. I tried to broach the subject with them one early afternoon, when we met in the kitchen. They'd left the rent, as usual, in an envelope next to the kettle. I hadn't picked it up for two days.

'Need to be increasing the rent, guys,' I said, 'now that you'll soon be rich and famous.' But they had grown cool, got used to status, albeit minor city-wide status. Mick shrugged.

'Probably be moving out soon, anyway. Ventura thinks we'll be set with a deal in the next few weeks. Mostly be recording in London, he says.' Keith said nothing. I'd desultorily listened to the two demo tapes the band had produced in local studios. They were good, I thought. But what did I know? I'd blunted my sensitivity to the emotional thrill that was in music through too many bad bands, too loud, in too many late-night clubs, too drunk. One afternoon, I put on a Hank Williams tape, but it sounded thin and rattly and irritating. It was something you had to listen to, and I'd lost the habit.

The Maestro's gig was a triumph. There were 15 A&R men there, including four heads of slave purchasing from major record companies. The band played a blinder, with a top-quality, hugely loud PA system. The three months since I'd seen them had taken them all over the country to poxy provincial gigs which had honed their set to a controlled ferocity. Ventura was in hyper, but expansive mood. 'Hi, scum,' he said, smiling. 'Gave you a career, eh? Where's my fucking percentage!' I wobbled on liquid legs. 'Party, afterwards. In the Holiday Inn. If you can make it without falling over, you should come.' He leaned closer, whispering, hissing into my ear. 'You fucking useless cunt.' I nodded agreement, leaning against the bar clutching a bottle of yellow beer with some fruit in the neck. Then Ruth was in front of me, looking self-possessed and utterly excited and utterly beautiful, dressed to perfection in expensive black, fashionable amid fashion victims, but above the youthful excesses. 'Well, hallo,' she said.

'Proud of your boy, then, Mrs Grant?'

'I am, actually. I never thought it would go this far. And how are you? Long time no see. As people say.' Tough. Always tough. Tough and gentle and suddenly the cancerous tumour of my rock'n'roll illness began to tear away, and beyond it, far away, I could see something glinting, beautiful, like a dawn mountain morning, the Highlands, mist clearing . . . but lost. Gone. Unattainable. An unbearable bleakness. Suddenly it all began to slip away from me. I began to speak. I wanted to explain about needing to dive into this sparkling ocean of rock, and swim down and down, further and further in search of the jewels I knew were somewhere and would comfort and keep me forever. And about the night staring out at the pile in the filthy, putrid Clyde, wondering if I should leap for it. I wanted to tell her that I loved her, about the clearing fog, the mountains glistening with dew; about the tumour that was ripping away too late, but that I was young, still, young at heart, a rebel, really, with big dreams of . . . something. That I'd felt, but not any more, that old, stupid cliché, tied down. But instead I fell over.

I remember, dimly, what happened then. Ruth picked me up, helped by Keith, and as they were going to the Holiday Inn, that was where I went too. Once there, Ruth took control, booked a room, and got a reluctant porter to help her and a grumbling Keith ('My fucking guitar and stuff are back at the club, and the roadies are pissed as farts, and this bastard's been running around town like a randy skunk for the last three months. Fuck him, or rather don't fucking fuck him.' No way to speak to your mother) to manhandle me into a lift. Everything was spinning. I tried to speak, but formulating words was taking hours. At least I hadn't been sick; that was a relief. And then I was, all over the porter. I remember that. I remember the look of anguish and contempt on his face.

I woke up the next day about noon. I was alone. The bedside telephone was ringing: the reception desk, wanting to know if I was checking out. I said no. Nothing was going to get me out of bed for at least two hours. I ordered a room-service breakfast of orange juice and coffee, and waited for the ceiling to stay in one place. That took a long time.

I finally left that night, by the tradesmen's entrance. Miraculously my clothes, though dirty and dancehalled with smoke and sweat, were not encrusted with vomit. My aim had been true. That poor porter. I sneaked out to avoid paying. I was fairly certain that Ruth's name had been on the room booking. She had, after all, taken care of it. But I couldn't face finding out.

There was nobody at Ruthven Street. Mick and Keith's rooms were empty, with a month's advance rent left next to the kettle. I went out for a fish supper, changed my mind and had smoked sausage instead, with pickled onions, letting the spicy taste and grease cut into the pounding hangover. Then I slept for a solid 14 hours. I still felt crap. In the mirror I looked swollen, grey and red, blotchy. I bathed, dressed in some Ruthclothes and went over to Losers, where Andy was glad to see me, he said. That cheered me up. It was a long time since somebody had been glad to see me. I telephoned Ruth over a fresh orange and lemonade. She picked up the phone, and said, 'Hallo?'

I said, 'Ruth, listen . . .'

For the first time since I'd met her, she told me to fuck off. It was not a Ruth thing to say, but she did it quietly, curtly, definitely. She said it well, as if she'd been practising. I finished my fresh orange and lemonade, and the next morning I called a dealer acquaintance, took him to the lock-up and we agreed a truly shitty price for the entire contents and the lease. Cash deal, of course. I packed some clothes – funny how nearly all of them had become Ruthclothes – the Yamaha guitar, the music centre, my tapes and a box of half-decent saleable books I'd forgotten all about, and drove the VW north out of Glasgow.

Success

People thought I was a New Age traveller, a hippy, an urban gypsy. I parked the VW in lay-bys, grew dirtier; didn't care. The remnants of my expensive Ruthhaircuts grew tangled and greasy and long. I was shunned by official caravan sites where I might have been able to wash. The money in my Giro bank account and the cash I had with me was gradually eaten and drunk and driven away. I stopped drinking, virtually, simply because I didn't have the cash. Three days of jittery, teeth-grinding panic, then the taste for it was gone, in the past. Like so much else. I kept the box of books I'd taken away with me for emergencies, or a particularly rainy day. A flood, perhaps. Three Graham Greene first editions, some *Dandy* and *Beano* annuals, later ones I'd been unable to get rid of to Andy's pal, an obscure Victorian illustrated bird book, which was worth about £100 to the right buyer. I kept them underneath the VW's back seat, with the sleeping-bag and the typewriter. After all, I was a rock journalist. I drifted through Argyll, tried to camp with other rootless refugees, the proper New Agers with their dreadlocked hair and dogs on strings, then just discovering Scotland after the determined police break-ups of the Stonehenge and peace convoys. But they shunned me too. I was halfway between motorised tramp and bourgeois tourist. Not dirty enough. I half-heartedly checked out the occasional jumble-sale, and that new-fangled import from America via England, the car-boot sale. I turned over a few quid, but there was little enthusiasm, let alone what had once been the thrill, the joy of the chase, the deal. One Pringle-sweater-and-pearled old woman, a well-heeled pillar of the Scottish Women's Rural Institute in whose name a sale was being held in Taynuilt, had a mint-condition Dinky Toys 1960s Fab One, Lady Penelope's pink futuristic Rolls Royce from *Thunderbirds*, still boxed. I could have it for £2.00, she said, sitting in a deckchair beside the open tailgate of her VW Polo and regarding my lank personage with distaste. I wondered where she'd come across it. Maybe she'd stolen it off a grandchild. But there was a wee boy of about seven standing next to me, watching every move of my grimy fingers as I pored over the model car. One fist was closed tightly over coins; I could hear them grinding like an adult's teeth. At last I put the car back on the picnic rug which covered the back of the Polo. He snatched it up, looked despairingly at the old woman, who had a distinct resemblance to the politician Norman Tebbit, only with more facial hair, and said, 'One pound fifty. That's all I've got.' She pursed her lips so that they appeared to have been swallowed.

'Two pounds is the price. This is for charity, you know. Go and ask your mum for another 50 pence.' A lipless smile. He put the boxed car back, smiling politely, but with an obvious, sad certainty that, whether by iron-fist fatherly dictate or poverty, there was going to be no more family cash forthcoming. I gave her the £2.00, took the box and handed it to the boy. 'There you are. Give me the £1.50.' Silently he did so. Then, loudly so that the Tebbitesque old bat could hear, I said: 'Congratulations, son. You just made a profit of about £50. Tell your mum or dad that car is worth between £60 and £70 at auction, or if you like, don't bother. It depends how much you like it. If you want to keep it. But it's good to know the value. And don't take sweeties from strangers.' I never spoke to children, and I could feel that my words were making no sense to him. He looked at me like I was indeed the kind of man his parents had warned him against accepting cinnamon balls from, and ran off. The old woman was frowning at me. In her agitation, her lips looked like they'd disappeared halfway down her throat, then been regurgitated.

'You weren't serious, were you? It's only a toy car. Found it in the loft with a lot of stuff my son Roger had.' I assured her that I had been completely serious. If I had been less bored, I would have lied, and suggested I take a look at the rest of Roger's stuff, maybe give her a few quid for it, as I had a friend who ran an orphanage . . . but I didn't.

Autumn's first golden chill saw me in Ullapool, watching the Russian klondikers collect in Loch Broom for the hoovering of herring from greedy Scottish fishing boats. There I sold the bird book to a local antique shop for £80, a hopelessly beaten-down price. I needed the money. Once or twice I'd sat at the camper's diminutive table with the typewriter and gazed at its keys, dreaming, wondering if I could write something and sell it for a profit, like I sold objects, things. Or used to. But the paper remained blank, like me. I wondered about claiming dole, but hadn't the faintest idea either how to go about it or even if I was eligible. Probably not. I spent a few weeks collecting mushrooms in the birch forests of Ross-shire, selling them to an agency in Muir of Ord who processed them for the Italian market. I had a pamphlet which warned you which fungi were poisonous and which weren't, and from that it was relatively easy to identify the psyllocibin variety. I collected them for myself, and one luminous October day I drove to Lochinver, in Sutherland, parked by the fishmarket there, where nobody took much notice of me, and as the sun set, I cooked a three-egg omelette using the chopped hallucinogenic mushrooms as a filling. Seasoned with black pepper, and Heinz tomato ketchup, it tasted fine, especially chased with a tin of Guinness, not the horrible, nitrogen- fuelled, pseudo-draught stuff. The hard-edged, tangy variety.

I'd never taken hallucinogenics. A New Age traveller I'd met briefly in Ballachulish had waxed lyrical about psyllocibin mushrooms, and about the ease with which they could be found in early autumn in the Highlands. At first, as darkness fell on the VW and the lights of the fish market came on, pink and yellow, I was conscious only of feeling slightly sick, as if one of the eggs had been off or something. Then I noticed that dolphins were flying in over the sea towards me, brightly lit dolphins, smiling. It was all completely natural; normal. Then each of them turned into Ventura Venissimo, and in unison they were chanting, 'Ruth. Fuck Ruth. That's what I'm doing, fucking Ruth.' Over and over again. Suddenly the dolphins were helicopters, and the light flowed and ran white and red and yellow, and napalm was spattering me, burning my skin, dissolving my body into black, acid slime, and Ventura was still there, huge above it all, shouting, smiling, his teeth glinting and growing into huge tusks like an elephant's. There was Ruth, old, grey and smiling too, but with such humour that I knew we shared a joke which was the funniest joke in the world, and I began to laugh uncontrollably, falling into the cramped floor of the VW, where I woke up, hours later, aching in every muscle, lying in a pool of rotten egg sick. Fortunately, due to lack of space, I'd assumed the foetal position, thus obeying one of the cardinal rock'n'roll guidelines, as enunciated by Ventura: always sleep on your side. As I thought of him his face returned, crisp and clear like a high-quality video being re-run, with the teeth growing larger and sharper and more tusk-like; then I was looking out at the harbour, now crammed with the fishing boats whose ghostly masthead searchlights had lit their way into the rock-bound port the previous night. I realised that the dolphins and the helicopters were explained by those lights. But that didn't make the hallucinations any less real. And they kept on being real for weeks, until, like remembered faces you never see again, they simply lodged in my memory as distant, factual experiences. I threw away the rest of the magic mushrooms, and was given a cheery welcome at the Fishermen's Mission, where I ate bacon and egg and drank tea. The Superintendent came and sat beside me. He was brief, and direct. For a second, I knew he was God, and almost fell at his feet. Then he wasn't. I ate the bacon. It tasted of dolphin. Whatever dolphin tastes of, that bacon was it. I felt my gorge rising, and then suddenly everything was clear, calm, and I felt so at one with the world and so overwhelmed with love for this smiling, uniformed Christian beside me.

'Shower?' he said. 'We cater for the body and the spirit here, but mostly the body. You can wash yourself and your clothes, too. There's a wee laundrette. Do you know how to work a washing machine?' I did. I certainly did. I smiled and smiled and smiled.

I left Lochinver that evening, having been given a small New Testament by the Mission Superintendent. 'Cleanliness of the mind and spirit will make you feel better,' were his only words of witness. I had just about returned to whatever normality was, I thought, but was struck by the sensation that some things would not be the same again. And that I would never try magic mushrooms again. I murmured my thanks, and put £2.00 into the donations box. All I could really afford. They had a second-hand bookstall, though, with a selection of yachting books at 40 pence each. I picked them out, and wrote an address in Edinburgh on a piece of paper. Then I dumped the lot, about half a dozen, on the Superintendent's desk. 'There might be £50 there,' I said. Then I drove towards winter and Inverness.,

There I set about cleaning up my act; slightly. I got rid of my Graham Greene at Charles Leakey's high-class second-hand bookshop down by the river, rented a bedsit on the edge of a rough area known as The Ferry, and began systematically haunting the auctions at Fraser's saleroom, along with scavenging forays into the hinterland. I returned to my fast-turnover approach, occasionally sending things south to Glasgow or Edinburgh, cash on delivery, to people who knew they could trust my judgment. There were one or two.

Inverness is a bastard schizophrenic town, offspring of the rural Highlands and Lowland entrepreneurialism, the douce early settlement crenellated by the Victorians and completely fucked over by moronic 1960s planners. In a breathtaking setting, with the Ben Wyvis massif towering to the north, the Moray Firth to the east and the river providing a magnificent centrepiece, the town was once lovely. Now, surrounded by concrete and tin warehouses and industrial developments, the centre features toilet-block architecture which has none of the poise and grace of great modernism. It is as if a deliberate attempt to ruin the look of the place has been made. A kind of aesthetic terrorism by the Philistine Republican Army. Or perhaps somebody arrived there to plan the new buildings and found, like me, that the locals are among the unfriendliest, rudest, most dismissive people in Scotland, and decided to take his revenge.

Invernessians are reputed to speak the purest English in the country. This, as anyone who has spent any time there will affirm, is untrue. Inverness is pronounced Inverknees, and 'right enough' pronounced, in whining, wheedling fashion, as 'rayyyit enaaafff'. Interestingly, the idea of the locals speaking a particularly pure form of English stems from the occupation of the town by Oliver Cromwell's troops, who imposed their very English English on the Gaelic-speaking population. The people of Inverness never spoke Scots. They learned English from the English, as a foreign language. An occupied territory. That sullen resentment against strangers has been handed down, gene by gene by gene.

I found one or two good things: the Castle Restaurant, near the Castle itself which is now a court and police station – the flock of women who run the upmarket greasy spoon which is the Castle Restaurant are possibly the nicest people in Inverness; and the Phoenix Bar – great interior, and the least unwelcoming town pub. Cash enabled me to begin drinking again, but this time without the headlong urge for oblivion and brilliance. I also discovered Highland Industrial Supplies' vast warehouse of cheap, high-quality working clothes. My leather Ruthjacket survived, restitched by Corvin Leather, where you can get stags turned into coats, but everything else had grown permanently dirty or worn out by months of van condensation and wear. I replaced them with hairy tartan lumberjack shirts, trousers which stood up on their own, and bizarre items like training shoes with steel toe-caps. My hair, shoulder length and alarmingly receding at the front, as if it was being pulled out, I had cut to a conservative length. I looked both younger and balder. And I began to read and write.

Inverness Library is a kind of mini Acropolis which looks on to the busy, diesel-drenched bus station, and there I spent day after day, reading. I had loved books for their smell, taste, texture and value, wolfing down paperbacks like cheap chocolate as a kind of temporary distraction, a buffer against boredom, until the *ennui* grew too big and tough to ignore. Now I set out to read books I could never own. Deliberately I did not take out membership, but just sat in the building and read, leavening serious literature with magazines and travel brochures and junk. All newspapers, especially the music weeklies, I ignored. I became a common sight in the library. I nodded to the attendants. None of them ever spoke to me. I was, after all, in Inverness.

At my bedsit, a clumsily converted room in an old stone house, with an illegal toilet and shower screened off from my sleeping-and-sitting room, visually but not olfactorily, I set up the old Olympia typewriter on the formica-topped table, along with a pile of recycled paper and a *Roget's Thesaurus* I'd picked up for ten pence in the Oxfam shop. I had the Yamaha guitar, and the music centre, which still worked after those months bumping around unused in the damp VW. I had my Hank Williams tapes. I began to listen to those songs again, those songs of bitter sadness and triumph and humour and hopes of glory. And the grim humour, the aching sadness and exultation of those tragic songs began once more to cut through, to touch me. I was beginning to be touchable again. And I began to hammer them out on the battered guitar, quietly so as not to disturb my neighbours, all 12 of them, sectioned away in the boxes which had been erected in the house by our landlord, a repulsively fat man called Gilfillan. He and his wife, Elsie, thin and dried out like an elongated raisin, ran a bed and breakfast for homeless DHSS cases as well as this 'flatted development', as he called it. It was dirty and full of families waiting for council houses, often noisily drunk and dangerous when crossed. But I got a special cheap rate because I was paying cash. He liked cash, did Gilfillan, for his weekly drinking binges. I never found out his first name.

And there, in the uneasy underbelly of Inverness, I began to write my great Glasgow novel, a novel which drew shamelessly on the stuff I was voraciously half-digesting from the library, which was going to pay back some of the people I'd had to deal with in the big, smoky, grey city, which was going to be tough and tender and thrilling and commercial and make me a lot of money. Having stumbled across Alexander Trocchi, whose novels and poems were kept in a locked cupboard at Inverness Library, along with things like *Last Exit to Brooklyn* and the original Noddy books (racist and sexist), I started with a title. I liked it. It seemed to resonate with possibility.

One evening I was staggering homewards from the rumbustious island-bar piece of Edwardiana called the Phoenix, having, as usual, been spoken to by no one and having, admittedly, tried to speak to no one, when something made me totter to a soggy halt outside Radio Rentals. The televisions in the window were all tuned to the same late-night pop programme, and the section being shown was of a band in concert in a medium-sized, standing-only rock venue, maybe Barrowland in Glasgow. Enough people were in the audience to make it obvious the band were heading famewards, had maybe had one or two hit singles. I could hear nothing, but as I swayed in the light Inverness breeze, I could see Mick and Keith distantly playing out the roles they'd always played ever since I'd met them. Their Mick and Keith roles. It appeared Truth Drug had made it. Or at least made something. I walked back to the bedsit. I had a book to write which would make them suffer. And everybody else. Everybody. Me especially.

The Rats of Fear

So
Build a broad stages
with many burrows off
into which the rats of fear may run.
ALEXANDER TROCCHI

If I may say so, it's a brilliant title. *The Rats of Fear: A Novel*. The epigram's pretty damn good too, a resurrected quote from Glasgow's great lost writer, heroin addict, first publisher of Samuel Beckett and cash-in-hand pornographer Alexander Trocchi. You can still get some of his fix-fuelled toss-offs in station bookstalls, pseudo-classical trash like *Sappho of Lesbos*, which isn't even particularly dirty. Quite different, however, is *Thongs*, an unbelievable cross between *No Mean City*, *Last Exit From Brooklyn*, *The Shorter Catechism* and the Marquis de Sade. I came by it in the first place, if you'll pardon the expression, in the Clarkston house of a professional arsonist called Leonard. Leonard was an arson broker, specialising in vehicles. Trouble with your repayments? For £100 Leonard could arrange the theft of your Reliant Robin and its reduction to a small pile of melted plastic in some forgotten corner of Drumchapel or one of the other housing schemes. And not just Reliant Robins. It's amazing, the flammability of valuable objects. Or buildings, for that matter. Anyway Leonard, like so many other fringe hoods in the city, had rock'n'roll stars in his eyes and liked to hang out in the clubs, telling people he was keen to 'get into management'. Of obscure middle-class origins, he was smilingly polite and, the word was, ruthless, dangerous, but pleasantly so. He was profusely welcomed at each and every disco in town, no matter how strict the door policy. Leonard could have turned up wearing a Pac-a-Mac and wellington boots and he'd have waltzed into the most fashionable night spot with ease, and perhaps a quick flick of a Zippo. Hey, my man, Lenny! What's cookin'? Nobody I know, I hope?

Leonard lived in his parents' old house in the suburban sandstone of Clarkston. His mother and father were both dead, but the house had been kept as a kind of museum to them. The kitchen didn't look as if it had been washed for years. It creaked with too-big antique furniture. 'Dad dealt in all sorts of old stuff,' said Leonard. 'Used to collect opium pipes. Best dope I ever had, I took the silver fittings off an ivory one, smoked what was underneath. Maybe hundreds of years old. I was ripped for days.' It turned out he was a Trocchi fan, both the porn and, of course, *Cain's Book*, the heroin tribute. 'You got to read *Thongs*, man, it's the ultimate. The absolute ultimate Glasgow novel. It'll make more than your fuckin' hair stand on end, man.' Actually, it made me throw up. I threw up in his house, too, in actual fact. Drunkenness and opium. Bad mixture . . .

Pronounced Trochy, as in Loch Lochy, Alexander of that ilk was a Glasgow Italian genius who became a publisher in Paris, skipper of a garbage scow off New York, beat poet, friend of Ginsberg and Kerouac, writer of dreadful poetry and two brilliant novels: *Cain's Book* and *Young Adam*, which is the ultimate Scottish novel, no question, if you're a certain kind of existentialism-fixated young man keen on Camus. My 'rats of fear' quote comes from Trocchi's weirdly ham-fisted poetry book *Man At Leisure*, where he's trying to be an urban Earl of Rochester. It doesn't work, but you have to admit it's a terrific epigram. The poem itself is simply called 'Fear'. I don't know about the 'broad stages' line, though. Should it be 'broad stage?' Maybe I'm ignorant of some blindingly obvious classical allusion. Then again, maybe the typesetter was drunk. Whatever, for a black, not to say *noir* thriller about Glasgow thugs, drugs and possibly mugs, it's a title to kill for: *The Rats of Fear: A Novel*. I like it. Still.*

Before the Great Glaswegian Novel, I had thought of a TV play, utilising my religious background to deal with the subject of premillennial dispensationalism. This was the plot: Jesus comes back to collect his saints and whisk them off to heaven. Or rather, he doesn't. Two wee boys, brothers, hear a preacher predict Christ's imminent return and come up with the idea, after much convoluted Bible study, that it's on Wednesday. They decide that

* *Man At Leisure*, by Alexander Trocchi, published by Calder and Boyars Ltd in 1972. It includes a poem called 'The Worldly Wisdom of Cdr T. Taskmaster Disaster, RN', a truly weird business, worthy of comparison with some of the strangest poems ever written. It's a kind of folk song about cruelty in the navy, written in Cockney.

if they know He's coming on Wednesday, they can commit as many sins as they like and repent of them fully just before the Son of God arrives to remove them from this mortal coil. I typed this out as a synopsis, and on reading it, I discovered what I should have realised earlier. It was all completely unbelievable. No one outside the small circle of believers and backsliders could possibly accept such a bizarre concept. So I binned it.

But this was to be a novel, a thriller, Chandleresque, though avoiding all the macho Scotticisms and po-faced one-liners of McIlvanney and his tendency towards pre- and post-masturbation Presbyterian guilt. Later that, as well as the look-ah'm-dead-literary-pal intellectualism, was removed by smart TV hacks, and the result, allegedly, was *Taggart*, meathead formulaic Agatha Christie with glottal stops and butchers' cleavers. I much preferred the Trocchiesque horror of Derek Raymond, or the sheer sordid viciousness of Frederic Lindsay. The rarefied, self-consciously literary work of Kennedy, Kelman, Gray and their ilk smacked to me of the urban kailyard so beloved, it seemed from their book-jackets, of London critics. No Scottish writers, as far as I was concerned, were hip, cool, rock'n'roll. Neither was I, but I wanted to write as if I was. Because that would sell, I was certain. I mean, hell, I'd read Alexander Trocchi. I could pronounce his name. I knew the chords to 'Brown Sugar'. Once I'd been able to by-pass the queues at the hippiest clubs in Glasgow, not even feeling like an arsehole doing it. Though I was. One night I sat down with a half bottle of Grouse and a packet of Berkeleys, and began living the legend. Hammett, Big Ray . . . cancer, cirrhosis, genius and self-abuse. If only I'd had a hat, a snap-brim homburg. Tipped back on my head, wreathed in smoke as the typewriter snapped and tinged and zipped and clunked. A hat would have made it perfect. Besides, I was receding. A vanity hat could be called for, like the ones rock stars wear. Spot a rock musician in a hat or a headscarf, and you know that baldness lurks underneath. Fact of life.

THE RATS OF FEAR: A NOVEL.

Chapter One: Homecoming

Forehead cold on the window as we judder over Glasgow's old, guttering switchboard of streetlights, the Airbus's left wing flexing like one of Rolf Harris's didgeridoos. Turbulence. I hate it.

Maybe outside the wings are making that AWIBAWOOO-

HAAAOOOAAHWIBOO noise, like Rolf's bloody wibbly wobbly board, which wasn't, come to think of it, called a didgeridoo. That was a huge long Aboriginal drainpipe think thing he made strange metallic farting sounds down. SUN ARISE, HE COME IN THE MORNING ... AFFFRRROOIINNGGOINN-GOINNGGG ... Hey, world music, man! Indigenous fucking Australian culture! God, I loved that show, those 1960s fish-and-chip television Saturday nights. Those dancers ... was it Pan's Pepole? No, the Young Generation, that was it. Or was it Younger? Anyway, Val Doonican was even better, all Rafferty's Motor Car and Aran-knit Jim Reeves with Dave Allen telling jokes even my parents found funny. Jokes we kids didn't understand...

What was that fucking* thing called then? Not a wibble board, surely? Anyway, the wings appear to have settled down to a steady tremble. Surely those engines are too heavy for them?

'Ladies and gentlemen we will very shortly now be landing at Glasgow. Please keep your seatbelts fastened until we reach the terminal building and have come to a complete halt. There may be an increase in engine noise as we land. This is normal procedure. Please do not be alarmed.' No more plastic crap red wine, then. I drain the dregs in my flimsy tumbler.

Alarmed! OH SHIT WE'RE FALLING, falling like a seagull's turd towards the streets and the houses and the roads and the cars and the playgrounds and the pigeon lofts and the dogs and the cats and the people below. BAAANG! The Airbus hits the bottom of the airpocket like some unsuspecting midfielder meeting a tackle from a pre-retirement, pre-menstrual, pre-heart-bypass Graeme Souness. The seatbelt's given me a hernia. Look left. My wing still has its big Rolls Royce engine attached, one of those gigantic motors they make down there somewhere near the airport, at Hillington. Or is that shut

---

* Foul language, and I mean really foul, is obviously essential in the world of the hip, cool, far-out and generally happening urban thriller. I mean, this is how people REALLY TALK, right? I was simply reflecting the World Out There, How They speak. How They think. At least, that's what I'd tell my father, I decided. Except, of course, he was in New Zealand ... 'Foul language is the sign of a bankrupt vocabulary,' he said. Used to say. But in the world of art, of the author, you can use swear words ... wait a minute. Who am I trying to convince here? I don't have to pray for forgiveness everytime the word 'fuck' slips into my consciousness. I don't have to prove I'm a nice, articulate, thoughtful guy and that I don't swear any more. OK, so the swearing in *The Rats of Fear* is contrived and silly and self-consciously naughty but I'm allowed to swear. I'm a big boy, and God isn't waiting to lightning-zap me for every fuck. Or every 'fuck'. So fuck it. (But just to be on the safe side, sorry God.)

now? But the wing I can see is wobbling, up and down, and I try desperately to think of Rolf, of one of his ghastly paintings which we only ever saw in black and white, of anything other than the absolutely certain fact that I am going to die, horribly, if quickly. And soon.

'Did you know that when they analyse the black boxes, the voice recorders, after crashes, the last thing they hear before impact is always, always screaming?' The second most beautiful woman in the world had told me that, a PR person for St Kitts Airways I'd met at a cocktail party in Anguilla,* one of the let's-invite-a-bit-of-rough-for-a-giggle ex-pat dos that abounded out of season, when it was summer everywhere else. Now, in February, Anguilla's near-perpetual sunshine was at its tourist-hooking zenith, hauling the cellulite and gooseflesh charters in from New Jersey and Toronto and Frankfurt. Jesus, it seemed a million miles away, instead of just a few thousand and 12 fear-wracked aeroplane hours. I could still hear her tinkly voice, casually conversing: 'Nearly everyone is dead by the time they reach the ground, most of the passengers anyway. Heart failure, you know.' Good to know that, I'd told her. Now I won't be so worried about it, so I probably won't die of a fucking heart attack and just get mashed and mangled when we hit the ground. Because I know I'm going to die in a plane crash. And statistically, the more I fly, the more likely it gets.

* The problem for popular novelists, would-be, almost-was or never-in-a-month-of-Sundays, is The Glamorous Setting. Millport, Arran ('Don't they make those white jumpers there?' Actually a small but significant number of tourists each year go to Arran, the Firth of Clyde's wondrous jewel, thinking they are heading for the Irish Aran Islands. Sly shopkeepers make sure they stock plenty of Aran handknits for these travellers in ignorance) or the Isle of Man may be glamorous if you come from Orlando, Florida, but not if you're a beleaguered publisher in Islington who probably thinks Shetland is next to Skye and Barra somewhere off the coast of Perth. The reason I chose Anguilla was simple. I'd once found myself getting drunk one Wednesday grab-a-grannie night in Henry Afrika's, in the newly acquired company of a jet-lagged *Evening Times* journalist, just back from a press jaunt to the Caribbean. First he bored me into a state of comatose acceptance of his expense-account alcohol by droning on and on about dusky Caribbean maidens, rum punch and fried flying fish with cannabis, a dish over which I think he was being somewhat misled. Then a granny grabbed him and he disappeared, presumably in a taxi to Easterhouse or some such, where his next-morning's awakening in the wrinkled, bacon-and-egg arms of Senga or Jean or Betty must have provided at least something of a counterpoint to the Caribbean fleshpots. At any rate, he left the word Anguilla resonating around my hungover mind with some glimmers of voodoo-converted English hoteliers, drugs, music, hints of rebellion, and his press party's encounters with the ruling British colonialists. A sift through Inverness Library's travel section, some brochures from AT Mays, and my glamorous setting was, well, set. It was only after my Inverness researches, however, that I realised Anguilla and Angola were two different places.

Down, down below the rough air, coming in over the brief glitter of water amid utter blackness, the Clyde. Then landing as smooth as a bikini-line after electrolysis, the engines reversing in a sucking, whooshing roar, yellow lights blurring past, and I was home. A gnawing depression began in my guts, all the tension of the flight giving way to thoughts of the immediate future.

One shoulder bag, some duty-free Daniel Finzi rum from Jimmy's stall at Antigua's Coolidge Airport, plus some throat-dissolving Susie's Hot Sauce, sold on the main concourse at Coolidge in old Lucozade bottles. They'd stopped me going through the green channel at Heathrow, inevitably. No explanation, but the complete works. A body search, external and internal, impersonal and polite and degrading. Bags, bottles, opened. One Customs prick almost choked on the hot sauce, from just a fingertip's worth. Bastards. The most corrupt uniformed service in any country, always, but do you hear about it? Do you fuck.

I walked from the Supershuttle gate slowly along the endless finger of glass and steel which leads to Glasgow Airport's main concourse. I half-expected one of those upper-arm apprehensions from a second wave of Customs pricks, or maybe some of the sharply besuited funny handshakers in Glasgow's very own force of civil obedience enforcers. Nothing. The tired, overbellied businessmen and rumpled, power-skirted women hurried past me, rushing to their tattered home lives or some Friday night social stumble. I tried to collect myself, put the jet-lagged, fear-frazzled, wine-dulled bits together, as home and past and Glasgow waited at the end of this corridor and some motorway tarmac to ... what? Kick my teeth in? My spleen? Kidneys, testicles or worse? Possibly. That would fit with some stupid arseholes' No Mean City hardman vision of themselves. Or maybe my own. The red-carpet treatment? Hardly.

There, past security, in the anonymous public bit of this most anonymous of airports, waited all the lifts home, all the sweethearts and reluctant amateur taxi drivers. There were a few embraces, some of them apparently genuine. I dodged slowly through the milling crowd, then downstairs to the baggage carousel. On a there-and-back-in-a-day February shuttle, last of the evening, there were few luggage-loaded travellers. I waited for my second-hand, dynamite-proof Revelation suitcase to appear, and it was then the hand gripped my right triceps.

I was glad Nigel himself had taken the trouble to come to the airport. If it had just been some of his lowbrow assistants, walk on, self-parodying thugs straight out of Taggart central casting – Jesus, do they still have Taggart after three years? Surely nothing that bad could have survived – I might have faced their delegated desire to live the fucking legend and give me a wee, forceful, *de rigueur* talking to. The fact that Nigel was here was an encouraging sign. He was smiling, though. That wasn't.

'How're ye doin', big man?' Nigel was the perfect off-the-peg Glaswegian size, five foot eight, a red-haired, mid-thirties Ally McCoist with a better haircut. And a different religion. Why he'd been called Nigel I could never work out. Nigel Francis O'Donnel. He claimed his mother had named him for an upmarket break-out from the confines of Castlemilk. Thus his schoolmates had simply called him wankie until – according to him – he'd earned their respect by derailing an electric commuter train just outside Rutherglen station with an off-cut of rail. One old man had died of a heart-attack. Nigel had been seven. How the fuck had he moved the rail? Delegation, boy, delegation.

Now his clothes were off some very expensive pegs indeed: Armani, Versace. A Cartier tank watch flopped on a pale wrist. The thin, indoor face was freckled, the green eyes big and blank. The wide coral scar over the right cheek had been plasticked, but not well enough.

'Fine, Nige. You're looking in the pink, anyway.' He frowned, wondering if I was joking about his face. He fingered the scar, an old habit, and smiled.

'Still can't keep the evil member under control, eh? And I don't mean your dick, man, I mean this.' He flicked the tip of his tongue as if ridding himself of a piece of snot. 'You better be careful' – he suddenly leered up close into my face, a manic smile. 'The bogey men'll get you.'

Behind Nigel I could see two of the inevitable entourage. Next next to his Armani, one was big, one was wee. The wee one's nose was so broken it had virtually disappeared into his face. I wondered why he didn't get it fixed, then realised it wouldn't be worth it. That nose was in a constant firing line. The big one had a scarred chin. I'm six foot two, and I'd have had to stand on a soapbox to reach the rest of his face. Must have been Weetabix in the genes somewhere.

'Aye, fuck off Nige, and take Pinky and Perky with you.' I looked down at the still-smiling face, dropped my voice so it didn't echo round the airport like a last call. 'I am finished with you, and your poxy imports and exports. I nearly got thrown into the Caribbean with a lead aqualung because of you and what you didn't fucking tell me. Three years of antiques, clean as a whistle, Scotland to Anguilla then on to America, a good wee earner and a good wee Electrolux for your ill-gotten gains. But oh no, you have to up the ante, don't you. And I'm the one facing the fat guys in black hats.' I was lying, of course. I'd known all along what was really going on with Caledonian Collectables. I just hadn't wanted to admit it to myself. And Nigel knew that as well.

Nigel's expression changed into a mockery of sorrowful concern. He patted my shoulder. I shivered, and it wasn't just the cold. I'd come prepared in an old leather bomber jacket, black polo neck, pure fucking Jean-Louis Trintignant via Lloyd Cole. Neither of them famous anymore, probably, and me lagging behind this city's eternal fashionability. Always the carving knife of style, Glasgow.

'Hey, remember the old alma mater, boy.' He smiled, stepped back, everything overplayed as usual, but sinister for all that. Cartoon psychopath. Gesturing to Pinky and Perky, who obediently shuffled closer, he opened his hands in innocence, looked at me with a faraway, nostalgic expression in his eyes. 'We were at yooni together, remember that? Those were the days, eh? Boys' — he turned to Pinky and Perky — 'best days of my fucking life, I'm telling you.' His expression changed again, became a parody of care and concern. 'Look, man, I know things went a wee bit ... awry out there. I just want you to tell me what happened. Exactly what happened. So let's get your bags and I'll run you into town and we'll have a wee natter about it. All right?' Pinky and Perky had moved in closer. I could see, out of the corner of my eye, my battered Revelation case sitting alone at the end of the now-static carousel. The other passengers had gone.

'Look Nige,' I said in a bored voice. 'We'll talk here. Don't fuck me about, because I haven't come back here without insurance. You know me better than that.' I could see two of the armed plainclothes policemen who patrol the airport concourse, as inconspicuous as Woody Allen in a mosque. They were eyeing our little group curiously. Maybe they even recognised Nigel, the former student. Student for half a term, before the brighter-than-bright boy from Castlemilk got picked up for hustling hash, on the campus, and was busted out of the groves of academe for good. As far as I knew, it was still his only conviction. Nigel was a quick learner, and he'd graduated from that experience with distinction, if not honours. Or both, maybe, depending on how you looked at it.

'Brilliant to see you back safe, son!' Nigel shouted it in that half broken Gorbals pavement, half playing-fields of Kelvin-side accent of his, his wee joke against what he sardonically called 'Glesca classlessness', slapped me on the back and grinned. 'Let's have a drink to celebrate your return to God's own city, then. C'mon.' Pinky and Perky shrugged, relaxed. I picked up my lonely suitcase, felt the clank of the duty-free and we headed for the bar. The two policemen sauntered past this old pals' act trying to look both bored and tough, their identical increase-your-maturity moustaches twitching disdainfully. We've got pistols and fuck the size of our dicks, pal. We know how to use them. The guns, that is.

I had indeed been at university with Nigel. His brief fling with academic life as a first-year Moral Philosophy, English and Economic History student, procurement of mind-altering substances a speciality, had coincided with my own arrival at Gilmorehill to commence becoming a lawyer. Even as a fresh-faced first year I was giving it heavy middle-class rebellion, straight from the privileged arsehole bright-boy status at Ayr Academy, acting hard. I was in the market for some dope, and had bought some stuff off him, complete shite as it turned out, dried and compressed sage or onion or something. I hunted Nigel out to demand my money back, we did some blow together, and he asked me, nicely, why he shouldn't get some of his Castlemilk pals to reduce my skull to chipboard. I told him I had no idea. He laughed, handed over some decent Lebanese Red, and the next I heard he was out of university and in the glasshouse at Glenochil, still only 17, too young for Barlinnie.

Next time I saw him, I was a law graduate without a job, turned down by all the sensible Glasgow firms – in fact, all the Scottish firms – on account of what was undoubtedly a bad attitude and some probably even worse references from my lecturers. Solicitors with earrings and tattoos, even ones who spoke reasonably Ayrshire posh like me, even ones who made sure Terry's needlework rarely popped out from my suit sleeves, were not wanted on board. So I was farting around doing precognitions for one or two criminal lawyers I'd met in pubs, interviewing witnesses, sometimes tracking down the kind of elusive characters whose interests weren't best served by a court appearance of any sort. The money was crap – most of the time – so was the company I kept. One of the witnesses to be called in a murder trial, a messy but strictly tribal south-side one, was Nigel. He was heading upmarket by then, with a co-ownership flat in Pollokshields and a BMW 325i. He remembered me, we did some blow again. He was hilarious, I thought then. I mean, how many middle-league Glasgow gangsters quoted lumps of Sartre's *Existentialism and Humanism* at you when stoned? Few. Later, I pretended I hadn't been able to find him, some brainless footsoldier went down for a decade and that was that. Except we kept in touch. Ethics, doncha just love them? Well. Not really.

Pinky and Perky went for the drinks, while Nigel lit a Marlboro Light with a ridiculous Zippo in what looked like real gold. Across the too-varnished table in the hideous fake Edwardian bar, all brass, bow-ties, whorehouse stained glass, he was smiling that manic little private smile, looking at me. I was red-wine headachy, jet lagged and, yes, frightened. But I felt sure Nigel wouldn't hurt me. Much. I wondered when he'd last done any of the coke he was so obviously well acquainted with, and if he had any on him. I could have done with a line or two to hose out that red-wine heaviness.

'What insurance, then?' He blew some smoke over at my face in a steady stream. 'What have you got over little old goody-two-shoes me, then, Monsieur Merleau-Ponty?'

I wondered what lies to tell him. We had always lied to each other, Nige and me, second guessing all the time, usually about small things, things like who I was screwing, who was HIV-positive, which of us might have screwed somebody the HIV-positive person might have screwed, which policeman was bent ... that sort of stuff. Sometimes it got tortuous, not to mention dangerous. But that had been before the little antique showroom in Anguilla, set up three years ago by a sexually-on-the-run non-lawyer – me – to handle the flogging of Scotland's historical detritus to the Yanks, had moved smoothly, as intended, into catalogue mail order, with an expanding list of regular customers right across the States. The tourists would come, look around the air-conditioned shop, buy a stone hot-water bottle or a fire iron or a mirror-and-mahogany pub gantry and put their names down for lists of what was in the six-monthly container from Greenock. And of course, the drugs went back and forth too. All I had to do was let Ferdinand in the Valley know when some bigger stuff was heading to, say, Long Island, and things would presumably be put inside the stone hot-water bottles. I didn't like to think about it too much. In fact, I didn't like to think about it at all. I was strictly antiques, after all. Strict as fuck. My own habits were inexpensive, too: locally grown ganja at the weekend and a bit of Colombian Ajax for special occasions. Mr Moderate, that was me. The Richard Neville tendency: like good wine, to be savoured occasionally. And if you can't handle it, pal, if you've lost every ounce of ambition and energy you ever had getting blasted, or spent all your cash and self-respect on smack or coke ... well, fuck you. Me, I was Mr Unambitious. Mr Fucking Self-Deception, and why not? Mostly I stuck to the Red Stripe and Finzi's Spiced Reggae Rum, sometimes doing some Guinness as a ganja chaser according to local custom. Pure fucking genius.

It had been fun. There was the sun, the inevitable and mostly safe sex. I kept single, got sunburned, forgot Glasgow and the events which had forced me to leave so very, very quickly, courtesy of Nigel's considerate wee offer of a job in the Caribbean. The bastard had known I couldn't turn it down.

Anyway, after three years, things started going wrong. Anguilla might be a British colony, but its status as a tax-free offshore banking centre with company secrecy laws stricter than the Channel Islands or Masonic ritual had attracted some funny people, not to mention the serious Miami shit with aerodromes on private atolls and half-laundered cash going into hotel developments. That Caribbean *laissez-faire* developed an edge. Strange new Brits with hard wee faces arrived to work at the tiny Government House, where a genial governor's job was to hold frequent and lavish cocktail parties. A fortnight before my sudden arrival back in the motherland, Ferdinand had vanished. Completely. Then a container-load of antiques, fresh from Scotland, had gone up in flames. Then I'd had the visit from the three fat bastards in linen suits, all heavily influenced by repeat showings of *Godfather II*. At that point I'd deposited a file of receipts, shipping documentation, Polaroid snapshots of furniture and customer lists in the Anguilla branch of the Royal Bank of Scotland, sent off a note to my solicitor in Glasgow, another to Nigel, hopped the LIAT flight to Antigua and got the hell out of the sunshine.*

---

* My thinking was: MOVIES! De Niro playing the (significantly unnamed) narrator, maybe with the entire action shifting from Glasgow to New York. You could still use the Caribbean, but I quite fancied turning the whole thing around, so that instead of Anguilla, we had, for example, a hippy commune on, say, Arran. Or perhaps somewhere a bit more romantic like Orkney. But De Niro was really too old for the part.

'All right, Nigel, and this is not a wind-up. Two solicitors, three banks, letters and receipts and names and files, one set of originals, the rest photocopies. It's simple, just like the movies. Anything happens to me, it all goes to the *Sun* and the filth.' Not so much a lie, just a wee exaggeration. I mean, who needs two solicitors? The rest was almost true. I looked at Nigel's Marlboro, felt a twinge of desire for that asbestosis rasp at the chest you only get from Marlboros, even the slightly slower-death versions, and forced my mind away from fags. It had been five years since nicotine had departed my personal list of approved drugs. I even mixed my hash with herbal mixture, that tobacco-free tobacco stuff, Honeyrose. The Celestial Wind Health Food Shop in Anguilla had imported it specially for me. Health. Health and Efficiency, that's me.

'Och, boy, this is just unnecessary.' Nigel had his palms outstretched, all Arthur Daley innocent, as Pinky and Perky arrived with the drinks: a large malt whisky for Nigel, something from the islands which smelled like creosote, Perrier for the two spear-carriers and a glass of brown fizzy shite for me, complete with red tin and enough chemicals to sterilise an elephant. It was time to get back into the Scottish way of life: crap beer in a horrible pub with a bunch of dangerous criminals, one of whom was probably mad and whose nose was beginning to run suspiciously. And I was hardly off the fucking shuttle yet.

'Just tell me the story. Your wee eh ... valentine didn't ... elucidate too clearly what had made you panic like a turkey meeting Santa Claus. And just you remember who got you that wee job out in the fucking sunshine. You weren't complaining three years ago, were you? I think you owe me for that.' This time he was serious. The green eyes were still, the half-smile less manic and even more dangerous. 'But listen, listen to me – you don't have to worry about having your balls shoved down your throat or anything ... crude. Let us proceed without unnecesssary violence.' Pinky and Perky sipped their Perrier and said nothing.

So I told him the story. Told him about the men in linen suits, about Ferdinand, about the container fire. I'd a feeling he already knew it all, but I told him anyway. I even told him the truth about the proposition I'd received, the offer I had not exactly refused, but hightailed it away from. The big, sunburned, quiet American saying he was sure, once they'd taken 'this little operation' under 'our people's' paternal wing, a place could be found for me. Damn right a place would be found for me, off some fucking coral reef or out the back door of a Cessna. And no horse's head in the bed either. Not that I'd ever understood how the film producer in the film didn't die of a heart-attack when he woke up with Shergar staring at him between the sheets. Maybe it happened to him all the time. No accounting for taste. You want horse? You got horse. There was a guy in Antigua who fucked dead fish, but only imported mackerel. Sick, but harmless. At least you didn't have to wine them and dine them.

Nigel nodded, smoked, sipped his malt whisky. When I'd finished, he looked at me and said: 'Seventeen-year-old Port Ellen, from Islay. This bar may be shite, but it's one of only two places in Glasgow you can get it.' Oh great. I really wanted to know that. He sat staring at me, eyes unfocused, seemingly far away.

'Nigel?' He lifted a sandy eyebrow. 'Nigel, you don't happen to remember what Rolf Harris called that board he wobbled about to give that kind of WIBAWOHPAWIBAAWOOH sound, you know, like on, whatever it was, "Tie Me Kangaroo Down Sport" or whatever. Only I've been racking my brains ...'*

'Och yes, it was a didgeridoo, wasn't it?'

'No, no, that was that huge long drainpipe horn thing he blew into on "Sun Arise".' Nigel shook his head.

'Listen son, anyway, we have to go.' He rose, drained his malt, which he'd taken neat. Pinky and Perky left what remained of their Perriers and stood up with him. Nigel leaned towards me, whispering. 'I think you're probably lying to me, somewhere along the line. But I'm prepared to believe the emm, central thrust of your wee story, 'cause I've got some corroboration. But you should have stuck it out. Don't pretend you didn't know what was going down, you dirty piece of hypocritical dogshite, 'cause I know and you know that's just fucking wank.' He stood back, solemn, no smile. 'Hey, I'd have taken care of you.' Aye, sure. 'What are you gonnie do?' I shook my head, shrugged. 'Well, don't expect me to help you this time. Now you're on your own.' Then the smile flashed back across that scarred face, the pinched nose flaring out a wee bit, the pale green eyes flashing, hungry for the coke which awaited in the car outside, the Jag or the BM or the Merc.

---

* This Harris stuff was, you must remember, written long before Rolf made his astonishing comeback in the 1990s with a cover version of 'Stairway to Heaven', the Zeppelin classic, accompanied only by wobble-board – its proper name. Pretty spookily prophetic, eh? What an ability to spot musical trends. Next medium-to-small things: whistling records (as in 'I Was Kaiser Bill's Batman') and kazoos.

'Count yourself lucky. That is what I mean when I say that man is condemned to be free.' Off they went, leaving me to finish my stomach-ripping toxic beer, my heart pounding from too much Chateau Rouge de Supershuttle and the aftermath of fear. The planes hadn't crashed, Nigel hadn't had Pinky and Perky perform genito-urinary surgery on me without anaesthetic, and I was alone in Glasgow with a sun tan and enough money to last me maybe, oh, a couple of months. Never mind, though. Something would come up. Hopefully the reason I'd left this sandblasted town in the first place wouldn't, but that was probably a forlorn piece of straw-clutching. I left the red tin and the glass eating holes through the varnish on the veneered table and went to look for a taxi. I was sure Nigel had been wrong about the didgeridoo.

Thank God, the taxi driver was a taciturn, smoke-pickled man in his 50s without any apparent curiosity in me and my origins. He said nothing at all as I slumped into the front seat of his immaculate Ford Sierra diesel. 'Holiday Inn, mate,' I muttered in a West of Scotland brogue calculated to impart the information that I was local and not going to be fooled by expensive detours, scenic trips around housing schemes, garbage incinerators or razed docklands. Johnny Cash softly crooned some death, sex and home-cooking country anthem I didn't recognise as the car rattled its diesely way up the ramp and on to the elevated M8 for the motorway swoop into Glasgow.

We burbled past Paisley, then past the old Lumo building, a giant art-deco mutation of a control tower which I remembered best from the mid-80s with a huge, tawdry sign on it reading 'Caravanland'. Ricky Ross from Deacon Blue, then an English teacher struggling for fame with a band called Doctor Love, had done for it what Costello did for London's Hoover factory and written a song about the place. It got him his first TV exposure. Now the concrete-and-glass edifice lay unlit and abandoned, glimmering in reflected sodium light from the street below.

The driver remained silent as the smell of the former Gray Dunn biscuit factory hard by the Kingston bridge brought back a million childhood memories of tooth-rotting teatime treats. Blue Riband, pronounced Blue Rib And. He didn't say a word as we crossed the Clyde on the enormously high span meant to allow the passage of ships to the city centre. No ships ever came, and the docks were replaced by crass deco revival architecture housing Golf GTI drivers. The river had been cleaned up as the old heavy industries closed down, and these days you could watch salmon struggling upstream from your cappuccino balcony. At least you could three years ago. Maybe someone had killed off the salmon by now.

But it was dark, and all I could see from the taxi was the shadowy outline of the old *Daily Record* building, its lights extinguished like Maxwell's lies, and the shimmer of neon and sodium on the river below. Then down, down from the bridge and the motorway into Glasgow itself, Argyle Street, ground level at last. Not for long, though. The Sierra U-turned into the Holiday Inn entrance, and came to a halt outside. The driver still said nothing, and I wondered if he was dumb, as in tongueless, silent, Dalglish-at-a-press conference. He was a dead cert for big tips if he was. On the tape, Big Johnny was singing that he was going down into a burning ring of fire. Garrulous taxi drivers are real pains in the arse. Antigua was different. Somehow you didn't mind so much when the sun was shining and the guy was offering you cheap dope and smiling like someone had chibbed his mouth to twice its normal size.

'How much is that then, mate?' I said, over-gutturally. Jesus, be true to your middle-class roots, ya bas. YOU bastard. He turned toward me.

'On the house, pal.' A face which looked as if it had been rolled down a few flights of tenement stairs cracked into a gap-site grin. 'Nigel just wanted to make sure you got safely into town. No need for a tip. No doubt reception'll give us your room number, if we need it.'

I got out of the taxi and walked into the hotel, not looking back, heart fluttering painfully. Fear. Anger. Age. You bastard, Nigel. To hell, though. He'd said his piece. I couldn't see him doing anything more tonight.

I checked in under the name Wendell Gee, stolen out of an old REM song, and paid cash in advance for one night. Upstairs in the corporate anonymity of the room, I drank some crap house red from the mini-bar at hideous expense, watched some dreadful, interminable detective film about a bumbling, alcoholic policeman with an old Jaguar some idiot had fitted with a vinyl roof, and then there was nothing until the crash of the door flying open, the heavy, gloved hands lifting me off the bed, hauling me upright and throwing me against the wall.*

---

* Be warned. This is all exceedingly horrible for a considerable number of reasonably long paragraphs. You might think there's evidence of enjoyment in the writing, in the

There was an immediate flurry of muffled banging and shouting from the rudely awoken occupant of the room next door. I was bleeding from the nose down the textured oatmeal, too winded to speak, but mentally screaming 'Nigel, you bastard', over and over again. Then a high, sneering voice, not mine, said: 'Gone to the land of nod with all your clothes on, then? Expecting to make a sudden departure? Without visiting us? We would be most offended, young man. Most.'

I was released from the now red-blotched blandness of the wall I had become so unexpectedly intimate with, and turned to find myself gazing into the face of William Burgess, once a down-at-heel undercover drug-squad sergeant, now clearly something else. He was power-dressed in Hugo Boss with some fairly naff Marks and Spencer touches, like the cheap black shoes and the shirt with the squint, bulging collar. He'd filled out too. Now he was a fat rodent-featured cunt, an overfed guinea pig. His brutally spiky footballer haircut, complete with blond highlights, added to the messy effect of his failed sartorial attempt to go upmarket.

'Hallo there, Sergeant Bill,' I said, once I'd got my breath back. 'Been to the Barras for those gladrags?' The blow came from the side, and unless Burgess had sprouted an extra pair of arms, he hadn't thrown it. I fell back on to the bed, gasping from the kidney punch. A rumbling, chest infection noise: somebody else was speaking.

'It's Inspector Burgess to you, scum, or Mister Burgess. Have you got that quite clear?' Squat and even uglier than the other shitefucker, there emerged into my vision someone who looked like a tall dwarf: big head, lumpy features, long arms, short legs, beer gut. But then I'd forgotten that's what the typical Glaswegian of about 50 looked like, the ones born just after rickets and just before free orange juice. It was wearing one of those hideous padded Barbour jackets, buttoned at the neck.

'Meet Sergeant Flaws,' said Burgess in that sing-song whine of his. 'He's now my, emm, right arm, you might say. That right, Ernest?' Sergeant Ernest Flaws turned a devoted, shaggy-dog head towards his master and grinned, his mouth

---

descriptions of blood and snot and other bodily fluids unnecessarily expelled. Wrong. This is all completely cynical hack-writing. I just thought this is what was expected. Actually, I'm a really nice guy and the rest of this book, in case you're worried, is uplifting and wry and gentle and quite saleable to a very wide and respectable market indeed.

opening to reveal a black chasm. So much for National Health dentistry. I could smell the rot, the damage caused by Glasgow's wondrous diet: chips and abattoir pies and doughnuts and cakes and Chelsea buns and Macaroon bars and sweet, fizzy drinks like Irn Bru and cream soda, packet of boilings every morning from the newsagents, black-and-white striped balls, suck suck suck. Too scared to go to the dentist, let them suppurate to stumps like that little London—Irish intellectual punk—folk prick, what was his name Shane something, giving it cut-rate Brendan Behan, the wasted-artist trip. The Pogues. Dreadful band.

'What the fuck do you want, Burgess?' Flaws leaned closer, breathed on my face like hell in a waxed jacket. Bad breath as a weapon. 'Sorry. What the fuck do you want . . . Inspector?'

'What do I want?' He laughed, this pudgy shite who had once tried to hang out at clubs like New Drug (oh, yeah, very subtle) and Garvey's, pretending he was a happening sorta punter and failing as only a genetically mutated small-brained policeman can. He laughed in his new suit and his stupid shoes. 'What do I want? I want to hurt you. I want to hurt you very badly, you two-bit piece of half-arsed, half-educated turd.' He'd been practising his insults. I wondered if he taped them, then played them back to himself. 'I want to hurt you because of your little scam with the lovely Nigel, who has come up in the fucking world since you went off to be his lapdog among the niggers. He has risen to the top of this filthy pond like the shite he is, and I want to stamp on him. And I'm going to.'

'Well, you'll get wet and messy shoes, then, Inspector.' Flaws leaned in, jabbed a stiff set of fingers into my solar plexus. I leaned over the bed and threw up sour red wine on the beige carpet. That's what hotel carpets are for, after all. Gradually, whooping and coughing and spluttering while the stench of Flaws's mouth and probably all his inner organs filled the room, I recovered the power of speech. 'I'm not involved with Nigel any more. That is over. Completely.' And he laughed again, the bastard. A cold thread of anger laced its way across my heaving chest. I wiped the blood and snot and tears off my face. 'I'm here to live the quite life.'

Burgess shrugged. 'It doesn't matter. Nigel isn't going to let you out of his sight, is he? I mean, who brought you here? I'm going to hurt you in a big way, son. After all that shit I put up with from you before, you are going to get it. And hopefully that poncy-named Tim as well.' Tims and niggers. Aren't our sensitive, New Age, liberated policemen wonderful. Burgess exited suddenly, like the detectives on telly he no doubt videoed so he could imitate their every fucking move. Flaws followed, backing out of the room, that black-hole smile on his face, his stink left behind.

It was still there, grown stale and rancid along with the red-wine vomit, the blood and the sweaty fear, when I left in the darkness of morning, an hour later. I had showered away some of the pain and the anger and the mess, packed the bags, picked up the duty free and taken the lift to the first floor. The back route to the Holiday Inn's health club, deserted but open to residents, and I was walking out of the fire door into a deserted staff carpark. I was sore, scared and annoyed, confused and very tired, but buzzing at the same time with the jet lag and the adrenaline. Palpitations creased my rib cage, my heart pitter-pattering like an aged Vespa. I walked into the cavernous underground carpark of the old Anderston Cross shopping-centre, hoping you could still use it as a short-cut into Hope Street. In the fluorescent shadows, there were strange piles, rumpled and with soft angles, seemingly cardboard and cloth. As I passed, one moved, revealing itself as a Dr Who monster from the golden age of children's horror, a creature of rags and hair, stinking worse than I did of cheap wine. I wasn't alarmed. This was nothing compared to Flaws. It spoke: 'Price of a cup of tea, sir?' Without thinking, I handed over my duty-free Daniel Finzi rum, and walked on, following the underground roadway upwards towards my first Glasgow morning in three years. Home at last, brothers and sisters. Home at last.

And that's the end. Not just of the first chapter, but of the whole thing. I had obviously completed an outline of the plot, because after all, Structure is All in Detective Fiction, as Agatha used to say, so basically Nameless Narrator finds a flat, falls in with dubious rock band whose bass player is found dead with neck of guitar rammed up his bottom. As a former – hey! – private dick, he is hired by worried manager as death threats descend on other band members. Lead singer is an arrogant plonker name of Gary Zambesi. From Milngavie. Nigel keeps popping up. So do the horrid policemen. Hassle hassle hassle. After many dark, dangerous and disgusting adventures, including lots of sex of every sort, much of it utterly disgusting, Nameless Narrator finds out that Nigel's blind sister has been infected with HIV by the lead singer, Gary Zambesi. But he told her he was the bass player, and because she was blind, she didn't know what he looked like.

Obviously. So anyway, vengeful big brother Nigel sorted out the bass player in a nasty manner symbolic of how he may or may not have contracted the HIV virus he had passed on to Nigel's sister, whose name was Leonora. Except of course, it was the nasty horrible Gary. Gary gets electrocuted on stage. Nigel is converted at a gospel rally in a tent on Glasgow Green. The sister goes to a hospice. Nigel goes to the police, where Sergeant Flaws beats him to death in a cell as Nigel sings 'Oh For a Thousand Tongues to Sing' and 'Just as I Am, Without One Plea'. Nameless Narrator goes back to the Caribbean, having struck a deal with the Mafia, who decide there's more money in Scottish antiques than in drugs.

It took six painful weeks of many half bottles and countless fags to turn out *The Rats of Fear*, Chapter One: Homecoming, as well as the plot and plan, because, after all, structure is the secret of all great fiction, as Tolstoy once said. Once I'd sobered up, I realised that the time had come to stop writing fiction, once and for all. I did think, however, that a decent hat would have made all the difference.

Heaven

I became bored with writing fiction. I suppose. Or attempting to. Besides, it was too hard, all that making things up. Invention is incredibly energy-sapping. I would sit at the typewriter thinking, God, I wish I was out, I wish I was with people, I wish I was part of something, not just some wanker creating fantasies of revenge on a city, on people who probably wouldn't even recognise themselves if they ever read *The Rats of Fear*. So when I saw a classified advertisement in the *Inverness Courier* which simply said 'small private library for sale', with a telephone number, I was relieved to abandon my incipient authorial career, and take the increasingly mouldering VW west to check out a potential source of income: ready-made books.

In the village of Boirreannach, which, oddly, is Gaelic for woman, I found Mr Meldrum and his books. He was 80, spry if a little delicate looking, iron-grey hair combed meticulously, and was going south to Perth where his son and daughter-in-law had a house 'with what they call a granny flat. Which is slightly offensive, I suppose, as my wife died 20 years ago. But I suppose they don't see the importance of terminology.' He sighed. The house had been sold, and now his 1930s bungalow, complete with steel windows and Lutyens pitched roof with huge central chimney, was going to become a holiday home 'for perfectly nice people from Shropshire. I would rather it had gone to local folk, but . . . the money, you see. The granny flat needs some alterations. I suppose for it to become a grandfather flat. Actually,' he smiled a wintry smile, 'they neither have nor wish children, so the term is redundant. Grandfather. And now they're too old, probably, to breed.' A dark cloud passed over his snowy smile. His small library, more of a large-ish book collection, really, stretched across half a wall of shelves from the 1920s right up to the present. All hardback, literary fiction and biography. Some first editions, one or two of real value. I swallowed any sentimentality and offered him £1000 for the lot. He accepted immediately. It was a big purchase for me.

'I've taken the best,' said Mr Meldrum, complacently. 'Just one box, they said. So I've taken the best. You can have a look if you, like. See what you've missed.' In the kitchen was one cardboard whisky box. It contained a fine old Roget, a new edition of *Chamber's Dictionary*, a two-volume *Complete Works of Shakespeare*, and two other, older books. One was called *Irrigation Techniques: The British East Africa Experience*; the other was *The Desert Blossoms: My Life in Water*. Both were by E.W. Meldrum. One had been published in 1937; the other in 1955. 'Next,' said Mr Meldrum, 'the novel. Clear the decks, that's what you have to do. Get rid of the distractions, and write. I am a writer, you see. Water engineer and author, that's how I describe myself. This is a golden opportunity. Golden.'

It was late afternoon when I left Boirreannach; I couldn't face the drive back to Inverness, and so I headed into a setting summer sun along single-track roads and up over a wooded pass until I dropped down into the glen called Glen Oidchche, and the village on its coastal fringe: Mollydish.

Sometimes things just come together. There was a burnished, glinting sea, and the midges were bad, but not, on that summer night, flesh-boilingly ferocious. I parked the VW by the little harbour, next to the beach, and had a pint of Murphy's at what I would later come to know as the Incomers. I overheard bartalk about Mrs Tooth's daughter trying to rent out the bike shop, and found out that she, whose mother was the doddery owner of a shop with a flat above it, had been forced to come north after an ill-fated venture into bicycle hire had failed and the operators fled back to their native Aberdeen. 'Just as well,' said Algernon, in his twisted Scots–English brogue. 'Couldn't understand a bloody word they said.'

I caught Mrs Tooth's semi-female offspring, Mrs Ernestina Dalglish, as she was angrily sweeping out the shop, and did my polite best to strike a deal for a long-term lease on the doorstep. She was all for it. 'Well, I suppose that's all right. My mother has the final say.' She grimaced. Indeed, her mother did, as I was later to find out, through a tortuous exchange of letters with the venerable Mrs Tooth and the two five-pound-card telephone calls it took to convince her I was worthy to have the birthplace of her late husband under my husbandry. Ernestina was as much of a problem, with her mother-manipulating campaign to make me buy the place. Oh, she was sure her mother would agree. No problem. But all that came much later. That sudden, mysterious evening on the doorstep of Number Seven, Ernestina was anxious to go south and have someone else worry about looking after her mother's property, property she was uneasy about having the responsibility for, even though it was clearly in the hope that one day she would reap the financial benefit of her factoring. She saw an opportunity, and despite the knowledge that her mother would insist on prevaricating, she accepted from me a cheque for £150 I didn't possess, having left Mr Meldrum with a £400 deposit at his extremely sensible insistence. Next day, a Sunday, I drove back to Inverness and put the VW into the weekly car auction out at Dalcross. VW Campers seem to be desirable items, although mine had been more than through the wars, and it was knocked down at £1500. I then bought a hideous old Ford Transit 35 cwt with exactly a week's MOT for £350, leaving me £900 after commission and VAT. On the Monday I loaded the smoking beast with my meagre belongings, drove to Boirreannach and stacked Mr Meldrum's library in among the smell of engine oil and sheep shit which no amount of scrubbing would remove. And then I moved into Mollydish for good and bad and Mrs Tooth and Ernestina and so far, for ever.

The phone rings. These days I have a phone, partly because I'm so far out of the dealing mainstream that I need one, and partly because the public call box in Mollydish is constantly crammed in summer with backpackers, some of whom, pilgrim-burdened, get stuck within its confines and have to be rescued by amused regulars from the Incomers. And also, I'm less afraid of calls coming out of the blue, disrupting and tearing apart and bringing back memories and figures from the past. Ghosts. Ernestina and Mrs Tooth, unfortunately, both have my number.

But the ghosts do come back. The tiny television in that crappy old music centre long ago went grey, blank, sightless, but there's a mammoth projection TV, inevitably, in the Incomers, and I frequently see it. I never buy a newspaper, but catch the six o'clock news maybe three days in seven. And so it was that the great Truth Drug scandal hit me, on my first pint of the evening, just six weeks after I'd moved into Mollydish.

'Good evening. Top Scots pop group Truth Drug, whose hit version of "My Bucket's Got a Hole in it" was at the top of the charts for seven weeks, have been hit by a major drugs scandal. Guitarist Patrick Grant is in a Frankfurt hospital with a suspected drugs overdose, and the band's manager, Ventura Venissimo, has been charged with importing heroin into the country by the German authorities. This report from Pippa Fellatio in Frankfurt.' The Thunderbirds-puppet woman on the screen gave way to a smaller, tousled female figure in one of those Gore-Tex jackets all television reporters wear as a badge of their position. It was blowing a gale in Frankfurt, and her voice was rumpled by the wind and rain. I noticed immediately that she had a hand problem. Every sentence had a gesture, which was hypnotically distracting. It was as if she was conducting a choir.

'Patrick Grant, known universally as Keith Grant, is in a critical condition after apparently smoking heroin which had been contaminated with a form of toxic fertiliser. He is understood to be on a life-support machine and his mother is being flown out from Glasgow to be at his bedside. Lead singer Mick Merchison had this to say earlier today . . .'

A video clip of a drawn and stunned-looking Mick was played in. He could barely string a sentence together, and I hardly recognised him. He was thinner, harder, and clearly on or just off something. 'Tragic, you know . . . just tragic. Accident that could . . . you know . . .' Minders with shaven heads like concrete gravestones surrounded him. Finally one shepherded Mick away as dozens of cameras electronically strobed the scene. There was a brief trademark Mick flick of the hair, frozen by the flashguns, then he was in a long, black limo and speeding away from the glorious media. Back to Pippa Fellatio. That couldn't be her name, surely. Then the sub-titler flicked it up on the screen: Pippa Valaccio. Oh. Another Glasgow ice-cream family, like Venissimo. Or not, it seemed.

'Band manager Ventura Venissimo is being held in a police cell after a search of his room revealed nearly a kilogramme of a suspected illegal substance. This is currently being tested to ascertain if it is the same drug thought to have affected Mr Grant. The band's manager, who has a colourful reputation for his aggressive approach, was charged with police assault when he attempted to punch one of the investigating officers. He was charged under his real name of John Jamieson.' Then they played a glossy, pop-video version of 'My Bucket's Got a Hole in it', and gave a potted history of the band. Signed to Gorgon Records, released two unsuccessful singles to some critical acclaim, built up a strong local following, then broke through on both sides of the Atlantic with a soul version of the old Johnny Williams classic. Johnny Williams indeed. Poor old Hank. Fucked around to the end. I downed the Murphy's and went home, six pints lighter than my usual Wednesday night consumption. I didn't have to look up Ruth's number. It was there in my fingers without any conscious thought. It rang, and her voice answered, which I hadn't expected. It had been an unthinking reaction, stubbing out all the intervening time. But it was an answering machine. A normal, even-toned businesslike message. 'I can't come to the phone right now, but I'll get in touch if you leave a message.' That was to put off prospective thieves. I might be here, it was saying. I might be around, so don't take this as proof that I'm out, you bastards. I paused, then bridged the gap which appeared unbridgeable after that vomit-flecked night in the Holiday Inn, at Ruth's expense. Then I said, 'I was . . . sorry to hear about Keith. If there's anything I can do.' And my number. Ghosts.

Two days later I had to go to Dingwall to look at some old fishing tackle. I coaxed the smoky Transit beast that was still, unbelievably, my transportation, into an approximation of life, and headed east. In the Ross-shire capital I bought a copy of the *Daily Record*, which had a huge front-page headline over a picture of Ventura: TRUTH DRUG BOSS WAS DOPE GODFATHER. Jesus. I sat in the van and read it, totally incredulous. Sources had apparently revealed that Ventura's background was as a middle-weight coke and heroin dealer to the middle-class denizens of Milngavie and Bearsden. And he had done time for it. No wonder he had changed his name. I wondered if the band had just been a way of extending his powdered-susbtances operation into the international arena. The story was meagre on facts, very big on 'according to sources'. But it had an interview with Ventura's mum, described as 'an Anniesland housewife' who retained, at least from the picture, a certain latinate sultriness and was in her late 50s. She claimed that 'Johnny was always good to me. His dad was never here, and maybe he got in with bad company.' Shit.

I picked up the fishing reels, and two lovely wee silver hammers for bashing out salmons' brains. Salmon priests, they're called. Mollydish was an angling paradise, and I had quickly discovered that fishing books went well. But there wasn't enough in the shop alone to sustain me, so I had to continue my on-the-road dealing. I wandered along Dingwall's pedestrianised main street, mentally comparing the undeveloped little town with the hideous sprawl of Inverness, when I came suddenly across a tiny lane with, it seemed, a shop window far at the end where something glinted. I was drawn like iron filings by a magnet, and found myself gazing in the window of a small music store, where among the accordions and fiddles in the window display stood an old Fender

Stratocaster. It was red. Redder than red. I gazed at it from the street, transfixed, the years peeling away. I half expected to look around and upwards to see my father standing there with his big black Bible under his arm. I shook away the clutching fingers of the past, and realised that the only thing stopping me from going in and buying not just a red guitar, but the ultimate red guitar, a red Strat, an old, pre-1967 one, one with history and the patina of use on it . . . the only thing stopping me was money. So I went back to the fishing-tackle dealer and sold him the lot back, at a slight loss to keep him not unfriendly. He shook his head, but did the deal, a big bluff Englishman who seemed permanently unhappy. 'Bloody off yer 'ead, mate. Bloody off yer bloody 'ead.'

'Bloody right, mate,' I replied in my best Yorkshire voice, feeling happier than I had done in years.

I drove back to Mollydish with the red guitar and a practice amplifier, a tiny thing called a Pig's Nose, which I half-remembered as being a favourite of Carlos Santana. Was he still alive? I had no idea. I felt like it was Christmas, a childhood Christmas, when religion took second place to the mystery of Santa and presents; then I was swamped with guilt and melancholy about Keith and Ruth and Ventura and getting screwed – or rather screwing myself – over the fishing tackle. Then I reached out to the battered old guitar case propped up in the seat next to me, and felt an overwhelming sense of comfort. It was mine. Mine. At last. At last.

Ruth didn't phone.

Ventura was extradited back to Scotland, where he faced charges associated with a plan to export drugs which had been landed in Scotland, all over Europe. I wondered if any of them had been left in waterproof bags attached to creel buoys off Mollydish? I wondered if Ventura knew Malcie or Ross, who I still sometimes spot on his eternal twilight excavations. Searching. Surely not. Ventura got ten years, more than for murder. But then he probably had murdered people. Not Keith. He had only disabled him for life. Although it turned out that Keith had been getting the good stuff, not the shite which Ventura was planning to export. He was working according to good capitalist principles. Keith had, in desperation, broken into Ventura's room and helped himself. From the wrong bag. He'd got the export-only samples. Mick had been chasing the dragon too, apparently, nicely under Ventura's wing for as long as the fat bastard needed them. But he had loved pop music, that guy. He knew its history, its appeal, its spirit. He even understood about Hank Williams, for Christ's sake. That had been their hit single. 'My Bucket's Got a Hole in it'

. . . John Prine, what was that song he'd done, way back when he was another new Bob Dylan? There's a hole in daddy's arm, where all the money goes . . . I had even liked the wee pseudo-Italianate shite, had seen good in him that nobody else had. Had maybe seen myself in him, somehow. And he had turned out to be beyond evil. Or just a dealer. A runner. Cash only.

I had talked about evil, about sin, back in the evangelistic days. But someone like Ventura had been unthinkable then. The ultimate sinful person was the kind of man I'd become. A backslider. Someone who had known the truth and turned away, setting an example for others to be horrified at. But Ventura was beyond the devil. Talent, knowledge, a love of music . . . the ruthlessness, the deviousness, that business with the review. He had even got me hooked on something not quite as bad as heroin, although just as demeaning and life-sucking. Rock journalism. That tawdry, poisonous, second-hand glamour. Used, like so much else in my life. Somebody else's property, passing through my dealing hands. Keith had suffered permanent brain damage, and his lungs were wrecked. He was in a wheelchair. A mawkish, puke-making TV documentary went out about Ruth and him, and how she was devotedly looking after him and campaigning against drug addiction. A mother's story, it was called. She still looked beautiful, but maybe that was just the telly. And the Murphy's I was watching it through. Keith could speak only slowly, stumblingly. They had moved to a large, venerable country house, somewhere in southern Scotland. I recognised a few of the pieces inside. That papier-mâché tray. The Peter Howson picture. A ship model. That green, bubbly glass vase. The final shot was of Keith, the mean, moody look of yore shorn to a pathetic innocence, in his wheelchair, strumming hesitantly that old sunburst Telecaster, the one he and Mick had come into Ruthven Street with, so excited, so full of hope and joy and life. He was playing, of all things, Hank's 'Hey Good Lookin''. That night I discovered that you could, in reality, cry into your beer.

Mick, meanwhile, had launched a solo career. In the States. Or so it was said during the programme. He had a great voice, but somehow I doubted if he would ever recover from what had happened. Even with the best detox money could buy.

Winter. Evil-minded clouds overhead, and a glowering wind. I am returning along the beach from my morning walk, blowing away Saturday's hangover, and thinking about stopping drinking. Well, maybe for a week or so. I've been getting these back pains, and I'm afraid it might be my liver, or kidneys or something. As I stumble in the deep shingle, I see a figure toiling towards me. It is Doctor Mary. We talk, and I mutter something about my sore back. She is so capable, Doctor Mary, that you can forget how attractive she is. But her blue eyes are too intimidating for many. We Mollydish males content ourselves with telling dirty stories about her, weaving fantasies we know we are too weak to make reality. Besides, she knows about my piles. 'Come round to the surgery tomorrow and I'll check out your bloods and the colour of your piss,' she grins. Romance pulls down the shutters again, and I walk on.

As I walk along Mollydish's main street, the wind wheezes through telephone wires, and the houses are fortressed against the elements. Peat reek comes in gusts, from belching chimneys which I know to my cost can blow back in weather like this, showering you with sparks and acrid fumes. It is contained, Mollydish, a very inward place, and yet I do not feel apart. I am a transplanted tree in this ancient orchard. A lot, some would say most, of us here are. Yet the thin, tiny rootlets have taken a grip, and for the first time in my life I feel at home. I will buy the flat and shop, I decide. My hoarding deserves permanence.

As I near the shop, a strange thing happens. I can hear music, hymn-singing, strong and firmly accompanied by a piano. It brings me out in goose bumps which have nothing to do with the cold. The wind is increasing, and the music comes and goes, buffeted between the houses and with the sound of the sea and the gulls crashing over its cadences. But I am no longer in Mollydish. I am in Bittermouth, on a cold Sunday, the last Sunday of the summer that the open-air meetings are held by the prom. And men in black homburg hats are competing with the devil wind as huddled, rainwear-clad figures hurry by.

> Oh for a thousand tongues to sing
> My great Redeemer's praise
> My graaaaaaayyyyyaaaaayyyyt Redeemer's praise
> The glories of my God and King
> The triumphs of His Grace (the triumphs of His . . .)
> The triumphs of His . . . (the triumphs of His Grace)
> The Tryayayayaumphs of. His. Grace.

It stops, in a gulping yowl of technical disaster. I can see a car parked next to the shop, its front doors open. It's calmer here, away from the sea, where a prevailing westerly is going to blow for at least two days. Out of the car climb two figures, male and female; he has a cassette tape in his hands. It has spilled its innards in a black tangle, and he is helplessly spooling the mashed tape through his hands. But I can hear the next verse of that old hymn bouncing around in my head:

> He breaks the powowowower of cancelled sin
> He sets the prisoner free . . .

I only realise that I'm singing aloud when the couple's faces jerk towards me. They are heavily sunburned, fit-looking people, but elderly. They seem curiously caught, as if frozen by surprise at something. 'I'm just going to unlock the door,' I call out, 'if you see anything that interests you . . . the shop'll be open in a minute . . .' Then I realise I'm looking at my mother and father, and I'm trying desperately to remember what kind of state the flat is in. I think I hoovered yesterday. I'm sure I did. I polished the guitar, anyway. I do remember that.